Men With Broken Faces

by

James Ostby

Also by James Ostby

Jake Miller's Wheel

A Literary Novel

PART ONE

CHAPTER ONE

Morgan Feeney knelt in the dark with his face over the toilet hole, and he threw up. When his stomach was empty, he wiped his mouth with his shirt sleeve. Then he gagged and threw up again: a thin, acid drool. He was so sick from his three-day drinking binge that not even the stench of the outhouse affronted him. So sick he wanted to die, but not sick enough to want to die there. *Here lies Morgan Feeney - Sheepherder. Born September 13th, 1893, Rock Falls, Illinois. Died alone in a stinking outhouse, April*—whatever day it was—*1917, Miles City, Montana.*

Halfway up the rear stairway of the dilapidated Windsor Hotel, Morgan sank to his knees and crawled, oblivious to the grime and cigarette butts. Someone in cowboy boots said something to him, but Morgan didn't look up, and he didn't answer. He kept crawling, and as he reached his door, he put his hand in a glob of phlegm and tobacco juice. It felt like a raw oyster. He reached up and wiped his hand on the wall.

Morgan woke and found himself sprawled sideways across the bed with his clothes still on. There was a dry stream of drool down one side of his chin. He tried to lie still, but a shaft of sunlight through the open window blinded him through his eyelids. He turned away and fumbled for the pocket watch his father had given him.

As the locomotive huffed and belched away from the depot and gained speed, Morgan took one last look back, and he thought he saw his father on the platform, waving. But there was no one. His father was lying on a pile of straw in the barn, drunk.

The watch was the only damn thing his father had ever given him. The only good thing. Morgan hadn't been home since. No reason to. His mother had died a month before he left home, and he'd found out about his father's death too late to make it back to the funeral. Probably wouldn't have gone anyway.

Morgan squinted. Eleven o'clock. He pulled the pillow over his face and waited for the bomb inside his head to either explode or fizzle.

It took Morgan twenty minutes to get up, and when he did, he stood looking around the dingy room: a sagging wrought-iron bed, a small, unpainted, cigarette-burned table, and a green, paint-chipped chest of drawers. The red-and-yellow tulips on the faded wallpaper made him sick again, but he swallowed and congratulated himself on being able to stand. He went to the window and looked out. Just a miserable, dusty, dirty, prairie cowtown. A long main street and a couple of side streets, lined mostly with quickly-constructed wood-frame business buildings and a few homes. Most of the homes were farther out, in various stages of completion.

A grain wagon lumbered by, the driver holding onto his hat and hunkering against the wind and grit. A heavy lady in a long, pink dress hurried into the Red Rooster hotel across the street. She looked familiar. The hotel had a bad reputation.

Morgan rummaged in his traveling bag for his cleanest underwear, and padded down the hall to the washroom.

"What's your medicine?" the bartender asked. He was huge, and strong looking beneath his flab, and his eyes were so close together they scarcely left room for the top of his nose. His pasty face was lined with purple-blue veins, like a hog's stomach at butchering time.

"Peerless. And whiskey." Morgan flipped a silver dollar onto the counter. The Pearly Gates bar smelled like all bars: whiskey, stale beer, sweaty men, and tobacco. And other mixed and indistinct odors. Morgan turned and looked for familiar faces. To his relief, he knew no one. He felt the shakes coming on.

The bartender put down an overflowing beer mug and a shot glass, and took the dollar. Morgan picked up the mug with both hands and drank, gulping, with foam running down the sides of his chin. Then he poured the shot into what was left. Hair of the dog. The mug didn't look very clean in the bottom.

The room was long and narrow, with unpainted rough-lumber walls and a skylight in the center of the high ceiling. The bar itself ran half the length of one side. It was nothing more than planks, as were the liquor shelves behind. The only embellishment was a large mirror on the wall above the shelves, with a stuffed buffalo head above. The buffalo looked down at Morgan and winked.

The bartender brought Morgan's change, then he went to the other end of the bar and sat staring sullenly at the opposite wall.

Morgan forced himself to look down from the buffalo, into the mirror, and he was uncomfortable with what he saw there too. It had nothing to do with the ravages of his dissipation; it was the pain underneath. Why did they always put mirrors in bars? To mirror pain and misery? Probably to let people know who was coming up behind them. There'd been a gunfight in the Pearly Gates three days before, Morgan had heard. The men—a rancher and a no account—had killed each other. The rancher—guy named Hayes—had been shot in the back, but he had been tough enough to draw his gun, turn, and shoot the rounder in the face. You'd have to be tough to do that with a .45 hole in you. The rancher's funeral had been well attended, but they'd just thrown the rounder into a shallow grave, like a dog. Word was the rancher had caught the rounder stealing his wife's jewelry, but someone had said he had caught him stealing his wife.

Morgan had no gun. He didn't like guns.

In back were two tables of poker players. Between the tables—sleeping on the floor with a spittoon between his legs—lay a drunk. A short, stout old man with a red beard. The players were laughing and spitting—missing their target on purpose—and the drunk was covered with thick tobacco juice.

Morgan waved for another beer, and he drank it slowly. As his shakes subsided, he dared to look into the mirror again. Not so bad after all. The outer part at least. Maybe his mother had been right when she had said he reminded her of the fair-haired, strong-featured Harvard types in magazines. If only his nose were smaller. But he had a strong chin, broad shoulders, and a calm, stoic look. That's what his eighth grade teacher, Mrs. Pringle, had called him. A stoic.

"Haw, haw, haw!" came from in back. The card players ordered another round of drinks, including one for Morgan. Morgan took whiskey and tipped his glass to them before gulping it down. But now what? Better to starve than to go back to tending sheep, day in and day out, summer and winter. He felt the self pity well up again. The gnawing reminder that life isn't fair. And the crushing, grinding loneliness.

"They didn't have to kill him!" Morgan cried. He was on his knees in the dirt, holding his dog, Wolf. Wolf—riddled with buckshot—had made it home to die.

"What the hell else they gonna do?" his father sneered. He had been drinking again. "Can't have a chicken killer runnin' loose."

"He wasn't a chicken killer."

"Yeah? Then why's that feather stuck to his tail?"

Morgan's mother, Hortense, knelt by him. "Leave him be, Albert." She put her arm around Morgan. "I'm sorry," she said. "He was a good dog."

Wolf. His only friend. Morgan was so tired of being alone he felt like crying, but you cry in a bar just once and you're through. You're lumped in with the rummies forever. You're no good in that town again.

———————————

Morgan forced down the greasy bacon and eggs. As he finished his coffee, two young men approached.

"Mind if we sit here?" the tall one asked. Morgan motioned. "Thanks, chum," the shorter one smiled.

They pulled up chairs. Morgan concentrated on his plate. He didn't feel like talking.

"Say, how's the grub here?" the short one asked. He was light complexioned and stocky; a little soft looking.

"Not bad," Morgan mumbled. "I'm just about done. I'll get outta your way." He swigged the last of his coffee and started to get up.

"Hold it. Don't hafta hurry on our account. Here, have another cup. Waiter, a little more java for this gentleman."

A tall, thin waitress with blond hair falling out from under her hairnet filled Morgan's cup before he could stop her, and she plopped down two menus. Morgan slumped back, remembering he had nowhere to go anyway.

"Name's Sydney Berman." The talkative one held out his hand. "This here's Jake Hermann."

"Morgan Feeney."

The tall, dark man reached across the table. He had a firm grip. "How do you do?" he said. His voice surprised Morgan. It was unusually deep, and soft.

10

"Glad to meet you." Morgan noticed a scar under one eye, and the man's nose looked like it had been broken, but he was still good looking enough.

The two studied their menus. "Steak, well done," the short one said. His friend took the same, and the waitress bustled away, not bothering to write down the order. Morgan gazed at her butt as she went back to the kitchen, but his attention was instinct.

"You from around here?" the short one asked.

"Worked on a ranch," Morgan replied.

"A cowboy." The short one smiled approvingly at his friend.

Morgan decided not to mention sheep. Miserable damn job. He had always been a loner, but two years was enough. Sun, wind, rain, heat, cold, snow . . . . Sagebrush stretching on forever, mosquitoes, flies, rattlesnakes; every perdition possible. Alkali dust so thick you had to wear a bandana over your face to breathe. And always the goddamn dumb sheep.

"We're from New York," the short one went on.

That explained the funny way they talked. Morgan held his cup in both hands to take another drink. He was starting to shake again.

"This isn't New York City, I can tell you that," the short one observed. The tall one smiled.

Morgan felt he had to say something. "Never been to New York."

"Suppose not," the short one said, looking at Morgan inquisitively. "Funny, and don't take me wrong, but you don't look like a rancher. Guess I thought they all wore big hats and had guns." He laughed, and Morgan shrugged.

"Well, I guess I'm not on a ranch anymore," Morgan said. "I quit the other day. Kinda wonder'n what to do now." He glanced at the tall one—Hermann—half wishing he'd say something, and all the time wishing the short one would shut up.

11

"You're outta work?" the short one asked.

"Yeah."

"Well, we're army men."

"You're in the army?"

"Will be. We're gonna sign up today."

"There's a war going on," Morgan said.

The short man sat back. "Yeah, we know, but we got tired of things."

Morgan looked at them anew. "Things?"

The short man pointed at his friend. "Jake's a fighter, an' I'm his manager."

That didn't surprise Morgan. Hermann wasn't all that big—maybe a hundred and eighty-some pounds—but he was hard looking. "Fighter, eh? Where?"

"Fairs, mostly, or anyplace there's somethin' goin' on," the short man replied. "Takes on all comers. Keeps us in the money till we get the big match."

"But what about the army?" Morgan asked.

The short man's face fell, and he was quiet for a moment. "To tell the truth, times ain't been too good for us lately. Oh, Jake wins alright—lost one fight in the last year an' a half, an' he only lost then 'cause he got hit low—but there's not much money in it, and we have trouble getting professional fights. He's too good. So we figured we'd take a break for awhile, that's all."

The short man seemed disconsolate. His friend was impassive as he ate. Hermann was the one who should be down in the dumps, Morgan figured. He was the one taking the lumps. Morgan ordered another cup of coffee. He was beginning to like his acquaintances, but there was something strange about them. The way they acted toward each other. Not that they were faggots or anything, but——

"So you're outta work, eh?" The short one studied Morgan.

12

"Yeah. Oh, well, something'll turn up. Boy, have I got a head. Out too late."

"Ever think about the army?" the tall one asked.

"Army? Naw, I don't think——"

"Say, that sounds like a swell idea," the short one said. "What the hey; you ain't doin' nothin' anyways. Why don'tcha come along?"

"Well, I never saw myself as an army man," Morgan hedged.

"Maybe you should think about it," the tall one said. "You could come with us and see the sergeant, just to talk."

"Yeah, what would it hurt?"

Morgan agreed, mostly because his head throbbed and he didn't feel like arguing.

"Fine. Let's go and see Sergeant Stimson," the short one said. "He seems like a decent fellow, an' I know they're lookin' for good men."

Sydney led them up the stairway of the courthouse to the second floor, then down the musty-smelling hall to a room marked 163rd Infantry. The door was closed, and as Sydney knocked, Morgan saw he was nervous. The closer they had come to the courthouse, the quieter Sydney had gotten. It was hard to tell how Jake Hermann was.

"Come!" a voice bellowed.

Sydney opened the door, and they shuffled in.

"Well, come in and close the goddamn door! Yer lettin' in the flies."

They hurried the rest of the way in, and Jake shut the door behind them. There, seated behind a desk, was the roughest man Morgan had ever seen. Sergeant Stimson was huge, approaching middle age, with dark hair and a pockmarked face. He stood, and Morgan saw he was even bigger than he had first appeared. He held out his hand to Sydney.

13

"Glad tuh see yuh, boys! Who's the fine young man yuh brought with?" The sergeant had a puffy pink scar on the left side of his face, from the hairline down.

"This here's Morgan Feeney. Thinks he might wanna join up," Sydney answered. His voice had gone high on him.

"Feeney. Good Irish name!"

Morgan's ancestors on his father's side were Scottish, but he kept quiet.

"Feeney, eh?" the sergeant continued. "My name's Stimson. I'm outta Fort Harrison. The One-sixty-third's been ordered to active duty. President Wilson's orderin' most of the guard units federalized, and we're gonna be among the first. Know what that means? It means you guys are in on the ground floor, that's what it means. I can sign yuh up right now if yuh want. Course yuh hafta pass the physical, but you look healthy enough tuh me." The sergeant straightened and looked them over again. "Well, what-cha gonna do, boys? I ain't got all day," he thundered. "Ya wanna fight the Huns or not?"

"We, well, we decided to sign up," Sydney stammered.

Sydney spoke for Jake, who nodded, and the sergeant apparently assumed he spoke for Morgan as well.

"Alright, here, sit down and fill these out, an' sign 'em. Yuh can read, can'tcha? I hate it when they sign with Xs."

He held out three forms. After they had filled them out and handed them back, Morgan felt as though he had not really made a decision. But it wasn't a bad feeling.

"Good. Now pass the physical exam and you're in the National Guard. Report here day after tomorrow at one o'clock for that, and yuh damn well better be here. If you're not here, and sober, yuh better be dead! Then we head for Fort Harrison."

He smiled, but Morgan didn't take it as a smile. As for the physical, Sydney had heard that anyone who could walk and breathe—and who didn't have consumption—passed.

As they left, Jake said, "Well, the fat's in the fire."

14

Four days later Morgan found himself with Jake and Sydney on a train bound for Fort Harrison, Montana. On April 7th, 1917, the day after the United States declared war on Germany, they were sworn into federal service, and they began basic training. By now Morgan had second thoughts about the whole thing.

On the morning of December 14th, 1917, the troops of the 41st Division boarded the U.S.S. *Leviathan*, bound for Liverpool, England. On the day after Christmas they left Liverpool for France. As Morgan lay in the hold of the old cargo ship *Andalusia*, he tried not to think. Thinking had always been his downfall.

CHAPTER TWO

Morgan looked around. Everything appeared as if he were seeing it for the first time, and he knew he had been away. The epilepsy his father had bestowed on him. Sometimes he felt refreshed, like waking from a pleasant dream. More often, however, there was little to remember, only wave after wave of some unknown dread. This time it had been the waves.

The French countryside was flat, with rows of beech trees between the fields. Nestled among the trees were houses—mostly brick—and they all had rust-colored tile roofs. Flowers decorated the lush grass along the road, but Morgan recognized only the poppies. It was all pastoral, with no signs of fighting, except for all of the American soldiers strung out along the road.

The morning sun hung low over the trees, and it was unusually warm, even for May. Morgan shrugged up the straps of his pack and adjusted the two crossed ammunition bandoliers that were eating into his shoulders. He was thankful that he wasn't in the machine gun battalion. He had enough to carry without lugging around a Hotchkiss. To his and everyone else's surprise, he had been promoted to corporal, and had been designated squad leader.

Epilepsy. The fits. Morgan couldn't shake the remembrance from when he was eight years old, of his father, in a drunken rage, striking him hard on the side of the head. Morgan hadn't remembered much afterward, but he had an image of his mother telling the doctor how he had fallen down the stairs. After the doctor had gone, his father had cried and apologized. So many years ago, but Morgan still had headaches, and . . . But what the hell? His parents were long gone, and what was done was done.

The only sounds were the tramp of feet, the squeaking of leather, the clinking of metal, and occasional complaining. After months of tedious front-line training near Sommedieue,

16

southeast of Verdun, they were at last on the move; part of the 2nd Division—the Indian Head Division—one of the best. Sydney Berman had been assigned to the 1st Division, and Jake—his fighter, and maybe more—to the 42nd. Morgan tried to forget. Never see them again. Excess mental baggage. Enough to worry about himself.

"France ain't what I thought it would be," a sergeant complained.

"These farms sure are small," someone toward the rear of the platoon said.

"Don't look much bigger than gardens," Alvin Maxwell called back. Alvin, from Fort Benton, Montana. Short and egg shaped, with arms and legs that stuck straight out like sticks on a snowman. Even his head was egg shaped. Grew up on a farm, and ran away from home right before harvest. "Wonder what kinda sheep those are?" He pointed to his right.

"Rambouillet," Morgan said.

"Huh? How come you know so much about sheep?"

Damn. Morgan hitched his rifle sling higher on his shoulder. It was obvious that every man knew his destiny was to be revealed that day, or sometime soon. Even Alvin, who apparently found some relief in chattering. This was finally it, and as they marched, Morgan imagined their inner preparations. Most were undoubtedly making peace with their Maker, atoning for past sins; hoping they would live to sin again. Some were clinging to reality, steeling themselves. And those who had no such preparations to make were comforting themselves with thoughts of home, or just concentrating on putting one foot in front of the other.

"Sooner or later it's gonna be party time, boys!" Sergeant Remington shouted. He was hard jawed and athletic, with graying hair, and eyes that turned steel blue when he gave orders. A twenty-five-year veteran. "Probably sooner," he added.

17

Morgan tried to think of a prayer, but he couldn't. His mother had tried to pound religion into him, and he had fought her. Not that he didn't believe in something. He just didn't like memorizing prayers, and going to church, and all of the other foolishness. Now the best he could do was the old standby from Psalms: *Yea, though I walk through the valley of the shadow of death, I will fear no evil. . . .* Better than nothing.

As the morning dew left the ground, choking dust from thousands of marching feet billowed into the still air. Morgan heard an airplane high above the dust, flying eastward. A few minutes later Archie guns cut loose. The plane sputtered, caught, and resumed its normal drone. There wasn't a man Morgan had talked to who wouldn't have given his right nut to be a flier. They had often discussed it, and the consensus was that most would give one, but no one would give both. They'd all rather be dead.

As he marched, Morgan was able to leave his physical form. Unlike his short, unanticipated epileptic flights, his imaginations were self-imposed escapements to times and places of his own choosing. Back to his childhood, before——

"Shit." The complainer was a round-headed, baby-faced youngster from Fort Wayne, Indiana, named Bill Baldwin. Next to him marched Ivan Ivanka, a huge Polish steelworker from Pittsburgh. Ivan was older than the others, and beside Bill, the age and size differences were even more apparent.

"That's what I say. Shit." It was Max Stuller from North Dakota. He didn't look German—with his black hair and sallow skin—but he had a German accent, and Morgan wondered when the others would come down on him for being a German sympathizer. Probably when the shooting started.

As Morgan's company crested a hill overlooking a vast, shallow valley, a gentle murmur arose. Before them lay a panorama of total devastation. Every tree for as far as they could see stood leafless and splintered, and the ground had been

18

pulverized, as if by a giant plow. The field of battle was littered with tin cans, helmets, clothing, rifles, and all other refuse of war: the seeds of Death and Destruction, to be harvested by the next generation of men.

Philbert Stanford came alongside Morgan. "How's it going, old sport?" he asked.

Philbert Wisdom Stanford. He talked like a banker, or a schoolteacher. Looked like one too, with his round wire spectacles and his delicate features. But he was tougher than he looked. Three days ago he had thrashed the hell out of Ivan, the steelworker, over a poker game.

"Fine. A delightful outing," Morgan replied. "I think they're gonna throw a picnic for us when we get there." From beneath the heavy stench of war, Morgan picked out the odor of death, like that of a dead cow on his father's farm, only sweeter and more sickly.

"Huh. I'll bet."

Philbert was an enigma. He wouldn't tell anyone where he was from, or anything about his background. Nothing, and if pushed, he became furious.

They met a group of poilus. Hairy ones. The French soldiers were a bedraggled lot, already beaten, and many had an unnerving, vacant look about them. Their only succor was their ration of pinard. Cheap wine. The poilus called it bull piss.

Morgan looked back to see if anyone had dropped out. Just behind him was Thorvold Vilander, a tall, rangy, Scandinavian youngster from northeastern Montana. Thorvold was homesick, and Morgan had spent several evenings talking with him about farming. It turned out that Thorvold was an expert horseman. Not racehorses, or riding horses, but farm horses.

A command car stopped, and Lieutenant Stafford—the lieutenant in command—got out and approached Morgan. "Feeney." Brusque—trying too hard to convey authority—he looked like he had just graduated from some fancy eastern college. Maybe captain of the rowing team.

"Yes, Sir," Morgan saluted.

Lieutenant Stafford took him aside. "I just wanted to check with some of you squad leaders. Keep in touch."

The lieutenant's weak, sea-green eyes flickered from side to side, and both of his pale cheeks twitched, like a cat in a room full of mongrel dogs. Morgan said nothing.

"Anything you boys need?"

Several suggestions popped into Morgan's head. "No, Sir."

"Um. Well, this evening, during stand to, you'll be getting the word. We may see some pretty good action. Keep it quiet until the sergeant breaks it."

"Yes Sir."

"Alright then, carry on." The lieutenant got back into the car and drove off.

Someone groused, "Damn ninety-day wonder. Yuh can tell he's not gonna get his ass shot off."

Morgan ran to catch up with his squad.

The men of the 2nd marched on, against the flow of retreating civilians struggling toward Paris on wagons, in two-wheeled carts, and on foot. As the old people and children moved to the side of the road to let the Americans pass, most of them cheered, and some knelt to pray. An old lady in a black dress touched Morgan's arm as he passed. Tears ran down her face and dripped off the whiskers on her chin.

And more ragged poilus came. Morgan recognized in their faces the distant look of those who had seen too much. "Hey, the Huns are thataway," someone hollered, but the poilus didn't understand.

Sergeant Remington stepped out of the column. "Alright men, keep up! Tomorrow we're gonna get our feet wet. You ready?"

A cheer went up. Sergeant Remington was their rock.

The next day, early in the morning, the 9th Regiment of the 3rd Infantry Brigade reached Meaux, a village on the Marne River, forty kilometers east of Paris.

"Mercy." Mike O'Donnell pressed his face deeper into the bottom of the trench.

Mike—a young Irishman who had immigrated to Boston with his parents just before the war—was on Morgan's right, Thorvold Vilander on his left.

"Oh, Mother," Mike cried, louder, in his Irish accent.

The men of the 2nd had been hurried helter-skelter into hastily-dug trenches in a desperate effort to halt the massive German offensive, and for two days they had been under artillery attack. Now, on the morning of the third day, Morgan knew the bombardment would last throughout eternity.

Morgan lifted his head, and his eyes met Thorvold's. Thorvold forced a smile, his big mouth gaping as they took courage from each other. Morgan shouted, but an explosion cut him off. It shook the ground, lifting him, then it let go and he fell, and clumps of dirt hailed down on him. He heard a ringing in his ears, and the crashing, thundering sounds of the barrage faded to a dull roar in the background. He lay still, waiting for the ringing to stop, then he carefully moved each arm and leg to make sure he was unhurt. After a few minutes his hearing returned.

At mid morning the firing stopped. Morgan and the others used the opportunity to take a quick drink of water, if they had any, and perhaps to eat a bite or two of cheese. They had cans of hardtack, but it was nearly inedible unless it could be

21

soaked. Besides, it just made them thirstier. Morgan threw his away.

The break in the shelling was also a chance to stretch, to take care of bodily functions—those who had not already done so involuntarily—to check on their companions, and to brace for the expected ground attack. Even the few old-timers like Sergeant Remington—the ones who had seen combat in Mexico and Cuba—had never encountered anything like the sustained bombardment to which they had been subjected.

Again the shelling came, heavier, and everyone burrowed in. Morgan's pants were full, but he didn't care.

At noon the shelling stopped, and again the men scrambled to take care of the immediate necessities of life. Then the count started.

"Al's hit!" someone in another company shouted. "Help."

Morgan started the roll.

"Gray."

"Here!" came a call from thirty yards to his left. Horace Gray, the genial all-American boy from Montgomery, Alabama. The stereotype of tall, dark, and handsome, except one eye was crossed. But it wasn't his shooting eye, so the army had taken him.

"Stuller."

"Here," from the right.

"Stanford."

"Yo!"

The check continued.

Finally, "Ivanka."

No answer.

"Ivan."

Again no answer.

"Where the hell's Ivan?" Morgan shouted. He had last seen him about three places to his right. He stood, cautiously looking toward the German positions far to the east. Then he started to where Ivan should have been.

Before he got there, Horace called out. "He's dead, Morgan."

"C'mon," Morgan murmured to Philbert.

Horace was kneeling over Ivan, and several others had gathered.

"What happened?" Morgan asked.

Horace shook his head without looking up, and pointed at a sticky patch of blood on the lower part of Ivan's back. Philbert squatted and lifted Ivan's shirt. There was a hole the size of his thumb.

"That Ivanka?" Sergeant Remington came huffing up. He had a pencil and a small notebook.

"Yeah," someone replied. "What the hell happened to 'im?"

Sergeant Remington squinted. "Some sorta fragment. Coulda been anything: a piece of metal, a rock, even a stick of wood. I'll send someone to pick him up as soon as I can. You guys had better be ready, the Huns aren't done yet. We've got orders to hold the line, and that's what we're gonna do." He continued down the trench.

The men stared at Ivan, and Philbert rolled him over.

"Looks like he's smiling," Max said.

They all looked at Max, and Mike O'Donnell couldn't help himself. "Coulda been one a' your Heinie relatives that pulled the cord on that artillery piece."

Max didn't reply. His sullen face flashed red, and Morgan saw his hand reach for his bayonet. Max had confided to Morgan that he had knifed a man once, back home in North Dakota, over a stray cow. The man had lived, but . . .

23

"None a' that now." Morgan stepped between them. "We're in this together." He turned toward Mike, and they glared at each other.

"Aw, what the hell," Mike said, his voice low, and flat. He took one last look at Max and walked away.

Horace lifted Ivan's head out of the dirt and stuffed a filthy shirt under it. One of his tears fell on Ivan's cheek.

Morgan found Ivan's helmet. He knelt and put it over Ivan's face to hide the smile that was already turning into a grimace. Big, tough Ivan, who hadn't been so tough at all.

The expected German attack never came, and again the 9th Regiment received orders to move. Now they were in a race to relieve the French at Bois de la Morette, another place neither Morgan nor anyone else had heard of.

The movement of the 2nd Division was disorganized, as always. The closer the trucks drew to the front, the more frantic their drivers became. Sometimes one of the Model T Fords would sputter to a stop, to be pushed off the road by its passengers. Again Brigadier General Lewis, commanding officer of the 3rd Infantry Brigade, had relayed orders to hold the line. As the pace accelerated, a determined—though temporary—euphoria set in; euphoria nurtured by the immortality of youth. Morgan, Horace, and Lansing Rhodes— squeezed together in a truck near the front of the column—were less enthusiastic.

Lansing was a robust, athletic, personable stoic whose dark, open-eyed features suggested to Morgan a certain intelligence. Lansing had grown up in a small Idaho logging town, and at age eighteen he had left home, bound for California, where he had worked as a carpenter before enlisting in the army. Lansing was older than most of the others, and Morgan valued his quiet maturity. He knew Lansing could be trusted in a tight spot.

24

Unlike most of the others, Lansing had liked the army from the start, but now he was having second thoughts. "Hell, you'd think they were going to a turkey shoot," he observed dryly. His low western twang quieted some of the closest, noisiest revelers.

Others had heard him but were unmoved. They were on the way to kill Germans, and, as one remarked for Lansing's benefit, "Anybody who don't wanna fight shouldn't be in the army."

Lansing ignored him. He and Morgan and Horace sat silently for another kilometer.

"Well, at least they're fulla vinegar," Horace said.

"Why, this is gonna be easy as pie," Lansing remarked sarcastically.

Morgan remembered what Lansing had said the night before, about "seeing the elephant." When Lansing was a boy, he had been regaled with battle stories by a hoary veteran of the Civil War. And once the old soldier had told him of how it had felt to see the elephant. To experience combat for the first time—not skirmishes or raiding parties; not sniping or potting away at each other from trenches or from behind trees and rocks—but real combat, in which legions of men advance into withering fire. Now Morgan knew that he, and Lansing, and all of the others were about to see the elephant.

The countryside was mostly wheat fields with rows of trees between. It all looked the same to Morgan. He felt around to make sure he had all of his equipment, then he reached down and began tightening his puttees. It was almost time.

A half kilometer later the trucks stopped, dropped off their human cargo, circled in a field, and started back in the direction from which they had come. The men of the 9th marched toward the fighting, and Morgan knew that, again, each was strengthening himself in a different way. Some cast off their fears through brash outbursts, while others took courage from the bold determination of their comrades. Morgan was thinking about Ivan. Poor, dumb Ivan.

CHAPTER THREE

Morgan had prepared the others as well as he could. Now, waiting for the German onslaught, he braced himself. He lay in the road ditch fingering his Springfield-pondering his conception of miracles-for it would take not one miracle, but a series, for him to survive the war.

The plan was to meet and repel the next German attack, then to counterattack before the enemy had a chance to regroup. With fixed bayonets, they waited. The enemy shelling had stopped, but the French were still returning heavy mortar fire. Morgan lifted his head and peeked over the road, but all he could see were wheat fields and scattered trees.

From far away, across the fields, came the enemy. Artillery eruptions laced them, but still they came—an unbroken line of gray—advancing at a fast walk. Morgan stared, terrified. He shrank back and looked at Horace Gray on his right. Horace looked back, and his bad eye was worse than ever. Morgan turned to Bill Baldwin on his left, but Bill was frozen. Morgan knew he was alone. They had all been alone since their first time under fire: the artillery barrage at Meaux. Morgan inched forward and gaped again at the apparitions before him, and as he did, several of them tumbled backward, but the line continued its advance, undaunted. Then, to Morgan's greater horror, they broke into a slow, ponderous run.

A Hotchkiss erupted somewhere down the line on Morgan's left, then another off to his right. Soon their staccato hammerings were muted by rifle fire. Morgan aimed and squeezed. The figure in his sights fell, but he couldn't be sure if it had been by his or someone else's bullet. The rest of the attackers crouched at the waist and came faster, and more of them fell, and Morgan fired without aiming. Then his rifle was empty, and he fumbled desperately for more ammunition. Bullets sang overhead as he reloaded, but when he looked again the German advance had stalled, and there, under the scant cover of the newly-grown wheat, they were being cut to pieces. After a few minutes, those enemy who could, sprang to their feet and ran, and the Americans stopped firing and cheered. Shooting fleeing men in the back was not part of their character. Morgan knew it was a chivalry they would soon find they could ill afford.

Morgan pulled back from his firing position and looked up and down the line, appalled at the cheering. How could they? Wasn't it obvious that now it was their turn? How could they be so stupid? "Damn fools," he growled under his breath.

Sergeant Remington came, half running, up the ditch. "Get ready, men. Let's give 'em hell boys!" He continued shouting encouragement, and most of the men responded enthusiastically. "Payback time!"

Morgan turned. A grotesque look had come over Bill's face; a murderous mask. Morgan started to say something, but it was too late.

"Jump-off time, men! Move out!" Sergeant Remington shouted. "Over we go! Form a line and give it to 'em."

All along the road, men stood and charged.

Morgan stumbled and fell, but he felt no pain, and he picked himself up and struggled on, whooping and yelling like the others. Fifty yards out he fell again, out of breath, and as he lay panting he noticed most of the shouting had died, and he heard bullets singing overhead. From directly in front of him he picked out the rapid "tat-tat-tat" of a machine gun. He tried to lie still.

"C'mon men," Sergeant Remington called above the din. "Get up! If you're gonna die, do it right, not lying here." He ran back and forth, kicking those who wouldn't move. "Stay here and you die like dogs."

Morgan jumped to his feet and pushed on. He could feel puffs of air from the bullets, and it was all he could do to keep from falling to the ground and burrowing in. Still he kept going, spurred by unexpected inner strength. As he ran peace descended over him, and time was no longer relevant. He felt himself floating, and he knew he had triumphed over mortality.

Carried by the tide of events, Morgan looked around at the others, and he was surprised to see some of them go down. He heard the familiar "thum-thum" from his deer-hunting days—of bullets striking flesh—and he turned to see Sergeant Remington sprawled on his back. Morgan calmly walked up to him. The sergeant lay still with his arms and legs outstretched. His eyes and mouth were open, and blood oozed from his chest and stomach. He was dead, but his mouth was moving. Morgan felt nothing.

"Wham."

Morgan saw a flash of light, and he clung to his rifle as he fell. He lay still, drifting back and forth between light and darkness.

Morgan woke fitfully, and he was lost and confused. By evening, however, he knew where, and who, he was. He was in a field hospital, lying in bed with a bandage wrapped around his head. People were bustling about, but he had trouble catching their attention. Every time he tried to move, bright lights flashed and his head throbbed even more.

"How are you feeling, Morgan Feeney?"

She was a young nurse, perhaps Morgan's age. Morgan tried to return the smile, but even that small effort sent pain shooting through his head and down the back of his neck.

"What happened?" he whispered.

She leaned closer. "I didn't understand. You'll have to say it again." She was pretty, with auburn hair, strong cheekbones, and vivid green-blue eyes.

"What happened?" Morgan repeated. Her skin was the color of his mother's alabaster statue of Venus de Milo.

"You have a scalp wound on the back of your head. Those who brought you in from the dressing station said you were grazed by a bullet. There was a hole in your helmet. See here, they even brought it in for you." She took Morgan's helmet from a stand beside the bed. "You're a lucky fellow, Morgan Feeney."

She poked her finger through the hole and wiggled it at him.

Morgan winced. "How bad is it?" he whispered, lifting his arm and pointing in the general direction of his head.

"Oh, pooh, not bad at all. It must feel worse than it is. The doctor says you'll be fine in a few days. He'll be around to see you in the morning. He calls you the one with the hard head."

She laughed. Morgan lifted his hand again, and she took it and held it for a moment. Then she was gone.

Morgan rolled his head sideways and looked at the rows of beds. Most of the men were quiet, but nearby someone lay moaning. The man's entire head was bandaged—even his eyes—and he kept trying to get up. Each time, he fell back and sobbed. In the other direction, at the far end of the room, another bad case cried out in pain, then lapsed into a babbling, sobbing groan.

The hospital was a barracks-type building with windows along each side. There was an outside door at one end, and a room on the other end, from which doctors and nurses emerged, and into which they disappeared. Coal-oil lanterns hung from the rafters above the center aisle, and the flies that were not attached to bleeding bandages or to bits of filth on the floor buzzed about looking for something better. Occasionally a doctor called and orderlies with a stretcher carried someone out. They always returned with a live replacement.

That night sleep came fleetingly to Morgan, but through the pain, the pretty young nurse's face hovered, sustaining him through the long hours. She sat by his bed wiping the fever from his face with cool, wet cloths, and giving him water to quench his deep thirst. At times they would hold hands, but more often their bond was incorporeal. They talked, quietly and with singular understanding, sharing their secret hopes and dreams.

In the morning she returned, and Morgan knew her name was Evangeline. She took his hand again and comforted him, and again they talked, and before she left she leaned over and gently kissed his forehead. Then Morgan slept peacefully.

Morgan fought to stay asleep, but he lost. Someone was calling to him from far away. He opened his eyes, and a nurse was standing over him. She was young, but not pretty.

"Time to wake up, soldier. We have to get you out of bed and get you cleaned up. Doctor's orders."

Short, stout, and abjectly homely—big-toothed and big-bellied—she was all business. She started to pull Morgan's blanket away.

"Wait. Where's Evangeline? I thought——"

She stopped. "Who?"

"Evangeline. She was here yesterday, and last night."

"There is no one here named Evangeline."

"But I——"

"I should know; I've been here for over two weeks." She softened. "I'm in charge of this section, and I know you've had a rough go of it since you came in. That was quite a knock on the head you took."

Morgan protested, but she quieted him. "Things happen in here, Morgan Feeney." She smiled. "It's been me watching over you, though I didn't expect you to remember."

Morgan looked numbly at her. It couldn't have been her.

31

She pulled his blanket the rest of the way off. His filthy underclothes were the same ones he had arrived in, and the smell sickened him, even though he was used to it.

"Now, let's get you up and into the showers. Can you sit up?"

She helped him. As he swung his feet to the floor, his head spun and the bright lights flashed again, and he started to fall.

"There, that's alright." The not-at-all-pretty nurse let go of his hands and moved to his side, steadying him. "Wait a minute. You'll be fine."

She stood with her arm across his back. Morgan kept his eyes closed until the flashing stopped.

"Feel better now?"

Morgan nodded and leaned down to pull on his shoes, then he tried to get up. He made it on the second try, and the nurse threw the blanket around him. Then she grabbed his wrist and drew his arm across her shoulders. It was apparent that she had done the same thing many times before. She reached down with her free hand and picked up the clean underclothes she had brought.

"Ready?" she asked, stepping out.

Morgan followed unsteadily, but after they had passed a few beds he found his legs. He tried to take his arm away.

"Not so fast, Morgan Feeney. You just hang on till we get there, then you're on your own in the shower."

They went outside and across a rutted dirt road to a corrugated metal shack.

"Here we are." She handed him the underclothes. "Throw those rags out the door when you're through. Keep the water off your bandage. Can you make it back to bed alone?"

Morgan smiled self-consciously as he turned to enter.

"Wait, there's one more thing," she stopped him. "When you're through here, go next door to the delousing room." She pointed to another metal shed. Morgan flushed as she walked away.

That evening Morgan lay trying to sort things out. He was haunted by his vision of Evangeline, and in his time of need he felt her nearness more than ever. It was a feeling akin to a religious experience.

Morgan trudged along the dusty road with his helmet hanging at his side. He felt inside the top left pocket of his tunic for his travel pass. He had been walking for only three hours and already two military police units had stopped him. Both times the back of his head and the mangled helmet had been more convincing than the pass. Besides, he was heading to the front, not away from it.

As he walked, Morgan was surprised at how deserted the road was. Occasionally he met a French soldier or two, or a farmer, but that was all, and there were no Americans other than the military police. He assumed they were all at the front, though he couldn't understand why there were no supply columns with which he could catch a ride.

Morgan could see for several kilometers in every direction, and ahead he heard heavy artillery. It reminded him of the thunderstorms back home in Illinois. The storms had come so slowly they could be seen for hours before they were heard, but when they got closer they seemed to signify the end of the world.

On a slight rise, Morgan stepped off the road and made for a clump of birch trees. He entered the thicket, cautiously peered around again, and unbuttoned his trousers. When he was finished he went to a tall Lombardy poplar tree beside the road, threw off his pack, and lay flat on his back with his helmet over his face. The grass was soft, and the rumble of the artillery faded.

Morgan heard someone say something, and he knew he had been asleep. He sat up, clenching his rifle in both hands, and his helmet rolled down his legs. There stood a scrawny American, and he too had a rifle.

"Jeez, don't do that to me!" Morgan shouted as he jumped up. "Why you damn near . . ." The man looked familiar. "Say, do I know you?"

The man didn't answer. Morgan squinted against the sun.   "Barry? Barry, from Montana?"

The man raised his eyebrows. He was young, but he looked old and frail. "You from Montana?"

"Barry Saul?"

He was only skin and bone, and his cheeks were sunken, like he was sucking them in.

"Morgan. I'm Morgan Feeney! Christ, don't you remember me? It hasn't been that damn long." Barry, the company quimp during basic training, who had turned out to be the best shot in the regiment. Barry, always talking about ". . . shooting some Huns."

"Morgan? I . . ." The young man's shoulders sagged, and he seemed to relax.

Morgan grabbed him by the shoulders, and there was nothing there. "Well how the hell are you?" Morgan asked.

"Alright. You?"

"Good. Here. I found a nice place to rest."

They sat in the shade of the tree.

"Things going alright?" the skeleton asked. He looked like a skeleton.

"Sure. Nothing to write home about, but I'm still kicking. Still in the Second Division. You?"

"The Forty-second."

"Doing what?"

Barry lifted his rifle from the grass. It had a long tubular sight.

"Oh. Well, I remember you always were a good shot back in training."

"I'm better now. Real good."

Morgan saw the change. There was something missing. Morgan couldn't think of anything to say, and all that came to mind were Barry's words from back in training camp the day they had left: *Aw, shit, the war'll be over by the time we get there. Anyways, I hear them little French girls is runnin' outta men over there, an' I'm just the guy that can help 'em out. Wa-hoo!*

There was nothing left of Barry. It was like he had been used up and was dead, but still moving. Morgan groped. "Have you seen any of the others? From the Montana bunch, I mean? Jake Hermann, the fighter? I heard he's in the Forty-second."

"Montana?" Barry shook his head. Morgan tried for another fifteen minutes, but he got nowhere, though Barry did seem to enjoy listening. Then Morgan had to go.

They stood, and Morgan reached out his hand. "Hang on Barry. This thing won't last forever."

Barry looked at him in a strange way. "Maybe it will. I think maybe it will. Say, how come you keep callin' me Barry? Who's Barry?"

"What d'yuh mean?"

"My name ain't Barry. It's Francis. Francis James Carroll, from North Carolina."

CHAPTER FOUR

Morgan sat surrounded by the men of his squad. Their trench was in a flat, open area, and behind it ran a row of dead trees and stumps. The ground in front had been chewed up, and there was not a living thing between them and the enemy three hundred yards away. The lines had been held, but at a terrible price, and now they were on the offensive, taking ground by day, and forming defensive positions at night. Sometimes, like now, they found shelter in already-dug trenches.

"Hell, Morgan, we thought you went west," Mike O'Donnell boomed in his thick Irish accent.

"Yeah," echoed Max Stuller in his trace of German. "We sure 'nuff thought you was dead, Morgan. They said yuh didn't look so good when they hauled you away." He thumped Morgan on the back a few times, evidently to make sure he was not an apparition.

Lansing Rhodes and a replacement named Mudd sat off to the side looking at Morgan's helmet. Clarence Mudd was a short, heavy, red-cheeked youth from Virginia who had been with the unit for only a week. He had the raised-eyebrow look of one who is perpetually surprised.

"I do declare," Clarence drawled. He felt the helmet where the bullet had gone through. "You must be the luckiest man in the army, to take one in the lid like that and live. I'll bet yuh had one helluva headache."

Morgan pushed through the circle of men and sat off to one side, on a wooden ammunition crate. The smell of unwashed bodies and rotting corpses was bad, but not as overwhelming as the stench of infected wounds in the hospital.

"Yuh hear any news?" Thorvold Vilander asked. He was pale, with red cheeks, and his mouth seemed bigger than ever, with too many teeth.

"Naw," Morgan replied. "Don't get much news lying in a hospital." He saw their disappointment. "Well, I did hear some officers talking, and it sounds like the Boche are getting pretty sick of it."

"Yeah? What else?" James Walker asked. James, who had grown up on a farm in Nebraska. Who had lied about his age to get in.

"Oh, that's about all, just that they're runnin' outta food and things like that. We don't have it so bad compared to them."

"Well, then, let's do our best to put a little more hurt on 'em," Bill Baldwin piped up. He was sitting on the lower step of the front wall, cleaning his rifle. "Might as well give 'em what for and get it over with."

Morgan felt like exploding. Damn dumb, round-faced kid. Then he saw Bill's resignation.

"Well, I dunno," Lansing said. "It looks to me like they're doing alright. I'm not getting my hopes up until they start waving white flags at us."

A general discussion followed. Some were hopeful, but most were skeptical. Morgan, the bearer of good tidings, had no opinion. After several minutes the argument died, and they all sat silently. It was a rare moment of reflection; a reverie none wanted to be the first to break.

Then an unease came over Morgan. "Say, where's Philbert?" he asked. No one answered, and Morgan saw that they were annoyed. He felt like an outsider. Some of the men looked down, and others exchanged furtive glances.

At last Lansing replied. "He took the duckboard trail, Morgan."

"The what?"

"He got bumped the day after you got hit. Machine gun cut him in half." Lansing paused. "An' you already know about Sergeant Remington." He said it matter-of-factly, and Morgan waited for him to continue, but Lansing looked away.

They sat, uncomfortably, and Morgan tried to think of something to say. Horace Gray and several of the others pretended to check their rifles, and the rest shuffled and mumbled, trying to shift the mood.

Finally Bill came to the rescue. "I declare, Morgan, you forgot to tell us about the nurses! Why, what a queer duck you are. Here you go off on vacation and come back without a word about the nurses." He winked at Max and the others.

Morgan shuddered as a vision of Evangeline passed before him.

"Shoot," Bill said, "I'll bet my bottom dollar he's in real good with the prettiest one he could find." A red-lipped, white-toothed grin crossed his grimy baby face.

They laughed as Morgan tried to smile.

"Yeah, Morgan, what about it? Was it worth gettin' shot in the head?" Horace chided.

"Shucks, he ain't gonna say nothin'. He's keepin' 'em all to himself," Mike added. "Why, sure enough, I thought there was somethin' different about him. Just lookit him, sittin' there like the king of Siam. Bet he was just as sorry to leave that hospital as we are to have him back."

They all had a good laugh. Morgan had given them what they wanted, and one by one they wandered away; all except Lansing, who had filled in as squad leader. Squad leader was a responsibility not shirked, but not sought.

"Glad to have you back," Lansing said.

Morgan detected a special genuineness in the way he said it. "Glad to be back."

Lansing took him down the line to meet Sergeant Remington's replacement.

That night when the shelling started—first the Germans, then the French—sleep was impossible, even for those who had been awake for days. Morgan, sitting with his back against the

38

damp, sticky soil of the parapet and his feet on the duckboards, saw the fatigue and the awful revelations of war in the faces of those he had rejoined. But there was more: a chilling bitterness that had replaced their brash self assurance. And a callousness toward each other, beneath the surface.

Throughout the night the bombardment continued, diminishing at times, only to increase to deafening, crashing crescendos.

Morgan sat beside his mother at the kitchen table, wiping the blood from her face with a wet rag. One of her eyes was already blackening, but the bleeding from her nose had stopped. "It's not as bad as it looks," she said. "He pushed me down, and I hit my head on the stove."

His father had been drinking for a week.

His mother took his hand—the one with the rag—and held it to her cheek. "It's not your fault. I don't want you getting hurt. Don't fight him, Morgan. You're only thirteen. When he's like that, it's best that you stay away. Go out to the barn until it's over."

"I can't leave you."

"I'll be alright." She took the bloody rag and wiped a tear from each of her eyes. "Oh, I wish you could have known him before the drinking."

———————————

It was hard to keep track of the days, but after some arguing, Thorvold and Horace decided that it was June 8th. They knew they were near Chateau-Thierry. That was all they knew, except that there was a big attack scheduled for the next day.

The trench in which the 9th Regiment sat was from a previous battle, and they had enlarged it as best they could, knowing that an artillery bombardment could come at any time, but also knowing that in the morning they would be abandoning it. That afternoon Morgan and Lansing, while digging, had hit a body. The stench had nearly overwhelmed them, and they had quickly covered it again, not knowing, or caring, who it was.

As darkness came, Morgan felt both relief and foreboding. The shooting had stopped, but the waiting had begun, and in the morning they would jump off. They had all aged years since the first time they had charged, shooting and whooping like savages toward the German lines, and they had acquitted themselves courageously. But Morgan had noticed that he and the other survivors had lost something that first time, and each time thereafter, until there was little left—no duty, no honor, no glory, no valor—only the determination to survive.

Morgan also saw that each man in his platoon reacted differently. A few still sustained themselves through comradeship; most withdrew, refusing to make ties with those who would surely die. And there were some who, defying the others, thrived on army life and combat. To them it was a vicious game in which they cared not whether they lived or died. They were like madmen. Some suspected Victor Steele was mad.

Victor's past was unknown, and he wanted it that way. He was a short, thin, dark, wiry man with a bad complexion, who spoke with a strange accent that some thought was Armenian. He had always been a loner, though he was amiable enough, and he always did more than his share. But there was, in Morgan's mind, something sinister about him—a coldness—and a fury that sometimes bubbled to the surface. Word was that during training he had nearly killed a man from another company over a joke taken as an insult, and thereafter he had been given a wide berth.

When it was dark, normal nighttime activities began. In more permanent positions there would have been patrols into No

Man's Land, to scout, and to string wire, but now that was futile. The positions were too fluid. Safety lay in the senses of those on watch, and in the star shells put up by both sides. Night attacks were rare but not unheard of.

As the darkness deepened, Morgan and Bill sat together trying to ward off the dread that had been theirs all day, and that would follow them into the night. There had been sporadic fighting, and as the result of a minor skirmish, an enemy soldier had been wounded and trapped between lines. He lay in a shell crater, and all afternoon his cries for help had gone up from the otherwise quiet battlefield. The Germans always tried to retrieve their dead and their wounded, and by late afternoon a rescue party had been sent out, only to be driven back. That evening the German waved a white flag, but someone, to the disgust of the others, had met the attempt with three well-fired shots. Now, in the darkness, the cries from the wounded man, though weaker, were all the more unnerving. Several more rescue attempts were made, but always a star shell went up, forcing the rescuers back. The Americans were obligated to fire, but they aimed high. All except one.

"Jeez, I can't stand listenin' tuh that guy anymore. What's he sayin'?" James had crawled down the shallow trench to be with Morgan and Bill.

"I dunno," Morgan replied. "Guess we should ask Max. He speaks German."

"Max says he's crying for his mother," Bill said flatly. "And he wants water."

"Jesus Christ," James moaned. A tear trickled down each dirty cheek, like a child who had been spanked. He saw Morgan looking at him in the moonlight, and he turned away.

They sat listening, and for a while everything was quiet. Then the cries started again. Another star shell lighted the area and the sentries ducked and closed their eyes to preserve their night vision. When it was dark they resumed watch.

41

Morgan leaned sideways and pulled something from beneath his buttock. It was a brass shell casing of some kind. He tossed it over his shoulder. Then he sat, knowing that he should try to sleep; knowing he couldn't. He wouldn't until he toppled in exhaustion later that night.

A French Chauchat sputtered a few rounds, then died. The wounded German was quiet. Morgan took a drink from his canteen, then passed it to Bill. Normally each rationed his own water, and it was unheard of to ask another for more, but Morgan had plenty, and he knew Bill had been running messages back to the command post all afternoon. Bill drank sparingly, and when he handed back the canteen, Morgan gave it to James, who also drank lightly.

"Sergeant Shepherd thinks it's gonna be a big day tomorrow," Bill said. Bill's big, round, baby face had turned rough, like boot leather, and lean.

"Damn, these fuckin' cooties are drivin' me nuts." James squirmed and scratched. "I just went over everything with a candle too. Yuh can't win."

"Well, they don't seem to like me as much as they like you," Bill said. They could barely see him smile in the dark.

"They deloused me at the hospital, but it lasted about a day," Morgan put in. "Guess they like me too."

"Yeah, well if you want some more, I've got plenty," James grumbled.

"I heard the First got gassed the other day," Bill said.

"That right?" Morgan said.

"Yeah, I heard them talkin' about it back at command. Said it wasn't so bad though, the wind shifted and blew most of it back on the Boche. They lit out like bats from hell."

They laughed.

Bill lowered his voice. "I dunno, though. A captain said he saw some of our boys that got it. Said they was all covered

42

with green blisters. Sounded pretty awful. Mustard gas, he said. Lord, gettin' shot's one thing, but I'd sure hate tuh get gassed."

"Aw, we ain't gonna get gassed," James assured him. "I heard about that stuff. Like you just said, it ain't reliable. Anyway, serves them Krauts right. That ain't no way tuh fight a war. The way I see it, if you're gonna fight, fight. Don't fiddle around with stuff like that. It just ain't right."

"Is that so, General James Walker? You think this is right—what we're doin' now—killin' each other this way?" Bill asked. "If you're gonna kill a man, what's the difference how you do it? I just don't see what it matters whether you shoot him, bomb him, stick him with a bayonet, or gas him."

"I dunno," James said. "I guess there ain't no difference. It just don't seem fair though."

"Fair?" Morgan broke in. "What the hell's fair? I bet those Boche over there don't like this any better'n we do. You give them a chance to throw down their rifles and walk away, an' they'd do it in a minute. So what's the sense in it? I wish I could figure out what started this whole mess in the first place."

The other two had no immediate answer. Then Bill spoke up. "Well, we all volunteered, didn't we? Guess we got ourselves into it."

"Hogwash," Morgan grunted. "It isn't that simple."

Eleven-year-old Morgan floated on his back while birds chirped happily in the trees along the creek bank. The creek had stopped its spring flow, leaving a chain of pools that was just right for swimming: warm, but still fresh and deep, before the stagnation and drying of late summer. The sun beat down from directly overhead, and now and then a gentle breeze swept over.

Morgan's mother, afraid he would go into one of his states and drown, had done all she could to keep him from swimming alone. Nevertheless Morgan swam, knowing that he had nothing to fear in the tranquility of his special place.

43

A cow came to drink, and when she was through she stood dumbly, watching Morgan. He lifted his head and stared back. He had never won a staring contest with a cow, so he lowered his head and closed his eyes. A few minutes later he looked, and she was gone.

Tired of floating, Morgan rolled over and started to swim, slowly, to the other side, then back. After a few trips, he climbed out and dried himself. Then he went to a large willow tree, spread his towel on the grass, and sat waiting for the sandy mud on his feet to dry. From where he was, high on the bank, Morgan could see their farm, with its white two-story house, barn, silo, and outbuildings. Off to his left an old wooden bridge crossed a dry section of the creek, and beyond that, a half mile away, was the school. To his right were more farms.

Someone was shaking him. "Hey, wake up, Morgan." Lansing.

"Ummph. What the hell now?"

"Shhh."

"Well, what?"

"It's Victor. He's out there." Lansing pointed with his thumb.

Morgan jumped up. "Out there! What the deuce is he doing out there? Nobody gave any orders for that!"

"Shhh. Pipe down. Yuh wanna get him killed?"

"Well what's he doing out there anyway?" Morgan croaked.

"He must be after that Fritz."

"What?" Morgan gasped.

"Shhh, dammit. That's what it looks like. During the last star shell he was heading straight for him."

"The damn fool, is he balmy? Even if he gets there he'll never get back. Anyway, why the hell does he wanna do in

44

some poor guy who's gonna die anyway? He must have rocks in his head."

"What now?"

"Nothing. What can we do? Just pass the word so our own boys don't shoot him."

"Maybe they should," Lansing said.

As Morgan groped and stumbled down the trench, he was sick of the dirtiness of war, and he half hoped Victor Steele would get what he deserved. Then he stepped on something soft.

"Ouch, what the hell yuh tryin' tuh do, kill me?" It was Max.

"Sorry."

"Oh, it's you. Well, since it's you, feel free tuh step on my stomach any time yuh want to."

"Alright, lie down again and I will."

"Huh."

"You hear about Victor?"

"Sure. That guy's queer."

"Lansing thinks he's after that Boche."

"Sure."

"Tell the men not to shoot 'im when he comes back."

Max passed the word.

"You seen 'im?" Morgan asked.

"Who, Victor?"

"Yeah."

"I saw him. I don't see how he made it that far." Max drew closer. "Tuh tell you the truth, Morgan, I wouldn't care if he got it himself. What he's doin' is wrong, if yuh ask me. Don't yuh think it's wrong?"

Another star shell went up. The sentries ducked, and those off duty peeked over the top. They could see Victor clearly, and they were surprised that the Germans couldn't. He was nearly to the crater when the light faded, and they heard the wounded German moan something.

"What's he saying, Max?" Morgan asked.

"He wants someone to kill him," Max answered sharply.

Max stared into the darkness, and a sickness welled up in Morgan's throat. Then Max looked at him again. "He wants someone to kill him, and to write to his wife and mother when he's dead."

Revulsion filled Morgan. Until then he had felt nothing but contempt for Victor. Now, however, he knew, and he hoped for a quick end. "Looks like he's gonna get his wish," he said.

Morgan and Max waited, silently. From time to time there was a moan, but mostly it was quiet. Then it was quiet all the time. Morgan went back to his position and waited. An hour and several star shells later, Lansing crawled over.

"What's going on? It didn't take 'im that long to go out," Lansing said. "Yuh don't suppose he got bumped?"

"Naw, there hasn't been a shot fired since he left, and that Boche wasn't about to bump 'im."

"Well he sure is taking his time."

Five minutes later they heard a voice. "Hold on, boys, I'm comin' in."

"Who's there?" James quavered.

"It's the kaiser. Who the hell yuh think it is?" Victor rolled over the edge of the trench and fell flat on the bottom. He picked himself up and started brushing dirt from himself.

"Where's your rifle?" James asked.

"Left it with Horace."

"Then how———?" James started to ask, but Morgan came up behind him and squeezed his arm.

"You better get cleaned up and get some rest," Morgan said to Victor.

"Yeah."

Victor felt his way back to his place, and Morgan heard him cry softly. Victor cried for a very long time.

46

CHAPTER FIVE

For weeks Morgan's 9th Regiment attacked, gaining ground a yard at a time under shredded beech trees, over fields and meadows, and through rock-strewn thickets. Sometimes they had artillery support; often they did not. There were heavy casualties, and always more replacements.

Thorvold Vilander had been dead when he hit the ground, struck in the mouth by a bullet from a German rifle. Or from a machine gun. It was all the same. Word of his death was whispered through the company, but that was his only requiem, and no one spoke of him again.

Two new men arrived. One was George Armstrong, from somewhere in Wisconsin. The other was Simon Madsen from South Dakota. George was huge and soft looking, with a quick smile and a cheery disposition. Simon was his counterpart: small and dark, dour and pessimistic.

In the morning, early, Sergeant Shepherd briefed the key men of his company. "I been talkin' to the first lieut and the major, and it looks like the only direction is straight ahead." Sergeant Shepherd was bigger and tougher looking than Sergeant Remington. Broken nosed and square jawed, with several small, jagged scars running down each cheek, he looked like he'd been caught in barbwire. But it was his eyes that caught Morgan: dark, and deep set. The deepest Morgan had ever seen. "It's not gonna be easy, but it's gotta be done, and we're gonna hafta do it." The sergeant held up a map and tried to make it out in the dark. "We're here, in the middle, and the Twenty-third's way over there." He pointed to his left. "The leathernecks are right there." He lowered the map and pointed again. "Now, we're supposed to attack here. Chateau-Thierry's southeast of us. It's gonna be an all-out attack, and we're gonna try to cross the Marne. That's a river, right here." He jabbed the map.

Morgan could see his finger in the darkness, but not the map.

"I hope to hell we get across," Sergeant Shepherd said. "A lot's ridin' on whether the engineers get the pontoon bridges up in good shape. But that's not our job. Our job is to get to the river and get across if we can. Any questions?"

"Yeah, when do we go over the top?" someone asked.

"Any time now, so you'd best get back to your places."

Morgan and Lansing started down the line, crouching so as not to be seen in the predawn glow. Morgan had come to depend on Lansing.

"You know how to swim?" Lansing asked.

Morgan was behind him, and could not see his smile. "Nope."

"Me neither."

The first one hundred yards were easy, then the Maxims opened fire, and from then on it was the same leapfrogging advance as before. Morgan tried to concentrate on what lay before him, while maintaining contact with those on each side. He had seen Lansing on his left, and he was sure Mike O'Donnell was on his right, maybe twenty yards away. He crawled forward and positioned himself behind a rotting log. Ahead he heard the distinct sound of a potato masher going off. He put his helmet on a stick and lifted it over the log, waited, then peeked. He could see for thirty yards. He aimed at a clump of bushes and fired. There was no reply. He counted to sixty, then popped up and fired again. Still nothing. He counted to thirty, jumped up, and ran, crouching, to the next cover.

Morgan hugged the ground, breathing dust, waiting for the others to catch up. Lansing appeared, slithering in behind a tree stump, but Morgan didn't see Mike. Not wanting to waste a bomb, Morgan picked up a rock and threw it into the bushes. When there was no response, he stood and charged, bayonet waist high. His charge carried him through, and he fell flat,

48

probing with his rifle. Then he saw it: a foot sticking out from behind a boulder. He pointed without aiming and started to squeeze, but stopped. The uniform above the puttees was army khaki.

"You alright?" Morgan whispered. There was no reply. "Hey," he rasped. "You alright?" Again there was no answer. He reached with his bayonet and poked the hobnailed sole. The foot was limp. Morgan crawled forward. He looked up, horrified. The soldier sat with his arms outstretched on each side, tied between two small trees. From his stomach protruded a bayonet—his own—and his mouth was stuffed with rifle cartridges. Morgan lurched back, and even after all of the horrors he had seen, he went to his knees and gagged.

When he was through, Morgan wiped his mouth and looked again. The man's eyes were wide open, and he had the ludicrous look of a circus clown smoking a half dozen cigar butts all at the same time. Morgan touched the side of the dead man's face, and it was still warm. Then he noticed something. He pulled one of the cartridges from the man's mouth. The fronts of the bullets had been cut flat to tear through flesh better. Dumdums! He had been caught with dumdums! Damn fool. Nobody but a damn fool would do that. Musta been new.

Morgan cut the man's arms free, and the body slumped to one side. Morgan propped him up again and flipped the rest of the cartridges from his mouth with one finger, then he pulled out the bayonet and threw it to the ground.

Fear seized Morgan, gripping his throat. He picked up his rifle and cringed, checking himself to make sure he had not pocketed any of the dumdums. Then he crept on, to the next cover, and waited. It was only a matter of time.

"Crack!" Pain seared the right side of Morgan's face. He rolled sideways, clutching his rifle in front of him, until he hit something.

49

"Crack! Crack." Again the sound of bullets hitting rock, but no new pain. Morgan rubbed his cheek. It was bloody, and he could feel stone chips and grit embedded in it, but he could still see.

"Crack." He was trapped behind a boulder, and bits of it flew up and landed softly on him. Frantically he tried to see where the shots were coming from.

"Crack." Directly in front. Morgan looked desperately each way for an escape, but there was none. He fought back the panic that was squeezing his breath away, and tried to think.

"Crack." The firing had slowed. They were waiting.

"Whump!" A bomb went off in front of him, and Morgan struggled to remain conscious. His ears rang, and small points of light danced across the insides of his closed eyelids.

"Whump." Morgan reached for one of the British Mills bombs on his belt and threw it hard, knowing that whoever had the strongest arm would win.

"Ka-rump." Through the ringing in his ears Morgan heard a scream. He forced himself to his knees and stared wide-eyed into the dust of the explosion. A German soldier stood in full view, staggering in a circle, holding his face in his hands, with blood streaming down the front of his gray uniform. Another crawled on his hands and knees toward the first. Morgan lifted his rifle and fired at the one standing, and he heard the "thud" of his bullet hitting the German in the back. The man on the ground tried to scramble away. Morgan cranked, aimed, and fired, and the man's arms and legs flew out, and he fell flat and lifeless.

Morgan lowered his rifle and hung his head, numbed by what he had done, oblivious to the danger surrounding him. He was dizzy, and he sank to his knees, dropping his rifle beside him. He fell forward. His head hit the boulder in front of him, and he toppled sideways.

Morgan sensed someone. He opened his eyes, and he could see Lansing's mouth moving. Morgan pointed to the side of his face, and Lansing wiped the blood away with his grimy hand.

"Not so bad. That all?"

That time Morgan heard him, and he nodded his head.

"Well," Lansing exclaimed. "You sure did a job on those two Boche over there."

The crossing of the Marne was a disaster.

CHAPTER SIX

"Where the hell are we?" someone asked. "Frogland still looks all the same tuh me."

"Seems like the trees are thinnin' out," someone else said. His head was too small for his body, and he had a wide, flat nose. "I'm from Pennsylvania, an' I feel naked without trees. Specially if someone's shootin' at me."

"How many times did yuh get shot at in Pennsylvania?"

Some of the men in the squad had been there since the beginning, yet Morgan hardly knew them. Men like John Dempsey. John was the sort of man who looked older than he was. There was nothing else unusual about him, except for his muscular build. And his dark, unfathomable eyes. He was one of the silent ones who followed orders, did his job, never complained, and never volunteered. He was a private man, and that made it easier for Morgan to avoid any special connection. Nevertheless, because it was a rare quiet evening, something prompted Morgan to try to break the barrier. All he knew of John was that he had spent a short time in the Montana State Prison in Deer Lodge.

"How are your feet?" Morgan asked. He leaned on his rifle, looking down at John, who had his puttees and high-topped shoes off and was rubbing his toes. Most of the men had foot trouble of some kind.

"They'll be alright I reckon. Clean socks wouldn't hurt any." He hung his socks on the edge of the trench where they would catch the last glimmer of sunlight. Then he sat back and put his feet on his pack, wriggling his toes. His feet were red and raw.

"Yeah, well, if they get real bad let me know. I can put you on sick report."

"They'll be alright."

"Um." Morgan tried to continue the conversation. "Did you grow up in Montana?"

John glanced up curiously. "Naw." He didn't volunteer any more, and there was an awkward silence as he leaned over and rubbed his feet again.

Morgan changed the subject. "Seems like we've been here forever."

There was no reply.

"I'll try to get some powder for your feet."

"Thanks. I'd appreciate it," John smiled.

Maybe he wasn't such a bad sort after all; just quiet. Morgan couldn't help wondering about his prison background though. Perhaps it was nothing. Morgan had once known a man who had spent two months in the clink for poaching a deer.

"I heard they're gonna give us some louse powder too, but I'll believe it when I see it," Morgan continued.

"Yeah, that'd be great. Damn cooties can drive a man batty."

"Yeah." Morgan itched all over, more from talking about it than from the lice themselves. They were plenty bad though, and as if they weren't enough, a large dark-gray rat poked its head out of a hole, sniffing nearsightedly. The rats were unafraid, and not particular about the company they kept. Morgan controlled the urge to blast the rat with his rifle.

"So Vincent wants to be a sniper," John said.

"Guess so."

Vincent Giardello was another whom Morgan knew only superficially. He was from New York City.

John cleared his throat and rubbed his feet again. Something seemed to be troubling him. "Remember that poor devil who was trapped in the shell crater?"

"Yeah," Morgan replied.

"Well, it was Vincent that kept 'em from gettin' him out."

53

"Coulda figured that."

"I was right beside Vincent. Yuh couldn't talk to him or nothin'. He just wasn't gonna let that guy go. I kept tellin' him to aim high, but he wouldn't do it. He kinda went into a trance, or spell, or somethin'. I don't think he even heard me."

"Some guys are like that. They like it. The killing."

"Then he oughta be happy if he gets a sniper job."

"I suppose so," Morgan said.

John reached over and felt his socks. They were still damp, and the sun had gone down, but he left them where they were. He wasn't through talking. "I had a run-in with a guy like that once."

Morgan waited.

"Happened in a saloon in Forsyth. A guy was beatin' up two sheepherders, an' damn near killin' 'em. He had been pickin' fights for years. He was a big cowboy who spent most of his time in the bars. Well, I had had a few too many, and I got into it. Next thing I knew the cowboy was half dead, an' I was in jail. Turned out somethin' happened to his head, and it took him two days to wake up, and there was still somethin' wrong with him after that. So they had a trial, and I wound up in the pen."

"Seems to me you did the right thing."

"Maybe, but I felt bad about it. Anyhow, I spent six months there."

"They let you out early?"

"Naw. The judge figured the cowboy had it comin'. He'd been throwin' him in jail for years. Had'da give me somethin' though, so he gave me six months."

"Then what?"

"Joined the army."

"They took you, after prison?"

"Didn't tell 'em."

"Didn't they ask?"

"Nope."

Morgan slung his rifle over his shoulder. "Well, take care of those feet. I'll see about that powder."

"Thanks."

In the morning Morgan made the rounds: changing the watch, rousing the men, and preparing for the short briefing.

"Rise and shine, men! C'mon, let's go. Fritz is waitin', and we can't disappoint him." He leaned down and shook Lansing, then continued along the trench. It wasn't like Lansing to be one of the last up.

"Hit the duckboard, Clarence." It was only another old, shallow, crumbling trench, and there was no duckboard. Just soft mud. Putrid, life-sucking mud. Morgan poked Clarence easily with the butt of his rifle, and saw him stir.

Farther down, Morgan noticed that John was still rolled up in his blanket. "Hit the boards, John. Big day ahead."

John lay still.

"John."

"Ohhh."

"What ails you?"

John struggled to sit up, and Morgan helped him. "What is it?"

"Oh, boy, I feel rotten. Been throwin' up all night, and I'm hot."

Morgan felt his forehead. "Yeah, you're warm alright. When'd it start?"

"Right after we talked last night."

"You shoulda said something."

"Not much we coulda done about it." He stayed wrapped in his blanket, shaking. "I think it's the influenza," John stuttered.

"We gotta get you outta here. Hang on." Morgan hurried back to put him on sick report.

Then Bill Baldwin came running up. "It's Lansing. He's sicker'n a dog."

"The hell? Flu?" Morgan asked.

"I think so. Or dysentery. Been throwin' up and shittin' all night."

"John's got it too. Tell you what, since you're here anyway, why don't you take 'em back to the aid station?"

"Yo." Bill bustled away to collect his gear.

Morgan took some satisfaction in knowing that Bill would waste enough time to miss jump off.

Two days after John and Lansing became ill, Morgan collapsed and was taken to a makeshift field hospital. He spent the first three days unaware of his surroundings.

On the first day, Evangeline returned, and Morgan wondered how she had found him. As before, she comforted him, and he knew he had been delivered; he had escaped the bounds of reality.

On the morning of the second day Morgan woke, and Evangeline floated up and away, arms outstretched. He reached for her, but she faded, and he was too weak to follow. He let his arms fall to the bed, and he closed his eyes.

Morgan first saw the heavy wooden cross beams and the high, peaked ceiling, then the stone walls and the stained-glass windows. The stench in the cathedral was overpowering.

Morgan lifted himself on his elbows and slid to a half-sitting position, leaning against the headboard. Close to him men were vomiting, and others lay still; lifeless but for an occasional moan. Across the aisle were the war casualties, and there the atmosphere was different. Most of the men in that section were alert, because of the pain. Directly opposite

56

Morgan sat a man with only one leg. The man stared coldly back, and Morgan lowered his eyes.

The queasiness in Morgan's stomach developed into full nausea, and he searched frantically for something to be sick in. Just in time he leaned over the side of the bed and lost what little he had, managing to deposit most of it in a bucket. He picked up a dirty towel and wiped his mouth. The vomiting had brought tears to his eyes, but he felt better.

Morgan looked around again. The altar area of the cathedral was now a nurses' station. Morgan could see no doctors.

"What's the trouble, old son?"

Startled, Morgan turned to his left. There, sitting on the edge of the adjacent bed, was a man twice his age.

"Nothing, Sir. Just a touch of the influenza."

"Huh. No need tuh be callin' me Sir. I ain't no officer. Yuh think they'd put an officer in with a bunch a' guys like us?"

"Guess not."

"Not damn likely, lemme tell yuh. Flu, eh? Same as me. Say, you look pretty good for a guy who just came in. I've been here for awhile, an' I've seen 'em carry guys outta here what died from it. What yuh think a' that?"

The grizzled old veteran was an outlandish sight, sitting with his skinny legs dangling. His hair stuck up in all directions, except in back, and he hadn't shaved for days. Morgan chuckled at himself for mistaking him for an officer.

"Name's MacIntosh. Sergeant Alfred MacIntosh. Al." A cloud came over his face. "Well, I used tuh be Sergeant MacIntosh, till they busted me. Now I'm just plain old MacIntosh."

"What happened?"

"Never you mind what happened."

"Sorry."

"That's alright. I popped off to the lieut once too often, that's all. Anyways, I'll get my stripes back. They need men of experience," he said proudly. "This is nothin' but an army of boys, that's what it is. Look at you. You can't be over twenty years old. It's a hell of a thing when they send boys like you over. You oughta be home with your wife, raisin' a family or somethin'."

"I'm not married. And I'm older than that."

"Well, then yuh oughta be home sparkin' some young skirt."

Morgan forced a laugh, but again the mocking loneliness enveloped him. "What outfit you from?" he asked.

"Fifth Marines. You?"

"Ninth Infantry, Second."

"Huh, I thought so. Where you guys been all this time we've been doin' the fightin'?"

"Haw!" Morgan guffawed. "We've seen a little action."

"Yeah, with the girls, more'n likely."

"Well what's wrong with that?"

Suddenly Morgan felt better, and they both giggled like schoolboys. An elderly nurse shushed them on her way by.

"She walks like she's got a rod up her ass," Al whispered.

"Ha."

"Yuh didn't gimme yir name."

"Morgan."

"Yuh got stripes?"

"Corporal."

"Ohhh." Al rolled his eyes.

"Don't gimme shit. I didn't ask for 'em."

"Gets tuh be the weeds sometimes, don't it?"

"You're lucky you got busted."

"Huh. I been in the Marines a long time. Now I'm busted again."

"You're gonna get your stripes back, eh?"

"Oh, yeah. Colonel says so." He paused. "Anyways, with so many guys gettin' bumped, they're gonna need me. Not that I wish anything bad on anybody, but that's just a fact. Helluva war."

"Yeah, helluva war."

The next morning Al packed his things.

"You sure you're ready to go back?" Morgan asked.

Al stopped packing. "If they say I'm ready, I'm ready. No use arguin'. You oughta know that by now."

"Yeah. I was just wonder'n though."

"I'm alright."

"You stayin' in after the war?" Morgan asked.

Al waved a towel at the flies that were buzzing around his head. "Damn flies. You'd think in a hospital they'd have some way tuh keep flies out. They near carried me off the other day. One more fly and they woulda." He threw down the towel. "Nope. I like the Marines, but when this tour is over I'm goin' back tuh Iowa. Gonna raise hogs. Not many, mind you, just enough tuh keep me goin'."

"Hogs?"

"Yeah. I always liked hogs. We had 'em when I was a youngster. Yep, gonna raise hogs. Nothin' like standing in the pen sloppin' hogs, havin' them look up at yuh like they do. I think that would be real nice." He was serious, and he looked back over his shoulder to see if Morgan was laughing. He wasn't. "Hogs. Always wanted a hog farm."

Morgan scratched his head. He hoped Al would get his hog farm. That wasn't too much to ask.

"I'd like to have a farm someday," Morgan said. "Maybe in Montana."

59

"Well, I'm checking out now," Al said. "You take care a' yirself, son." He held out his hand, and Morgan stood unsteadily.

"You too, Sergeant."

Al picked up his things and headed for the nurses' station. He signed out, stopped at the door, waved, and was gone. Morgan would always remember Sergeant Alfred MacIntosh.

CHAPTER SEVEN

By the time Morgan got back to his unit, he had missed some of the heaviest fighting at Belleau Wood, but his reunion party was short lived.

"Tsee-tsee-tsee-tsee."

The Maxims were singing again, their death song.

"Tsee-tsee-tsee-tsee."

Morgan, Clarence Mudd, and John Dempsey had been caught in the open with a half dozen men from the 3rd Squad. Three of the men from the 3rd were already dead, and the rest had panicked. One was crying, and another had lost control of his bowels.

"Settle down," Morgan shouted over the din. "Here, get those men laid out in front of us! Hurry up."

He and Clarence and two of the others struggled with the corpses. John returned fire in the general direction of the closest Maxim.

"Alright!" Morgan screamed. "Get that other one over here. Hurry up before they hit us again!"

With desperate strength they maneuvered the third body into place, and they all rolled in behind.

"Now what?" someone asked.

"Now we wait," Clarence answered. "We ain't goin' nowhere." His easy Virginia accent seemed out of place.

"Wait for what?" the one who had lost control asked.

"Just wait," Clarence growled.

"We've gotta hope our boys'll get around on the flanks," Morgan said.

"Thud-thud-thud-thud." Bullets slammed into the dead men, making them quiver.

"Oh, God!"

"Take it easy," Morgan ordered. "You wanna live through this, just take it easy."

"Ohhh."

The man who was crying threw down his rifle and clawed at the ground, trying to dig in, but the soil was hard and rocky, and after a few minutes he gave up. His fingers were raw and bleeding.

John lifted his rifle to fire, but Morgan pushed it down. "Better play dead for a while. No use asking for it."

John lowered his rifle, and they all drew closer together. "Ohhh."

"For chrissake put a sock in it! We ain't dead yet."

Morgan was on the left, and he took a quick look in that direction. He could make out khaki uniforms advancing through the splintered trunks of what used to be a grove of trees. "There go our guys. Just hang on for a while longer."

They hugged the ground. Twice more machine gun fire stitched the bodies in front of them, and Morgan felt a wetness ooze onto his hand. Blood and excrement. Then the firing stopped, and they cautiously looked. There was little to see in the dust and smoke.

"Looks like our boys came through," John said.

"Yeah. Better wait a few minutes though," Morgan said. They counted out five minutes.

"Let's get the fuck outta here," one of the men urged.

They heard something whisper overhead, and there was a tremendous explosion behind them.

"Ka-wham!"

"Mortar."

Morgan rolled onto his back and looked up. He could see another one coming, a minenwerfer, wobbling with a faint whooshing sound. "Ka-wham!" The second explosion was closer, lifting them from the ground.

"That's it," Morgan called. "They wouldn't be dropping shells this close unless they were pulling back. Let's get the hell outta here."

"Which way?"

"Straight ahead. We'll take their trench, then see what happens. Go!"

They sprang to their feet, leaped over their fallen comrades, and stormed forward. Two hundred yards later they were in the abandoned German positions. Behind them, where they had been, mortar shells fell, and Morgan saw one land directly on the bodies. Arms, legs, and other parts flew up, hovered, and fell.

"Everybody here?" Clarence asked.

They counted heads.

"Yeah. What now?"

"Gotta find out where we are," Morgan said. "See anybody?"

"Ka-wham!"

"Damn! I don't see anybody, but I don't wanna get caught sittin' here when they pull that mortar fire back on us," John said. "Seems like we'd be better off stickin' right on their tails as long as they're on the run."

"Right," Morgan said. "You guys with us?" He looked at the others, and they nodded grimly. "Alright. A couple of minutes to rest, and we'll head out. Keep your eyes open for any of our men." As he spoke he caught something out of the corner of his eye. He swung around and leveled his rifle. Bill Baldwin came running up.

"Take it easy," Bill said. "Oh, it's you. Where you guys been? We thought you got bumped."

"Bumped! Didn't yuh see us out there?" John shouted.

"Yeah, but we thought you were all bumped. Sure glad to see you guys are alright."

John stood, shoulders sagging, glaring at Bill. Bill started to say something, but stopped.

"You seen Sergeant Shepherd or the first lieut anywhere?" Morgan asked Bill.

"No. But I think they're somewhere over there." He indicated a thicket of trees far to their right. "That's where they were heading."

They rested for a while longer. The German trench—a quickly thrown-up shelter—was strewn with tin cans, cigarette butts, and spent ammunition. One of the men of the 3rd Squad picked up a pistol. "Some Heinie forgot his six-shooter." It was a strange-looking automatic.

"What kinda gun is that?" Clarence asked.

"Luger. The sergeant's got one just like it," John said.

The new owner wiped the dirt from it and stuck it in his belt.

"Don't shoot your pecker off," John said.

"Ka-wham!" Another heavy mortar shell fell, and they all ducked.

"They're gettin' too close," Morgan said. "Let's move."

They checked their weapons, and crawled from the trench. Morgan led the way.

Drawing closer to the sounds of small arms fire, Morgan again felt the terror he thought he had left behind in the open field. But he advanced, as he always had. Far to the front he could see the quickly-formed German skirmish line, and he could just make out the gray steel helmets bobbing. The Germans had not had time to dig in.

Morgan's only comfort in the familiar faces all around— the men of the 9th Regiment—was that he would not be cut off. There was no greater fear than that of being trapped alone or in a small group, to wither and die.

Morgan's squad had regrouped, and they were on their stomachs again, crawling ever forward into the spitting, probing fire. Mike O'Donnell slithered up to Morgan.

"We got the bastards on the run this time," Morgan said. He said it roughly, but impersonally. By now few of the men felt any great individual hatred for their enemy. Morgan tried to smile, but it came as a macabre grimace.

Mike was carrying a Chauchat that he had picked up somewhere. "I'm gonna take this up on that high spot an' see if I can clear 'em outta that brush over there," he said.

Morgan sneaked a look. "I dunno. How you gonna get there?"

"It's not far. I can make it."

"Yeah, well, be careful."

Mike checked his newfound weapon, slapped Morgan on the shoulder, and jumped to his feet. But before he had taken the first step, he fell. It happened so fast Morgan was unaffected, staring curiously. Then he reached out and drew Mike back into the shelter of the rocks.

"Mike?" Morgan rolled him over.

Mike lay with his eyes open. Then he groaned, and blood stained his chest.

"Mike!" Morgan screamed. He grabbed the front of Mike's tunic with both hands and shook him.

Mike gurgled, and blood ran from his mouth, but there was a flicker of recognition in his eyes, and he was trying to breathe.

"Jesus, Mike." Morgan leaned over him, oblivious to the rifle fire overhead. He ripped open Mike's tunic, and the blood pulsed out faster, in a bright red, gushing stream. Then the stream stopped, and Mike was dead.

Morgan closed Mike's tunic. He remained kneeling, patting Mike, trying to console him. Trying not to look at his face.

By late afternoon the fighting had subsided. The Germans had regrouped and formed new lines, and the Americans were, in any event, too exhausted to continue. They fell into any natural positions they could find. Morgan's squad crouched in a road ditch. There were scattered trees in the meadows behind them and on both sides, and in front lay open fields.

A lone cow—black, with a white face—grazed on the trampled oat crop. Presently a farmer waving a white rag on a stick emerged from a stand of trees. The man was shabbily dressed in a tan shirt and black pants, and he walked unsteadily. He waved his way to the cow, retrieved it, and led it away, back into the trees.

Bill crawled over to Morgan. "Mike?"

"Bumped," Morgan answered.

"Where?"

"Back in the rocks. Got it in the chest."

Bill crawled away to tell the others, and after that Mike's name was never spoken again.

"Feeney."

Morgan turned, and there was Sergeant Shepherd. "Yeah, Sergeant."

"You alright?"

"Yeah, why?"

"You didn't answer. You were just sittin' there, staring. I thought maybe you were sick." He looked at Morgan suspiciously.

"Naw, just thinking," Morgan said.

"Well, believe it or not, the field kitchen kept up with us. They're back there, behind that tree row, and they're gonna try to bring us hot stew, so be on the lookout."

"Right."

"It'll be cold by the time it gets here, but at least we eat tonight." The sergeant looked older than usual, and tired.

"Alright."

"Be sure the sentries stay awake, and I want someone on the Shoshos at all times."

"Alright."

"We really raised hob with 'em today, Feeney."

"Sure did."

Sergeant Shepherd shuffled away. Morgan passed the word to the others. Cold stew was better than no stew.

"Oh, yeah," Sergeant Shepherd called back, "sorry about O'Donnell. Good man. They'll be sending somebody up to replace 'im."

"Alright." Morgan checked the sentries, then settled in to wait for the cooks' helpers. They would carry the dixies in wooden boxes insulated with straw, but the stew would still be cold.

Morgan hoped Sergeant Shepherd hadn't thought he was sleeping. They had been coming more often lately. The *fits*, as his father had called them.

CHAPTER EIGHT

The already-hot morning sun steamed the excrement of thousands of men, giving rise to an invisible, stinking cloud that lingered gently over the still-exhausted men of the 9th Regiment.

Sergeant Shepherd and Lieutenant Stafford worked their way down the road ditch to where Morgan and Horace Gray were sitting. They had two men with them. One was Lansing.

"Feeney. We brought you a little help," Sergeant Shepherd smiled. He approached, bent at the waist to avoid sniper fire. Lansing looked like he had been on a two-week bender.

"Well?" Morgan put his hand on Lansing's shoulder. "How you doing?" Lansing, the only exception to his strict rule about not forming attachments.

"Fine. Got to see that nurse of yours."

Morgan saw that he was joking. He looked past him at the lieutenant and considered saluting, but he rejected the idea, and the lieutenant didn't press it. Lieutenant Stafford was carrying a thin wooden baton.

"Feeney, this is Samuel Robbins, and he'll be with yuh from now on," Sergeant Shepherd said. "I trust you'll take care of 'im."

"Right, Sergeant. We'll get him settled in." Morgan and the replacement shook hands. "Robbins, eh. Where from?"

"Virginia, Corporal." He stood almost half a head taller than Morgan, and it seemed that most of his height advantage was in his legs. His head was long and narrow, as was his nose. He was thin and pale, and edgy.

"Well, don't worry, we'll get you fixed up. Here, this is Horace Gray. He'll take you to your position and start briefing you."

"Alright, Corporal." The new man hitched up his pack. "What happened to the guy I'm replacing? How'd he get it?"

Morgan and Horace stiffened. Morgan tried to keep the harshness out of his voice. "Don't worry about it right now. Just go on down the line, and Horace'll set you up. Keep your head down, if yuh don't wanna lose your can."

Samuel Robbins looked so young. Morgan was appalled at how much the ones who had been with the unit from the beginning had aged. He couldn't even stand to look at himself in a mirror anymore. He pushed Robbins away. From now on Robbins would be just a name. Better that way.

"Now, the lieutenant wants to see Vincent Giardello," Sergeant Shepherd said.

"Vincent? Sure. Somebody get Giardello over here," Morgan called.

As they waited, Sergeant Shepherd apologized. "Sorry, we give one, and we take one, but that's the way it goes. The Lord isn't the only one that giveths and taketh. We'll try to get someone to take his place."

Morgan glanced at the lieutenant, who was looking toward the enemy lines, twitching nervously. Vincent came up.

"You Giardello?" the lieutenant asked.

"Yes, Sir." Vincent saluted. He was small, and dark—almost black—with a thin, hooked nose; and he always looked like he was smiling. Like his mouth was on upside down.

Lieutenant Stafford's return salute was more of a quick wave. "You're to come with us. Let's go."

Vincent looked at Sergeant Shepherd.

"Yuh got what yuh wanted. Get your gear together."

Vincent smiled and disappeared. A minute later he was back. "See you later, boys," he said.

The lieutenant tucked his baton under his arm and walked away. Vincent followed, but Sergeant Shepherd lagged behind.

"Sorry, Morgan. I know you're short."

"Yeah, well I can't say as anyone's gonna miss him much. He did his job though, can't complain about that." Morgan thought a moment. "I guess most of the men would say he did it too well."

Sergeant Shepherd studied Morgan's face. "Well, now, he'll get plenty of that with the sniper unit, won't he?"

"Yeah."

"That's the kind it takes," Sergeant Shepherd continued. "Back at headquarters they call 'em mad dogs. At least that's what the colonel calls 'em. They like the killin'. To them it's a game, like hunting, or a damn turkey shoot."

"Maybe they're right," Morgan said.

"I'd better get going," Sergeant Shepherd said.

"See yuh."

"Yeah. Keep your head down."

"Thanks." Morgan watched Sergeant Shepherd trot away, crouching as always. Morgan wished his father had been like him. Not that Sergeant Shepherd was that old; he just seemed old. And there he was, taking orders from Lieutenant Stafford.

That night Morgan crept along the ditch, one careful step at a time. "Lansing?"

"Over here."

Morgan followed the sound. "So, how you doing?"

"Never better," Lansing answered, but he didn't sound very good.

"It takes some people a while to get over the grippe."

"Guess so. But no use lying around in a hospital, even if they'd let me. Pretty depressing. There was this marine in the bed next to me. He'd been gut shot by a sniper."

Morgan grunted.

"He had an infection. It was horrid, and there wasn't anything they could do, except give him laudanum or something.

It didn't seem to help much. Anyway, I had to listen to him, night and day, for as long as I was there. The night before I left he was quiet, but I could hear him breathing, and in the morning he was dead."

"God."

"The worst part was the smell. Jesus, I never smelled anything that bad before. I tried to get 'em to let me move my bed, but they wouldn't. I couldn't wait to get outta there." Lansing stopped abruptly.

"Good to have you back," Morgan said.

"Good to be back."

They heard a muffled boom, followed by the explosion of a medium artillery shell. It was far away.

"Didn't think the Boche had any shells left," Lansing said.

"They've been saving them for us," Morgan answered. Immediately he was sorry. "I didn't mean——"

"I know."

Another shell exploded. Morgan got up to leave. "Well, I've gotta get the listening post relief squared away," he said. "The lieut decided he wants them out every night from now on."

"That damn shavetail. I thought he'd have made general by now. Need any help?"

"Nope. You better get rested up. We've been seeing quite a little action lately."

"Right."

As Morgan picked his way down the ditch, the danger of having a friend chilled him.

The sun blinded Morgan. He panicked and groped for his rifle. He had never slept that long before, and he felt something must be wrong. Lansing was lying beside him, peeking over the road.

"What the hell's going on?" Morgan asked.

"Hell if I know, but don't rock the boat. I'm in no hurry."

"John get back?" John Dempsey had taken a wounded German back to the field hospital.

"Sure, but he had quite a time. The password was *jackass*, and when he gave it, some MP didn't like his tone. He damn near shot him for calling him a jackass. John sure was sore."

"Haw, haw, haw," Morgan laughed. "It'd be a helluva note to get knocked off by an MP. Haw, haw, haw!"

They both laughed. When they were through Morgan felt strange, like he had laughed too hard and too long over something not all that funny. It had happened before—overreactions like that—and it was starting to worry him. He had seen it in some of the others too. Sometimes the slightest thing set them off; laughing and giggling uncontrollably, or going into dark rages. Most often, however, a deep, silent depression would set in. And some were starting to act just plain queer.

The respite was short lived. At noon orders came that all units were to push off no later than one o'clock.

Morgan fought the sickness building in his stomach. No one who had not faced such battle could ever know the feeling of rising from a trench and advancing to near-certain death. He and his comrades seldom talked about it, but they lived knowing that sooner or later *the* bullet would find them.

At five minutes after one o'clock the order came to stand to. Then the waiting began again, and it was excruciating. There, lying against the side of the road, Morgan knew that some were surrendering, some were praying, and others were blaspheming. And that some had lost control, functioning on pure instinct. But they held steady, rifles ready, bayonets fixed. And as always, each was isolated from the others.

The American gunners opened with their French 75s. Morgan found it hard to concentrate. It was always that way. He looked at Lansing on his left, then he tried to focus on the new man, Samuel, on his right, but he was met with a look of animal fear, and he had to turn away. He tried to conjure a vision of Evangeline, but not even that worked, so he gave in to the terror, and his body trembled.

". . . and if the Holy Spirit is with you, you will never be alone."

Morgan sat between his parents, third pew back, right side. He could smell his mother's sweat under her perfume.

"So, I say to you, cast your lot not with the sinners of the world, but with the blessed. Do good, and you will be rewarded in the life to come. Do evil, and you will be barred from the Kingdom of Heaven for eternity. It's your choice, and yours alone."

Pastor Lundmann stood behind the pulpit, glaring at the congregation. The longer he spoke, the more his thin, white hair flew in all directions, and the fiercer he became. Morgan saw his eyes flash, and he could hear thunder from above the altar. Morgan was afraid, and he snuggled closer to his mother. He closed his eyes.

"Morgan. Wake up, it's time to go."

His mother thought he had fallen asleep.

Sergeant Shepherd ran down the line.

"Steady, men. Any time now. Steady. When we go over our only chance is to go right at 'em. No stopping. Stop and you're dead. They're not that far away, and maybe we can catch 'em by surprise."

Morgan knew better. They all did. They had the overwhelming disadvantage of being the attackers, and the enemy was two hundred yards away over flat terrain. The sergeant continued down the ditch, and as he went, Morgan felt forsaken. He fingered his bayonet, and his hand shook. He looked to his right again, and Samuel was still staring at him, transfixed. Morgan tried to smile, but nothing happened. Even though it was Samuel's first battle, Morgan abandoned him, turning away, resting his cheek in the dirt. The dirt didn't smell like the dirt at home. It had a rotten smell to it.

Sergeant Shepherd returned. He looked at his watch. "Ready now. When the shelling stops, move out." As if he had signaled, the guns stopped. "Go!" he shouted. "Go, go, go!"

All along the line whistles blew. Men jumped to their feet and charged, and Morgan heard a rough cheer that turned into an unnerving, primal lament. He ran, doubled up, intent only on getting his bayonet home. Halfway across the field he heard the familiar, terrible "thud, thud, thud," and he saw George Armstrong fall backward. Samuel stopped, straightened, and looked at George's shabby, bloody form. Then he turned and stared stupidly at Morgan.

"Move!" Morgan screamed. "Don't just stand there, keep moving." Instead, Samuel sagged to his knees beside George. Morgan ran toward him.

"You can't help," Morgan cried. He grabbed the terrified soldier by the back of his belt, lifted him with one hand, and shoved him forward. Samuel's long arms and legs flailed in all directions, but he held onto his rifle. He stumbled, and Morgan gave him another push. "Move or die, you sonofabitch! It's up to you!" Morgan shouted.

They ran together. Then, one hundred yards from the German line, Morgan pulled Samuel to the ground. "We've got to split up and try to keep moving. Remember, there's no going back. We either take their position, or we lie out here till they pick us off."

Samuel's eyes bulged from his narrow head, but he seemed to understand. He and Morgan were in a shallow

74

depression, and Morgan couldn't see how the attack was going, but he heard a Hotchkiss start up somewhere ahead, with its steady "put-put-put." Morgan didn't know how anyone could have lugged a Hotchkiss that far under such conditions, but the sound was comforting. The gun sputtered again, and again, and then a bomb went off. Then two more bombs. Perhaps the German line had been broken.

Morgan called to Samuel, and to Lansing. "Now's our chance. Go!"

They stood and ran straight ahead until they were only fifty yards from where they had heard the Hotchkiss and the bombs. Morgan knew if he was wrong about the breakthrough, they were dead.

Thirty yards out Morgan slowed, trying to see better. Through the dust he saw the Hotchkiss hammering. The gunners were in a shallow, natural ditch, and the Germans were firing back; mostly rifle fire to cover the pull-back of their trench mortars. Morgan jumped down, and Samuel followed. Then Lansing rolled in, landing in a pile of empty tin cans.

"How the hell did you get here?" Morgan screamed to the gunners.

"Damned if I know. Just lucky I guess."

Morgan watched the loader. He was skinny, and he had a high-pitched voice. The gunner was swarthy and muscular. He stopped firing. "Damn," he said. "I can't keep this up or we'll burn 'er out. They're getting ready to counterattack. Boy am I glad to see you guys."

"Where is everybody?" Lansing asked.

"Two of our boys got it when we took this place," the loader said. "They're down there." He pointed.

"Samuel, go down and fetch their rifles," Morgan ordered. "Hurry up. And bring their ammo." Samuel scurried down a shallow ravine. "And bring their water, if they've got any," Morgan shouted after him.

"And the rest?" Lansing asked.

"Dunno," the gunner answered. "What outfit you guys with?" He kept his eyes to the front as he talked.

"Company D," Lansing replied. "They should be around here somewhere."

Samuel came back carrying two rifles, two bandoliers, and two canteens. He looked shaken. "Here," he mumbled. He held out the water to Morgan.

"I'll take those," the loader said. He snatched the canteens from Samuel's hand. "We need 'em to cool the gun barrel. We're all pissed out."

Morgan took the bandoliers. "Alright, this is where the cheese gets binding," he said to Samuel. "There's boo coo a' those bastards getting ready to come at us. You and Lansing each take two rifles. When they counterattack, let 'em have it. I'll be right between you, reloading. That'll give the rifles time to cool."

The three set up. There was sporadic rifle fire, and they could hear orders being shouted. It was almost time. A Maxim chattered, and rock chips flew up in front of the Hotchkiss gunners.

"Sheee," the loader whistled as they ducked. "Hold onto your balls, here they come. This is gonna be quite a scrap."

The Maxim stopped, and like specters the Germans arose and came toward them.

"Must be a hundred of 'em," Samuel gasped. "This is gonna be a ripsnorter."

"Give 'em hell!" Morgan shouted.

There were less than twenty-five, but they were closing fast. The Hotchkiss jumped, snarling and biting, and Lansing and Samuel fired, barely aiming. Morgan loaded, and he kept a bomb ready.

It was over in a minute, and only three of the Germans turned and ran. The rest were dead or dying.

76

CHAPTER NINE

The Allies took Belleau Wood, and on July 1st the 2nd Division captured the village of Vaux. Morgan and his companions—like all of those in the trenches—didn't know much, but they knew where they were. Two days later Morgan's division was pulled back for rest, and held in corps reserve near Montreuil aux Lions.

The 9th Regiment was camped in a meadow, surrounded by trees. Morgan lay under a huge linden, staring up through the branches. He relented, and allowed himself to remember again those who had fallen. First Ivan Ivanka and Sergeant Remington. Then Philbert Stanford, Thorvold Vilander, Mike O'Donnell, and George Armstrong. And just two days ago, James Walker, Bill Baldwin, and Alvin Maxwell. Bill had been hit in the face. His big, round, baby face, that was no longer young. James had been less fortunate. Wounded, he had lain alone for most of a day, trying to keep his intestines in. Alvin, the kid from Fort Benton, had been blown to bits by a blind pig. A trench mortar shell so big it had left only his egg-shaped head, and not much of that.

Morgan saw his dead comrades. Ivan, shocked and confused, wallowed through the mud in the bottom of a trench, until he reached the duckboards. He followed the duckboard trail skyward, until he disappeared. Bill smiled, but his smile dissolved and turned bloody red. James Walker sloshed past; the tall, thin farm boy who had lied about his age. Mike, Thorvold, and George; pulling themselves from the quagmire. Alvin, an egg-shaped head without a body. And when the last was gone, they came again, and again. Ivan, writhing in agony, his head lolling to one side. Thorvold, carrying his Springfield, bent under his pack. George, looking down and waving at Morgan; a grim and humorless wave. Again came Sergeant

Remington, shouting at those before him. Behind him was someone from another platoon who had been hit by a trench mortar. Half of his face was gone; replaced by a mask. The mask had tears painted on it. On they marched, out of the mire and onto the boards, dissolving into the clouds.

Morgan sat up, shaking. It was a beautiful, cloudless day, with a warm breeze and the smell of flowers. Roses perhaps, only he hadn't seen any. A mockingly serene day.

Someone was watching. There, under the next tree, sat a new man. The replacement looked down, embarrassed, but it was too late. He got up and walked away. His name was Tom Livingstone, and he was young and scared. That was all Morgan knew about him, and that was all he wanted to know. There were so few of the original men left.

Morgan went looking for Lansing. "Barn door," he called.

Lansing sat naked, picking lice out of his clothes. "Bonjour," he said. "Your French is getting better. Say, aren't we supposed to get deloused one of these days?"

"That's the word." Morgan itched from his own lice.

"Well, I sure am sick of these damn things," Lansing groused.

"Yeah."

"How many new guys?"

"Four."

"Any good?"

"Dunno. Probably not. Scared stiff. Guess I should talk to 'em. Don't know what good it would do."

"Yeah. You hear about that basket case over in the Third? They said he's still alive, but they never did find his arms and legs."

"So what does a guy say to the new meat?" Morgan sat down and watched Lansing pick lice.

79

"You know, old top," Lansing said, "it wouldn't be so bad if we knew what the hell we were doing over here. You ever think of that? I mean, sure, we're supposed to kill the Huns and all, but what for? How did this thing get started in the first place? Remember when we captured those Boche down in that ditch by the barn? There was the one who could speak a little English? Well that night we talked, and he showed me pictures of his family. Had a wife and a little girl. Hell, Morgan, he was just like you and me, except he talked funny. Doesn't that make you wonder?"

"You aren't becoming a pacifist, are you?" Morgan smiled.

Lansing looked around to be sure no one was listening. "Naw, I'm no pacifist. But dammit, I just don't know. Seems like if we could all just sit down and talk things over, without the kaisers and kings and presidents and premiers, maybe we could figure things out, and then go home. That's all."

Morgan sobered. "Well, not much chance of that, so no use going on about it. Anyway, you're not the first to think that. That's old stuff. People even write books about it."

"Guess you're right, but I'll tell you one thing. If I ever do get through this, I'm gonna go to college, and then get into politics. And I'm gonna do my level best to see we don't ever get into another mess like this."

"Good luck."

A truck stopped in front of the YMCA tent on the east end of the meadow. The driver and another man got out and began unloading boxes.

"I've come to believe in fate, like Napoleon," Lansing rambled. "I read about him. He believed in his lucky star. It's kinda that way with me now that I've got something to believe in. It's like I've got a mission in life that's too important to be wasted by me getting bumped. A guy's gotta have something to believe in. I know what's right and what's wrong, and I tell you,

I'm gettin' damn sick of watching people die, all because of a bunch of politicians and bigwigs. They're the ones who should be out here gettin' their asses shot off, not us. The average guy doesn't have a chance." He threw his tunic aside and looked at Morgan.

"Well?"

"Yeah, I guess you're right," Morgan mumbled. "Christ, you're turnin' into quite a philosopher."

"Maybe so, but I'm damn mad. This whole thing is nuts. It's like we're in hell, only from what I hear, nobody knows it. I just talked to one of the new guys—Melvin what's his name over there—and he said back home it's like a big, glorious game." He gestured across the way toward Melvin Dix, a thin, boyish-looking youngster who was standing watching the men unload the truck. "But believe me, when this is all over and people start counting how many of us didn't come back, things are going to change. They'll think twice before getting us into something like this again."

"Maybe," Morgan answered.

"No maybe about it. Jeez, you think we'll ever get mixed up in something this bad again? People are nutty, but not that nutty."

"Umph. Trouble is, most of 'em aren't very smart, and they're the ones doing the fighting, while the big boys pull the strings."

"Well, one thing I'd like to see is a law—maybe a constitutional amendment—that would make the president, the vice president, and congressmen be the first to the front lines in any war. Then see how many damn wars we get into."

"That's some rot," Morgan blurted. "Where do you get such queer ideas?"

"I've read. The ancient Greeks—guys like Plato—were always talking about the ideal government, and I think sometimes the simplest ideas that at first sound so goofy are the best. And Plato was right there in the front lines too."

"Well maybe so, but you're right, it sure does sound goofy. In the first place, nobody's going to pass a law like that. And in the second place, who'd run the country?"

"You just wait till people realize what they've done to our generation. All they hear now is propaganda, but how about when the truth comes out? And who'd run the country? The ones who were against war, that's who! Send the pro-war ones to put their lives where their mouths are."

"It'd never work."

"Why not?"

"Because people have short memories, and it'll always be the piss ants like you and me doing the fighting, while the windbags and business tycoons—merchants of death—play free and loose with our lives. That's the way it is, and that's the way it'll always be. It's just human nature."

"But it doesn't have to be that way," Lansing argued.

"Yes it does."

"Why?"

"Because those in higher positions are smarter than the rest of us. Look around." Morgan waved the back of his hand at the men who were scattered about. "Most of 'em are dumber'n sin. Regular guys, but basically stupid. The smart ones rise to the top like cream, and the rest of us—the masses—sink to the bottom. You think these guys, and the millions like them, are intelligent enough to do anything about their own lives? Hell, Lansing, ten years after the war most of the people back home won't even remember it. We will, if we live, but the average guy won't. And anyway, they'll be too busy trying to make livings. Trying to survive."

The discussion grew heated. Lansing stood and paced. He was a ludicrous sight without any clothes, circling Morgan and waving his arms, declaiming. "Don't you see? That's why

82

some of us have to stand up and make sure people remember, and that this never happens again. I have faith in people, Morgan. I still believe that humanity can advance. That's why, when this war is over, I'm going to——"

Morgan laughed. "You're a sight to behold, Lansing."

They argued for another half hour, until they were tired of arguing. In the end all Morgan would concede was that Lansing's ambitions were laudable.

Later, back under his linden tree, Morgan was disquieted. How superficially he had known Lansing. Or anyone else in the squad. And how little they knew of him. Of the barren, socially destitute life he had led.

Lila Gorman. Morgan had been fond of her ever since the first day of school. Then, when they were thirteen, something had changed. Affection had become infatuation, but after an initial flirtation, she had rebuffed him. Morgan had never known why, and still he wondered. Perhaps his affliction. But he had, through some inner deception, managed to preserve her memory, not as she was—married, with children, growing prematurely old on a farm—but as he wanted her to be. As he lay alone—a soldier of the Great War—he could see her as clearly as if she were there. She stood before him smiling, holding out her hand. She was beautiful, with fair complexion, dark eyes, and shiny black hair that fell to her shoulders, and Morgan still loved her.

Across the meadow a football game was going on, and on the west end of the clearing some of the men were constructing a boxing ring. Closer by, men sat playing cards. Most of them had no idea of the value of their money, and the object seemed to Morgan to be to lose as many francs as possible, in the shortest time, to the slickest shark.

Time off was on a rotation basis, and—money or not—all were eager for their turn to get to a town. Any town. Morgan

83

and Lansing had three-day passes for the following week, and until then they would have to worry about some military crisis interfering with their plans.

Morgan looked up at a bee that was buzzing around his head. Then, through the tree branches, he saw propaganda leaflets falling from a balloon, and as they fluttered to the ground, he picked one up. Out in the meadow men abandoned their card games and other pursuits to scamper, laughing and shouting like children. The German efforts were regarded as hilarious, and the leaflets made good toilet paper. Morgan crumpled his and tossed it aside. He got up and headed for the YMCA tent.

Inside, men sat at tables drinking coffee, eating cookies, and playing games; mostly checkers. There was standing room only, and the crowd spilled outside, where others smoked, read, or simply relaxed, trying to forget.

The Y men were paradoxical. The front-line troops saw them as slackers, a level below ambulance drivers. At the same time, they grudgingly—and privately—acknowledged that they should have done the same thing on religious grounds, whether they were religious or not. Morgan wished he were in the Y.

CHAPTER TEN

Morgan looked up. The early-morning sky was clear and blue, like the Montana sky on a warm summer day. The distant rumble of artillery could have been thunderstorms rolling across the prairie.

Morgan tested the tension on the top rope of the boxing ring. The fights were scheduled for that evening, and the only participant from Morgan's platoon was John Dempsey, who had been inveigled into fighting for the company. John weighed around one hundred sixty pounds, and he was supposed to be matched with someone his own size, but he was worried. He had heard the company was short a heavyweight. He didn't mind fighting, but he didn't want anything to do with heavyweights, especially if they knew what they were doing.

Morgan walked to the other side of the ring, glad he wasn't one of the company's sacrificial lambs. Most of the men of Company D had never even been in a bar fight. Lieutenant Stafford and the major had tried to talk Morgan into participating, but he had flatly refused unless ordered to do so. He had heard there were some professional fighters lined up, and he figured it would be just his luck to draw a pro, in which case his ring career would probably last about twenty seconds.

"How do, Morgan Feeney?"

Morgan jumped. "Well, I'll be switched! Jake Hermann." Jake, the prizefighter.

"Never thought I'd see you again," Jake said. He took Morgan's hand.

"What the devil are you doing here?" Morgan asked. Jake looked like he had just lost a fight, but on second glance Morgan saw something worse than physical pain. Whatever it was had contorted Jake's face, twisting one side up into a leering smile, and the other side down into a grimace.

85

"I'm with the headquarters staff. Orderly, mostly. You?"

"Front line."

"Oh." Jake looked at him curiously. "Rough go?"

"Yeah. Not much fun. Seen a lotta guys go west."

There was an awkward pause.

"But, what the hell," Morgan exclaimed. "Maybe the war'll end tomorrow. Anyway, you're looking good. Mercy, I never thought I'd run into you, out of all the millions of guys over here."

"Yeah, long way from Montana. Training seems like such a long time ago."

"Yeah," Morgan said. He put his back to the ropes and hung with his arms outstretched. "How's headquarters duty?"

"Fine. It's a good job." Jake thought for a moment. "Lotta nonsense though."

"What do you mean?"

"Oh, troops ordered this way, then that. Lotta bickering between officers, squabbles with the French, that sorta thing. Just seems like a helluva way to run an army."

"Oh."

"Still, I shouldn't squawk. I guess it isn't so bad."

They looked up to watch an airplane. French. Morgan guessed it was a Nieuport 28, but maybe it was a 27.

"That guy better watch out," Morgan observed. "Our Archie gunners brought down one of our own airplanes just the other day."

Jake didn't seem interested. They walked to the shade of a tree. "What outfit you with?" Jake asked.

"Ninth Regiment. Company D, right over there." Morgan pointed at a row of tents. "Finally got a little time off."

Jake started to say something, then stopped. As they both struggled to break the silence, a football landed nearby.

86

Morgan picked it up and threw it back. Then they talked about Montana, and about training camp. Finally it came out.

"You never saw any of the others?" Jake asked. The downward side of his face sagged even more, like it was melting.

"Well, I thought I ran into Barry Saul, but it wasn't him. It was some sniper. Looked like hell. Too much killing, like the guys in slaughterhouses who hit the cows between the eyes with sledgehammers. Eventually they can't take it anymore, even if it is just cows."

"I guess not. Anyway, I've been keepin' an eye out for Sydney," Jake said. "You remember him? My manager."

"Sure I remember Sydney." Poor Sydney. The army was rough on poufs. Well, Sydney wasn't exactly a pouf, but to most soldiers, guys like him were all the same. "You haven't seen him?"

"No. Thought maybe you had."

"No."

Jake turned away. "I guess I'll run into him sooner or later," he said softly. He looked back at the ring. "You fighting?" he asked.

"Me? Naw. I reckon I've got enough knocks on the head." Morgan rubbed the back of his scalp with his fingertips. It still hurt. "How 'bout you?"

"No, not likely."

"Why not?"

"Wouldn't be fair."

"I hear there are gonna be some pretty good boys entered. Maybe even some pros."

"Maybe so." There was no arrogance in Jake's voice. "A man knows how good he is at what he does. I'm good, Morgan. Maybe the best there is—at least I used to be—and there's no use hurting somebody just to prove it. Anyway, I'm gonna be the referee." Jake's voice was low, and he spoke slowly, like he was talking mostly to himself. Another wave of pain crossed his face.

"What's the trouble, Jake? Something eating you?"

"Could be worse. I mean, the job isn't bad, and all. It's just that . . ."

Morgan was uncomfortable. He was not used to people talking that way, and he wanted no more allegiances. Lansing was enough. Too much. "What? What is it?"

"Morgan, there's something wrong. I have headaches all the time, and I'm not thinking right." Jake rubbed his forehead with his fingers. "Something's gone haywire, that's all I know. Maybe I got hit in the head too many times. And the doctors won't believe me. They think I'm trying to pull a fast one."

"A fast one?"

"Yeah. To get discharged." Jake looked around to make sure no one was close. "Keep this dark."

"Yeah, sure," Morgan replied.

Jake's face hardened. "No, I mean really dark."

"Yeah. Christ, you can trust me."

"Alright." Jake looked around again, and then down at the ground, and Morgan could barely hear him. "I tried to blow myself up with a Mills bomb."

"You what?"

"You heard me."

"What happened?"

"It didn't go off."

"Didn't go off? I never heard of one not going off, and I've thrown plenty."

"Well, this one didn't."

"What did they think?"

"They think I fixed it so it wouldn't go off. They found a Tommy bar on me, so they assumed I'd fiddled with the fuse."

"You hadn't fixed it?"

"Hell no!" Jake looked up, and Morgan could see the desperation in his eyes. "They think I'm just another slacker."

"But why? Is it that bad?"

"Sometimes. I don't know what to do. Things look a little better today though. Maybe I'll get over it."

Morgan lay alone in his tent. From across the clearing came cheers as the first two combatants tried to beat each other's brains out.

Maybe Jake was right. Maybe he had been hit on the head too many times. Or maybe something inside had just gone haywire. Sometimes things just happen.

Morgan got up. Bullshit. He knew what it was. Jake couldn't get along without Sydney. A couple of poufs in a man's war. Well, at least they had each other. They would again, if they both made it through the war.

Morgan took a long drink of the pinard he had hidden in his pack. It was bitter, and acid tasting. He put it away, and went to watch Jake referee the fights.

Two middleweights were at it. One—large and muscular, with a strong chin and dark hair all over his body— was being pummeled about the ring by the other, who was smaller and blond, and less well built.

In round four the smaller fighter had mercy. He stopped, lowered his gloves to his waist, and took a right cross on purpose. He went to one knee and stayed there, while Jake counted him out. Then he got up and helped his unsteady opponent back to his corner. The winner sat with glazed eyes and blood running from his nose while the crowd booed.

The air was warm and fresh, and Morgan was surrounded by life, but he was afraid. Afraid in a different way than before. Before, he had been afraid to die. Now he wanted to live. There was a difference.

CHAPTER ELEVEN

Morgan, Lansing, and John Dempsey had found a place in the back of the tavern where it was dark. John sat with his elbows on the table, holding his head in his hands. His glass was still full.

"I tell you, a little wine'll make you feel as good as new," Morgan said.

John looked at him from between his fingers. "Ohh."

The tavern was dark and dirty, with brick walls and small, grimy windows. There was a thin layer of straw on the floor.

Lansing lifted his glass to propose a toast, and Morgan joined him, but John closed his eyes and squeezed his fingers together.

"Ohh, that guy nam near tooh muy heah uff."

"What?" Lansing asked.

"I said that guy damn near took my head off."

"He was no slouch. At least it didn't last long," Morgan consoled.

John glared at him through his fingers.

"Well, all I meant was, maybe it woulda been worse if it had gone on longer. This way he knocked you cuckoo right away and got it over with. Anyway, you gave it your best shot, and that's all anyone can ask."

"Yeah, then wha the heah weren't you thin there?"

"What?"

"I said, if you think it's so much fun, why the hell weren't you in there getting your brains beat out?"

"Maybe he wants to keep the brains he's got," Lansing offered.

"Shit."

Lansing waved to the girl at the counter. "Another." He held up their bottle.

Morgan stared. The girl was well endowed, with black, shoulder-length hair and a warm, genuine smile. Her long, straight nose and prominent cheekbones made her attractive.

Morgan emptied his glass, then he sat looking around. Mostly soldiers—French and American—but the glow of the wine made them seem distant, and it dulled their smell. In the corner near the far end of the bar an old man—the owner—sat dozing on a stool, and for more than an hour Morgan and Lansing had been speculating on which way he would fall.

The girl brought another bottle and took some money from the table. From close up she had a dull, peasant look. The remaining, well-worn five and ten franc notes before them looked fake, and the franc coins reminded Morgan of quarters. He and Lansing had been worrying all night that she was taking too much. John didn't care.

"I told Jake to help you out," Morgan said to John. "You know, the referee?"

"How could he help him out?" Lansing guffawed. "It didn't last long enough. He took one sock on the jaw, and that was it."

John took offense at that. He put his hands on the table and glowered at Lansing. "Did you have money on me?"

"Naw, but I didn't have any on the other guy either. I'm true blue."

"That was big of you. You're a fine fellow. A real pal."

"Thanks."

"Fuck you."

Morgan reached across the table and pushed John's glass closer. "Drink some more of that and you'll feel better."

John eyed the glass for a moment, then he took it in both hands and drank, gulping down the whole thing. He banged the glass down. "There. Satisfied?"

"Yeah. Have another." Morgan refilled his glass.

"I think he broke my jaw."

"Can you chew?" Lansing asked.

"Yes."

"Then it isn't broken."

"How do you know?"

"If you can chew, it isn't broken."

"How the shit do you know that?"

"A body snatcher told me once when I was helping him load his ambulance. Some guy claimed he had a broken jaw, but——"

"Oh, jeez. Come off it!"

The conversation and the wine were working wonders on John. Lansing held up his glass and toasted him.

"To you."

"Fuck you."

"That's the spirit!"

Lansing wasn't ordinarily a needler, but the cheap wine was taking hold. Morgan tried to change the subject. "Sure was good to see Jake again."

They both looked at him blankly.

"The referee. The guy who tried to blow himself up."

"Oh, yeah," John said. "Mercy, if I was gonna do myself in, I sure as hell wouldn't do it with a Mills bomb."

"Why not?" Lansing asked. He poured himself another glassful of wine. "It'd be fast."

"Ha! I've seen guys survive for days with their insides blown out."

"Just hold the bomb up to your head then."

Morgan was getting queasy. "Jake's a clerk. He wouldn't know to do that," he said.

"Then he shouldn't be trying to kill himself, if he can't do it right," Lansing countered. He was getting sloppy.

"That's my point," John smiled smugly. "He shouldn't be using a bomb."

Evidently John's head was better, but Morgan's was starting to hurt. Morgan sat back and listened to John and Lansing argue about the best way to commit suicide.

". . . and you put the barrel in your mouth, see, like this." John opened his mouth and poked his index finger in. "You aim up, like this, and pull the trigger with your toe."

Morgan closed his eyes.

"Thump!" Morgan opened his eyes and looked up. He was lying on the floor between his fallen chair and the table, and people were laughing. An elderly lady—possibly the waitress's mother—came over and began scolding him in French. She pointed at the door.

"C'mon, old-timer, she's inviting us to leave," John said. He helped Morgan to his feet, then he turned and pulled Lansing out of his chair. John and Lansing each flung one of Morgan's arms over their shoulders. Morgan groaned as they dragged him across the room, and as they departed, they were given a resounding round of applause. The irate lady let loose with one last torrent, waving both hands in disgust, then she turned to their table and began stuffing the last of their money into her apron pocket.

"Go to hell, you old dirty-neck bitch," John called back.

The late-morning heat of the tent woke Morgan, and by the time he got back from the latrine, Lansing was awake.

"Oh boy, have I got a head," Lansing moaned. He sat on his cot with his elbows on his knees and both hands on top of his head.

"Bad night all the way around I reckon," Morgan commiserated, though he didn't feel so bad himself. Then he remembered telling John and Lansing about Jake trying to blow himself up with a Mills bomb, and he was ashamed. Wine was no excuse for breaking a confidence.

"Ohhh," Lansing moaned again.

"We missed mess."

"Good. Oh, that cheap wine."

"Now you know why they call it bull piss."

Lansing didn't, or couldn't, answer. It was hot and stifling in the tent, but apparently he was too sick to move. Finally he had to answer the call of nature, and he staggered outside. When he got back he looked a little better. He started putting on his clothes.

"How's John?" Lansing asked as he pulled on his shoes.

"Dunno. Haven't seen him. If the fight didn't kill him, the wine should have."

"Killed who?" John stood holding back the flap of Morgan and Lansing's tent.

"You. We thought maybe you were dead," Morgan said.

"Heck no! Feel like a newborn babe. I guess I could go another five rounds."

"Huh," Lansing muttered. "Whaddyuh mean, *another*?"

"Well, Morgan was right; that wine sure fixed my head. Just what I needed, a night out with you rounders." He came in and sat on Morgan's cot. Say, d'ya hear about that friend of yours; Jake?

"No, what?"

"He got ahold of another Mills bomb."

"Oh, Christ."

"But, listen to this, it didn't go off either."

"What?"

"Another dud."

"No," Morgan gasped. "He's still alive?"

"Hell yes. Musta been a bad batch a' Mills bombs."

"Where is he? I better get over there."

"Yuh can't. He's gone."

"Gone? Where?"

"Well, I'm not sure, but the dope is that they thought he was fakin'—two duds in a row—and they sent him into a line company. Third Division I think."

"Oh, Lord. Just what he wanted." Morgan sat down hard. "I've gotta talk to the colonel."

"It won't do any good."

"I've still gotta try."

CHAPTER TWELVE

Morgan sat picking lice from his shirt—a futile but compelling pastime—while Lansing wrote in his diary. They had hunkered down along the edge of a potato field, behind a stone fence. The 9th was on the way back to front.

"What day is it?" Lansing asked.

"July 16th."

"Where are we?"

"Place called Montreuil I think," Morgan said.

Some of the men were munching on raw potatoes that they had dug. An old farmer in a blue uniform with red trim, and a tall hat, had chased them off with a musket.

"That old guy had an excellent command of French," one of the potato-eaters said. "I understood every word."

"He didn't sound like a Sunday school teacher," said another. "What kinda uniform was that? He musta fought with Napoleon."

"If he did, he's a hundred thirty years old."

Sergeant Shepherd hurried down the line, followed by a stoop-shouldered private.

"Feeney, see if yuh can get this man a beak cover. The Krauts have been gassin' heavier than ever. Oscar Benson, this is Morgan Feeney. He'll take care of yuh. Where'd you say you were from?"

"Oklahoma, Sergeant."

95

Morgan and the new man—really just another kid—shook hands.

"Get ready, you dust-disturbing pacifists," Sergeant Shepherd said as he walked away.

"Lansing, you wanna ramrod the new guys for a few days?" Morgan asked.

"Yeah." Lansing put away his diary.

Morgan looked back across the potato field and saw Lieutenant Stafford and a colonel studying a piece of paper. Probably a map. Morgan spat on the ground, and put on his shirt. "Alright men, toot sweet! We're gonna move out. No use crabbing about it. For chrissake don't forget your gaspirators, unless you like breathing hash. Check your ammo and your water. You have to shit, do it now, and don't take all day. We've got a long march ahead."

Morgan stopped and watched two other replacements check their gear. One was Elmer Sitwell, a butcher's assistant from New York City, and the other was Francis Cook, from some little town in Maine. Francis had just opened a barber shop when he was called up.

"Keep a stiff upper lip, boys," Morgan said. He made himself smile. The two were on their knees in the dirt, poking things back into their packs. Elmer straightened and returned the smile. He was short and blond; ordinary looking except that he didn't have a chin. The other, Francis, was also short, and he was heavy, with bulging eyes, like a frog. He was preoccupied, trying to decide what to take and what to leave.

"You'll be better off carrying too little than too much," Morgan said. "You think you'll be able to throw it away if it gets too heavy, but you'll be worn out by then. If it isn't absolutely necessary, leave it."

Francis pulled out a book and threw it into the dirt behind some bushes. It was a Bible. Elmer gobbled down two chocolate bars, gave two to Francis, and offered one to Morgan.

96

He also left behind a deck of cards and two tins of iron ration. Nearby, Horace Gray and Simon Madsen sat resting. They had not accumulated anything to leave behind.

"Well, it was good while it lasted," Horace said.

Simon's answer was a stream of tobacco juice through his front teeth.

"Whata sourpuss," Horace said. "What's eating you?"

"Don't seem tuh me like we got much tuh sing an' dance about," Simon answered. "Some rest," he snapped. "Don't do a feller no good a'tall, knowing that pretty soon yer gonna be right back in the meat grinder again."

"Every day off the line is a chance the war'll end."

"Bull! It'll go on forever, and we don't have the chance of a snowball in Hades of makin' it through. Just lookit those new guys over yonder. More meat for the grinder, that's all."

"Now, now. I suspect things'll be winding down pretty soon."

"Bunk! I told yuh, I got it from that guy at headquarters troop, that the Heinies are launching a big counterattack. Yuh just don't wanna believe me, do yuh?"

"Don't chew so much a' that damn snoose. You're gonna get thirsty on the way."

Simon spat again, and the glob landed near Horace's feet.

Morgan turned away from them and stood looking at Lieutenant Stafford and the colonel. He felt that at times like this he should have a premonition. Some dark, foreboding sense of what lay ahead. But he didn't. Nothing. Just the wish that it would all be over with. Maybe it would be better to be like Victor.

Victor Steele, Clarence Mudd, and John Dempsey all lay under a tree with their heads on their gear. Victor looked like he was sleeping, with one hand on his rifle. He moved only once, and that was to put his helmet over his face to keep away the flies. Everybody gave him an extra-wide berth, because of the rumors. Not to mention his mercy-killing of the trapped German.

Perpetually-surprised Clarence was fidgety. "Yeah, Simon got it from the top. There's somethin' big comin', and it looks like we'll be right in the middle of it." He waited for a response, but there was none. "What the hell's holdin' us up? This waitin' is worse than anything. Hurry up and wait. It's driving me to distraction. Can't anybody in this army make up their fuckin' mind?"

"Aw, quit kickin'," Victor said from under his helmet. "Ain't yuh gonna be satisfied till you're gettin' shot at again? This waitin' suits me to a T. I ain't keen on Jerry tryin' tuh blow my ass off again."

"Well, neither am I, but I just——"

"Why don'tcha quit beefing and relax? Stewing about it ain't gonna do yuh no good. You southern boys already lost one war."

"I ain't stewin', I just . . . Say, what do you mean, already lost one war?"

"You know damn good an' well what war I mean. So what's your hurry tuh . . . ?"

The new men, shunned by the others, were gathered in front of Lansing, who was trying to tell them what to expect. They sat apprehensively as he paced back and forth.

"Most of the time it isn't so bad. They shell us, we shell them. Once in a while there's action, but not as much fighting as you might think. As we go, I'll help you along, and you'll soon get the hang of it. Stick close to me, and we'll do our job. Any questions?"

There were none. There never were. Not about anything important. The new ones didn't know enough to ask about anything important.

Whistles blew and the company formed up. Morgan led the 1st Platoon into line, and after a few minutes they moved out. It looked like rain as they marched northeastward through the gloom, past fields of white clover, and—Morgan thought it strange—somewhere larks were singing.

The clouds had a strange lavender cast, and the gloom turned to drizzle. The men slogged on, rifles slung over their shoulders, muzzles down, and after the first few kilometers the banter stopped, and there was only grunting and complaining, and the slop of feet in the sticky clay. Behind them would be the rolling kitchens, followed by the water wagons.

Morgan's company crowded to the side of the road to let a group of French cavalrymen pass. The riders were elegant and aloof, mounted high on their horses; disdainful of their sullen-faced allies on the ground. The sun peeked out, and their lances glistened with heavy moisture.

"Those guys look like good targets," Morgan said.

When the French had passed, the men of Company D took the center of the road again. As he marched, Morgan tried to insulate himself from the discomfort: the wet stickiness, the blisters on his feet, and the fear of the unknown.

They swept across the dance floor as though they were gliding on a thin carpet of air. Evangeline was radiant in her white full-length gown, and Morgan was equally handsome in his black coat and tie. He led her in wide, sweeping circles, and she laughed joyfully. Then the other dancers left the floor, and they were alone, the center of attention. They whirled faster, in effortless delight, and when the music stopped, Evangeline took Morgan's face in her hands and kissed him.

"The new men are having a tough time keeping up," Lansing said.

"Well, they'll have to," Morgan replied.

99

Lansing fell in beside him. "Alright, but I don't think Francis is gonna make it if we have to go another day. His feet are going bad. Blisters as big as silver dollars."

"We'll check him during the next break. Maybe we can get him a ride on one of the howitzers. Trouble is, he'll likely get lost and we'll never see him again."

"Probably fine with him. What can you expect from a barber?"

They moved aside again to let a dozen 75-millimeter guns pass. The huge cannons were each pulled by six horses, and at the head of the procession was a gunnery sergeant. Each horse had beads on its head strap to keep off the flies. When the artillery had passed, Morgan's men continued, already too tired to care about stepping in the manure.

At noon the column stopped. There was hot beef stew, and lieutenants and sergeants major urged everyone to eat faster. Most of the men savored the stop more than the meal, but they ate anyway.

"Not bad," Morgan said as he chewed a lump of fat and beef.

They prized the fat almost as much as the meat. It quelled hunger pangs, and Morgan was eating it as insurance.

"Looks like you got yours from the bottom of the pot," Lansing said. "Lookit this. Mostly water."

He held out his tin bowl. Morgan could see the bottom.

"Here, take this." Morgan plopped a big lump of fatty meat into Lansing's broth.

"Naw, I wasn't begging, I just——"

"That's alright. I got more than I can eat anyway."

"Thanks." Lansing speared the lump with his fork and gnawed on it.

Morgan lifted his bowl and drank the rest, then he felt it coming: the feeling that had been with him since childhood.

Morgan heard someone speaking through a blue light, and whoever it was kept shaking him, though he could not actually feel it. His eyes focused, and it was Philbert Stanford. Then he remembered Philbert was dead.

"You alright?"

Morgan tried to sit up, but Lansing stopped him.

"Rest a minute. We aren't going anywhere just yet. There's another artillery column passing."

Morgan squinted at Max Stuller and the others who had gathered around him.

"He's fine," Lansing said. He waved them away.

"Oh, my head," Morgan moaned. "Was I bad?"

"Not too bad."

"Ohh."

"Damn you, I told you you could get out on account of this."

"And I told you I tried once, and it was just like with Jake. They told me I was faking."

"Well, if enough of us got together and vouched for you, you could——"

"Bullshit. Just drop it will you? I'm fine, so forget it. Just gimme a slug a' water." Morgan sat up, and Lansing opened his canteen.

"You don't want out, do you? That's what it is. This is making you queer, and now it's gotten to the point where you don't even know what's good for you. You just plain don't want out."

Lansing's voice had risen, and the others were looking at them.

"Hell, yes," Lansing cried, "you've lost control! You don't want out. You're nuts, that's what you are! Anybody else would kill to get out, but not you. Hell, you like it."

Morgan raised his hand to quiet him, but it was no use.

"Here we all are, looking for the bullet that's gonna send us home, and you've already got your ticket outta here, and you won't go! How the hell do you think that makes the rest of us feel? It's bad enough without someone like you enjoying it. It's guys like you who drag things out, because you like it. You like the mud, and the dirt, and the filth, and all of the killing, and——"

Horace handed his rifle to Victor and approached Lansing. "Settle down, old chum." He put his hand on Lansing's arm, but Lansing threw it off and continued his tirade.

". . . if we didn't have you to take care of all the time!" he shouted at Morgan. "You and your headaches, and rolling around on the ground! Who the hell do you think you are that you can expect us to put up with that? We don't——"

"That's enough," Horace barked.

John came over and helped Horace lead Lansing away.

"I'm gettin' sick of taking care of you all the time," Lansing screeched back over his shoulder.

They threw Lansing down, and John got ready to hit him if he tried to get up, but Lansing rolled over and sobbed into the wet ground. The others were embarrassed, and they turned away.

Sergeant Shepherd slouched down the road. "Time to move out, boys. We're keepin' the Boche waiting." He glanced at Lansing, who was still lying face down. "What's the matter with him?"

"Nothin', just played out. He's alright," John answered.

Morgan got up and came over. "Yeah, he's fine. He had a stomachache and threw up, but nothing serious. We'll take care of him."

"Yeah, alright, see that yuh do. If it keeps up, let me know. Could be dysentery. Let's go then." Sergeant Shepherd continued down the road, and John and Horace helped Lansing to his feet.

"Come on, old son," Horace said as Lansing steadied himself. "You're alright now. Let's get a move on."

Lansing slung his rifle over his shoulder and slinked to the rear of the squad. Morgan went to the front, and they started again, toward the east.

That night they stopped along the road and bedded down wherever they could: in barns, or under trees mostly. It was not raining, but the clouds hung low, and the air was sticky. There was more stew, but it was cold.

As darkness covered the forlorn group, Lansing crept up to Morgan, who had settled in on some heavy grass under a beech tree. Lansing threw down his things, but remained standing.

"This spot taken?"

"Help yourself."

"Guess I got a little out of line back there."

"Forget it."

"I don't know what got into me. I guess I've got a case of fedupness."

"I said forget it," Morgan interrupted. "You don't have to explain to me. Hell's bells, don't you think I know what happened? I'm an expert at it. For crying out loud, sit down and shut up. I don't wanna hear any more about it, and if I do I may get sore and give you a good goddamn punch in the nose. Now just shut the hell up!"

And Morgan knew, then, for the first time in his life, what it was like to have a true friend. And he knew the chance he was taking.

CHAPTER THIRTEEN

At 4:30 on the morning of July 18th, 1918, southwest of Soissions, a lone howitzer signaled the beginning of an Allied bombardment. A rolling barrage, behind which Morgan, Lansing, and Horace Gray advanced, slowly and laboriously, through the mud. The others followed, and they were afraid again; all except Victor Steele. They were counterattacking the Ludendorff offensive.

The early-morning sky cleared, leaving its sultry remains. There was little German resistance, and as the advance continued, Jack Smalley, a new man, slogged up to Morgan and Lansing. Jack was tired and haggard, but he was smiling. "I thought it would be worse than this."

"Cripes," Morgan murmured as he stepped over a German rifle.

"You'll get plenty of action, if that's what you want," Lansing said. "This is just a sideshow."

Jack's face fell. His loose, hanging jowls made him look like a bulldog.

"But then a guy never knows," Lansing added. "Maybe this is the beginning of the end for Jerry."

Jack would have none of it. He rejoined the other new men.

Company D pressed on through fields and hedgerows, past ruined farmhouses and burnt-out barns. The heat was stultifying, and the fighting intensified as German units regrouped. Waves of Allied assault troops pressed forward, supported by large and small tanks. The tanks clanked, sputtered, and churned forward until most of them either got stuck in the mud, or broke down. By late afternoon food, water, and ammunition were low, but the counterattack continued. Troops of both sides took sustenance where they could find it; often from the packs and canteens of the dead.

As darkness set in, the counterattack halted. Morgan and the other platoon leaders posted sentries, and those not on duty wrapped themselves in their still-damp blankets and sank to the ground. That night even the sentries slept.

Then it was morning.

"Get 'em ready to move out, Feeney." Sergeant Shepherd kicked Morgan's feet. Morgan tried to stand, but his legs buckled. The sergeant helped him.

"Rough go yesterday," the sergeant said.

"Yeah." Morgan looked around and tried to get his bearings, but the area was like any other. Colorless. Just more mud, shredded trees, and ruined farms. To the east he heard a German machine gun stutter.

"I hate to tell yuh, but there's gonna be hell to pay today, from what I hear," Sergeant Shepherd said. He said it like it was his fault. "So, better get your boys ready as soon as yuh can." He shuffled away, and Morgan noticed how thin he looked.

Morgan paused, clinging to the last quiet, until a plane flew along the lines. He didn't bother to look up.

"Let's go, boys." Morgan tried to summon enough energy to brave out the day. "Rise and shine," he called, louder, and those around him began to moan and cough themselves awake. "Hurry up, now. Sergeant says this is gonna be a big day."

Morgan opened a can of salmon and forced down a few mouthfuls. Goldfish, they called it. He checked his equipment, and sat waiting for the others to go through the same morning liturgy. They had been repeatedly warned about eating before a battle, in case they got hit in the stomach, but they didn't care.

Victor, always the first ready, sat quietly by Morgan. That was his way, and Morgan was used to it. Morgan had only recently gotten an accurate picture of Victor's inner workings. When they had first met, Morgan and the others had decided that

105

Victor was one of the few who actually liked fighting and killing. Then opinions had swung the other way, and most had figured his aloof hardness was a compensation.

Samuel Robbins joined Morgan and Victor. Samuel's long, thin nose drooped even more. "What's up, Morgan?" he asked.

"Same old thing," Morgan replied. It was the best he could do.

Samuel sagged down beside them. He was nothing but a loose connection of skin and bones, and he sat scratching his chest and groin with both hands. "Shee." He scratched harder, but Morgan and Victor paid no attention.

Sergeant Shepherd returned. "This is gonna be a big one, boys. They say we're gonna push the Heinies all the way back to Berlin." His old enthusiasm was gone, and he walked on without even slowing.

Morgan felt a personal loss in Sergeant Shepherd's malaise. A betrayal.

Samuel gave up scratching. "Darn it. I can't go this much longer."

Morgan didn't know if he meant the lice or the war, but he didn't ask. Neither did Victor, who sat gazing over the trampled wheatfields, eastward.

"I'm gonna check on those new guys," Morgan muttered. He got up and crept away, crouching in case there were snipers. He found the newcomers huddled together, and he felt sorry for them. Oscar Benson was with them; the young man from Oklahoma, who should have been at home. They all should have been home.

"You guys sure look down in the dumps," Morgan said.

Suddenly Morgan found something humorous in their fear as they looked up at him, and he started laughing. He laughed so hard he fell to the ground and held his stomach. Then the humor vanished, and he felt disassociated from himself, but

106

he couldn't stop. Lansing came running, and lifted him to his feet and led him away. Morgan was still laughing. Lansing waved the others off and tried to shield him from view. He took off Morgan's helmet, grabbed him by the ears, and shook him. "What the hell's the matter with you?"

Morgan looked at him, surprised. "What? Whaddyuh mean?"

"I never saw you on a jag like this before. What's eating you?"

"Did you see those guys, sitting there looking like a bunch of monkeys in a zoo, all huddled around? Ha, ha, ha! What a sight! Ha, ha, ha."

"Cut it out, Morgan! Just stop it." Lansing shook him by the ears again, then he looked back over his shoulder. The 2nd Squad had gathered, trying not to stare. "For Christ sake, Morgan, knock it off," Lansing growled under his breath.

"But there they were, and I . . ," Morgan started to protest. He knew what had happened, and he hung his head and was ashamed. He cried softly. Lansing gave him a dirty handkerchief, and Morgan wiped his face. Lansing picked up Morgan's helmet and handed it to him, and the onlookers moved away.

"You're alright, old man," Lansing consoled. "You just slipped a little, that's all. Happens to all of us at one time or another."

The counterattack was late in coming, and the troops of the 2nd Division waited. The day grew hotter, and still they waited. Lieutenant Stafford arrived, but it was evident that he knew no more than they. Far down the line a soldier leapt from cover and ran, screaming, toward the German positions. He ran until he was exhausted, then he fell. For a long time he lay, then he started to crawl back, and an enemy sniper killed him. Then it was quiet again, and the waiting continued.

107

By the time Morgan had convinced himself that the attack had been called off, the signal came, and as one, the men of the Indian Head Division left their meager cover and advanced. They had learned to walk, not run. Running only brought them closer to the death-spurting machine guns, and in any case they could not run far while carrying their equipment. Few failed in their duty, but they did not hurry.

They had not gone twenty feet when Morgan smelled the familiar odor of human excrement. Oscar had fouled himself, and so had others, but no one cared. Ultimately what counted was how well one comported himself when the fighting began. Only that was important in No Man's Land.

Morgan separated himself from the others so as not to attract fire. He pressed on, waiting for the din of battle to envelop him, as it always had. Instead of the usual detachment, however, there came a feeling more horrible than he had ever known.

The battlefield darkened, and smoke filled the air. The ground was a cauldron of seething, odoriferous slime, and Morgan clung to the duckboards and fought to keep from sinking. He looked at the heavens in supplication, caring not about Lansing, or any of the others. He only wanted it to end: the fear, the agony, the tiredness, and the despair. Anything would be better, even death.

CHAPTER FOURTEEN

Something was wrong. Morgan was surrounded by strangers, and whenever he asked a question, no one would answer. Then Lansing appeared, looking worried, and when Morgan tried to reassure him, Lansing started crying. Morgan struggled to stay, but someone led him away. He made a joke, but no one laughed. Strong, rough hands lifted and pushed him into the back of a truck, the engine started, and the ride began.

Morgan felt himself being dragged by the legs, and he opened his eyes just as he came to the end of the truck box. Two burly orderlies slung his arms over their shoulders and carried him to a building. Inside they threw him onto a bed and removed his puttees and shoes. They started to walk away, then they stopped.

"Think we oughta tie him?" one asked.

The other studied Morgan. "Naw. He looks alright. Let's get the others."

They went outside, and soon they returned with a large, heavy man with bushy eyebrows and no neck. Blood trickled from his mouth. They led him to the bed next to Morgan's. The man was struggling, and they needed help in tying him.

"Gosh, this guy's strong," one of the orderlies puffed as he finished tying the man's feet.

The large man saw Morgan and began screeching. Morgan tried to calm him, but his attempts only made things worse, so he lay back and blanked out everything: the shrieking, the moaning of the other patients, the orderlies, and the smell of illness.

It was dark, and the lanterns hanging from the rafters had been turned down. Morgan looked for his rifle, but he couldn't find it. He got up to look some more, and as he rummaged around, a nurse kept an eye on him from her desk at the far end of the room. She said something to someone, then she and an orderly approached. Morgan was on his hands and knees, looking under the bed.

"What's the trouble?" the nurse asked. She was young and frail looking. She didn't look like a nurse.

Morgan tried to explain that he had lost his rifle, but she didn't seem to understand.

"You'll have to get back in bed now," she said.

Morgan was about to soil himself, and he asked where the latrine was. Again she looked at him uncomprehendingly. Morgan pointed at his trousers and smiled embarrassedly.

"I think he has to go," the orderly said. "That it, soldier?"

Morgan nodded.

"I'll take him." The orderly took Morgan by the elbow and led him toward the door.

On the way back, Morgan asked what day it was, and this time the orderly understood.

"Tuesday," he replied. "The twenty-third, I think, but I could be wrong on that. Anyway, it's Tuesday, and you've been here for three days. How you feelin?" He didn't wait for an answer. "That big guy next to you; I don't know about him. He's really a nut. Suppose you noticed we still got 'im tied. Takes four of us to handle him."

He helped Morgan up the steps.

"You got it good compared to him, buddy." He steered Morgan down the center aisle. "Anything you need, just let me know old timer," he said.

Morgan fell back in bed.

Morgan and his father were in church. It was hot and uncomfortable, and the sermon was long: about suffering. There

110

was a wooden casket, painted shiny black, and on top lay a single bouquet of flowers. After much squirming and muttering under his breath, Morgan's father started to leave. Morgan grabbed his arm and pulled him back. "Do one decent thing for her," Morgan said. It was his mother's funeral.

CHAPTER FIFTEEN

The hospital was hot and fetid, and Morgan went outside. A shaded convalescent area had been set up, and there, in chairs, at tables, and on beds, the infirm struggled. Most of the soldiers were quiet, but a youngster in the chair next to Morgan was agitated by the sound of artillery fire. Morgan couldn't hear it, but he was no longer sure of anything.

"Damn! Don't they ever quit?" the young man whined. Well built and handsome, he looked like a varsity football player. He ran his fingers through his curly, brown hair and stared at the horizon.

"God. Yuh hear it?" He had a blanket over his knees, and he pulled it up to his chin. "Ohhh, on, and on, and on."

"Aw, for crying out loud, why don't you knock it off?" a large, dour-looking man at a nearby table protested. "You've been griping all morning, an' I'm gettin' sick of it. It's all in your head anyway, so why don't you keep it there?"

The young man moved away, to another chair, and carefully covered his lap with the blanket. He sat staring at the horizon, and sometimes he would shudder.

"You didn't have to be so tough on him," Morgan said to the large man.

"Is that so? Who the hell are you, and what business is it of yours?"

"It doesn't matter who I am."

The man got up and walked toward Morgan. He had short arms and a huge, red-veined nose. "You got a beef with me, mister?"

Morgan stood. "That's up to you."

"Well, then, maybe somebody should teach you to mind your own damn business." He started toward Morgan again, but a soldier with a bad arm jumped up and whispered in the man's ear. The large man looked at Morgan, and his face reddened to match his nose.

"Why, I mean, guess there's no reason to be at each other. No hard feelings?"

Morgan turned and walked away, toward the young soldier with the blanket. Morgan had no hard feelings. That was his trouble; he had no feelings at all. He didn't know what the large man's friend had whispered, and he didn't care.

The young man shook again, and pulled his blanket higher. "Damn! They're blowing some poor devils to smithereens. I can see it from here. Isn't that strange? Am I balmy?" He spoke to Morgan, but his eyes never left the horizon.

Morgan summoned what little strength he had. "I dunno. I guess we all are. Like a bunch of scarecrows. Nothing inside."

The young man broke his fixation and gazed at Morgan. "That's it, isn't it?" he said. "By golly, that's it. A fellow feels empty inside. Like a scarecrow. Like nothing matters anymore, and nothing ever will." The young man looked around to make sure no one was listening. "But you wanna know the worst of it?" he asked.

"Yeah."

"I've gotta get back to my outfit," he whispered. "If they don't let me outta here pretty soon, I'm gonna sneak back."

"Me too," Morgan said.

"You? You mean——?"

"Why not? What else is there?"

"Yeah."

That night Morgan tried to stay awake. He feared the night.

The battlefield was littered with the destruction and debris of war—shell holes, barbwire, discarded weapons, helmets—and bodies. It was quiet with the sound of death—the buzzing of flies on corpses—and Morgan was the sole enduring witness. As Morgan gathered himself to leave, a blinding light descended. Morgan covered his eyes. When he looked again, an angel stood before him: a figure in a white flowing robe.

"Morgan Feeney."

Morgan tried to speak.

The angel raised his hand. In it was a golden staff. "This is your great epiphany," he proclaimed. "I have come to grant you peace."

"Peace?" Morgan managed.

"Inner peace, and equanimity. You have paid dearly in life, but alas, you have not learned." The angel moved closer, hovering above the ground. He released the staff, and it hung in midair. "Are you prepared for supreme revelation?"

"Yes."

"Then you must renounce the most painful of your worldly values."

"What values?"

"Love, hope, charity, and compassion."

"Give up all human passions?" Morgan interrupted.

"Not all. Those that cause you pain. Only then will you know peace."

"But love, hope, charity, compassion. What else is there?" Morgan heard a moan. It was a soldier, still alive. Morgan moved to help.

"Stop!" commanded the angel. "Compassion will only bring more pain."

"But aren't you an angel from heaven?" Morgan quavered. "Aren't we commanded to show mercy?"

"You have given all you have to give. Now it is your turn to receive."

The soldier lay on his side with one arm outstretched, pleading for water.

"Never!" Morgan shouted at the angel.

A troubled look came over the angel's face. He retrieved his staff from midair and pointed it at Morgan. "Then you will suffer for it! For every passion you sustain, you will pay a terrible price!" The angel ascended, dimmed, and faded.

Morgan sagged to his knees and looked again at the man who had pleaded for water. The man was dead.

Morning came slowly, through a fit of dreams. When Morgan was fully awake, he lay in bed watching a nurse remove the bandage from a soldier's leg. The doctor beside her was young, dark, and handsome, and he looked like a college student. The doctor's colleague on the other side of the aisle gave the same impression, though he was somewhat older.

"Leg looks pretty good, soldier. Nurse, keep this wrapped for a couple more days, then I'll look at it again, and maybe we can keep the bandage off."

"Yes, Doctor."

The doctor walked past a man who was lying on a duck, groaning and passing mostly gas. The doctor's name was Stone. He had a three-day beard, and he looked exhausted. He stopped at Morgan's bed.

"Rotten business, those," he said, and Morgan guessed he meant gut wounds. "How are you feeling today, Feeney?"

Most of the doctors felt uncomfortable around shell-shock victims, but not Lieutenant Stone.

"Fine, Sir. I should be getting back, I——"

"Alright, Feeney, alright. Go. Not much more we can do. Real, er, physical wounds are one thing, but . . . Well, you know what I mean. Good luck." He patted Morgan's shoulder.

Morgan stood in front of the major's desk.

"Finally getting you outta here, eh Feeney?" the major said. He was a huge, beefy man with a pale complexion and reddish-brown hair. His teeth seemed to be permanently clenched, even when he talked.

"Yes, Sir."

"About time, isn't it?"

"Not soon enough for me, Sir," Morgan replied.

The major scrutinized him. "Whaddyuh mean by that, soldier?"

"Just want to get back with my unit, Sir."

"Well, if you were so damn keen on getting back, why'd it take yuh so long? To tell the gospel truth, I never did think there was anything much wrong with yuh. We got more to do than coddle guys like you who think they've had a rough time."

Morgan remained silent.

"Well? What have you got to say about that, Feeney?"

"Nothing, Sir. I guess you'd have to take that up with Dr. Stone."

"Umph! Damn highfalutin college kid. Oh, what the hell." The major scribbled his name at the bottom of a form and handed it to Morgan. "Take this and get the hell outta here, an' I don't wanna see your ass back here unless you're bleedin'. Understand? Now beat it."

"Yes Sir."

Morgan saluted. The major returned the salute contemptuously.

Morgan packed his few belongings. On his way out, he stopped at the convalescent area to see the young man who heard artillery fire.

"See you later," Morgan smiled. "They're letting me out."

"Oh, that's good," the young man replied. He straightened in his chair and motioned Morgan closer. "Did they say anything about me? They're lettin' me out too, you know,

116

any day now. I finally figured out that they don't like it when I tell 'em about the artillery, so I've been keepin' that under my hat."

"Don't be in too big a hurry."

The young man didn't hear. "Yeah, and the major said he couldn't wait to get ridda me. That's really swell news, isn't it, Feeney? I tell you, I can't stand it here. Half of these guys are all shot up, and the other half are batty. It's really depressing."

"Well, so long then kid. Maybe we'll run into each other."

"Yeah, that'd be nice, Corporal. I'll be lookin' for you. This afternoon I'm gonna see if they got my papers ready, and then I'll be right behind you. You didn't see my papers on the major's desk, did you?"

"No. Well, so long."

Morgan went down the hill to the road. There he waited for the next empty ambulance truck to the front.

CHAPTER SIXTEEN

That evening Morgan found Company D.

Sergeant Shepherd greeted him. "Well bless my soul! Morgan! How the goddamn hell are yuh, old son?" The sergeant seemed about to hug him. Men gathered, but Morgan didn't know any of them.

"Good to be back, Sergeant. Where are we?"

"The Pont-a-Mousson sector."

"Where's that?"

"Just about straight east of Paris I guess. We're a lot closer to Germany than we were a few days ago. How yuh feelin, old-timer? First yuh take a bullet in the head, then . . . Well, yer always gettin' sent tuh the doc. Couldn't yuh get 'em to keep yuh in a little longer?"

"As soon as you look like you can take a bullet, they kick you out," Morgan said.

"That figures."

It was getting dark, but Morgan could still see Sergeant Shepherd's face. He looked even older than Morgan had remembered. The men behind him were old beyond their years too. Old, worn, thin, dirty, and tired. Several of them had strange looks on their faces. They reminded Morgan of some of the men he had seen in the hospital. They reminded him of himself too, except he had learned to cope. If one had nothing to lose, nothing mattered.

"So, how is everybody?" Morgan asked.

"Everybody's still kickin'," Sergeant Shepherd said. "Except poor Oscar. Got clicked last week."

"What happened?"

"Sniper. Quiet—nothing at all going on—and they got 'im while he was on the latrine. Poor devil. Christ, they won't even let a guy take a shit."

"Well, that's the way it goes," Morgan said.

118

Sergeant Shepherd sized up Morgan. "He turned out to be a fine soldier. True blue."

"Yup, he was a swell guy," Morgan agreed without feeling.

"We got us a replacement already. Pat Fitsimmons. He's from Philadelphia. Used to be a policeman. And Francis Cook is back, so things are looking up. C'mon, First Platoon is down here. Lansing's been in charge, so I suppose we'd better keep it that way."

"Fine with me. I was getting tired of playing Little Jesus anyway."

"Don't hafta remind yuh to keep your head down, do I?"

Morgan looked at him disgustedly through the gloom, and the sergeant laughed.

"Everybody else alright?" Morgan asked.

"Good as can be expected."

They stumbled over something soft.

"Keep hearin' the Boche are about done," Sergeant Shepherd said, "but as far as I can tell, they don't know it yet."

"Lotta action when I was gone?"

"We've been raising hell now and then."

"How long you been here?"

"Not long. We were running helter-skelter all over the place, and the division got split up, but it's back together now."

Morgan was uncomfortable. He had always liked to get the feel of a position before darkness set in. He stepped on an empty tin can, then bumped into someone who was sitting alongside the front wall of the trench.

"Ow! Gosh, take it easy, buddy."

"Sorry."

"Yuh stepped right on my foot."

"Sorry. It's darker than the ace of spades."

"Dark? It ain't dark. What's the matter with you? You new or somethin'?"

119

"No."

"Ow."

"Oh, come off it," Sergeant Shepherd growled from up ahead. "You'll live. C'mon, we're just about there."

Soon Morgan was surrounded by Max Stuller, Horace Gray, and all of the others. They patted his back and shook his hand.

"I knew they couldn't keep a guy like you down."

Morgan recognized Clarence Mudd's southern accent.

"Good tuh have yuh back, Morgan."

Another slap on the back. It was Simon Madsen. Then Lansing pushed through the group. "Knew you'd be back," he said.

"Yeah."

Lansing stepped aside, letting the others talk, and for a short time Morgan was detached. He was glad to see them all, but except for Lansing, there were no special bonds.

The celebration went on for over an hour, and more than anything else the men were hungry for news. At first Morgan stalled, but as the demands grew more intense he began to recall snatches of conversations he had heard in the hospital. What he could not recall he made up, and he slanted every fabrication toward the optimistic side.

"So the major figures the Krauts are pulling back to the border and holding out for peace?" Samuel Robbins asked.

"Well I wasn't really listening," Morgan answered, "but I'm pretty sure that's what he said."

"And he got it from a colonel at division headquarters?" Jack Smalley persisted.

Morgan almost laughed at his hopeful, bulldog look. "Yeah, if I remember right, but don't hold me to it."

"Well, yuh musta heard it. Yuh couldn't a' imagined something like that," John Dempsey said. He said it with conviction, and all agreed, except Simon.

"I wouldn't put much credence in it," Simon groused.

They ignored him. "What was it that the doctor said about the Boche casualties?"

Morgan was tired, but he repeated the story patiently. "Just that they've had a lotta German wounded to take care of, and the prisoners are a pretty sorry lot."

"Yeah, but I thought the doc said they were about ready to throw down their rifles and quit."

"I guess one guy—some Fritz who'd had his leg blown off—said that. But then you can't go by what some poor mucker who——"

"Well, it sure enough sounds like they've about had enough," someone interrupted.

When they had heard what they wanted to hear, one by one the men of the 1st Squad slipped away into the darkness to find some small refuge in solitude. Morgan found a dry spot and sat down, exhausted from his lies and embellishments.

Lansing remained. "I wanted 'em to give you the squad again," he said.

"Naw. That's alright. You can have it."

An owl hooted, and it was answered by a Maxim gun that "put-put-putted" exactly three times. Morgan felt a rat scurry over his leg. He didn't know what to say next.

"What happened?" Lansing asked.

"They call it shell shock," Morgan answered.

"What's that?"

"That's when you get kinda queer, like I was."

"What's it like?"

Lansing was not embarrassed in asking, and Morgan was not ashamed to answer.

"It's hard to describe . . ." Morgan paused, and he and Lansing sat listening to the frogs. A German star shell went up and the frogs stopped croaking, and Morgan and Lansing saw each other clearly for the first time. Lansing's filthy clothes hung

121

loosely from his frame, and he sagged forward as he sat cross-legged, leaning both elbows on his knees. His face was grim and haggard, and his eyes glowed deep in their sockets. Morgan knew he looked better than Lansing. He had eaten well and he was rested, and he still had the clean blush of a noncombatant. He felt guilty for it.

"You don't know what it's like until it happens to you," Morgan said, "and you still really don't know what it's like until you start feeling better. When it happens, it's like you want to laugh and cry at the same time. It's kind of like being in a dream, and nothing makes sense. And the worst part is, you don't make sense to anyone either. You just want to climb back out of it some way, but the harder you try, the worse it gets. You know people are looking at you funny, but nothing you do helps. Finally you just shut up. That's all you can do."

"Sounds rotten."

"It is. It's not so bad till you come around again. Then you really know what happened. And the hell of it is, you wonder when it's gonna happen again." Morgan shifted, and he felt a rat sniff his hand. "Well, nothing to get maudlin about."

"You're alright now, aren't you?"

"Sure. How about you?"

"Fine. I'm fine, Morgan. You know me. I'm a rock."

Lansing had changed. Something was terribly wrong.

CHAPTER SEVENTEEN

"Hey, you alright?" Max Stuller approached. "Hey, somethin' wrong with you?" He squatted, looking quizzically into Morgan's face.

Morgan thought—because of Max's German accent—that he had been captured. "What? Oh, Max. What's up?"

"What's up? Whaddyuh mean what's up?"

"What are you talking about?"

"You was just sittin' there, starin' at the sky again, like you always do." Max sat down. He took off his helmet and put it beside him, but he kept his rifle. "You weren't even blinkin'. How long yuh been sittin' there like that?"

"Not long I guess." Morgan was no longer embarrassed.

"Yuh sure yuh weren't just sleepin'? One guy I used tuh know could sleep with his eyes open. Damndest thing I ever saw. I don't see how he kept from——"

"Naw, I wasn't sleeping. It's just something I do. It's nothing."

"Is it that there shell shock?"

"No."

"Do you remember it?"

"Sometimes." Morgan put his hand to his forehead. "Usually I get a headache. It'll go away in a few minutes." His explanations seemed to puzzle Max all the more, and Morgan tried to change the subject. "So you boys have been carrying on alright without me, eh?"

"Sure, but——"

"Poor old Oscar. What a way to go, sitting on the latrine."

"Yeah, them's the hazards. Anyways, I gotta ask you something." Max would not be put off.

"What?"

"Well, that shock, or whatever you had. I think maybe I got it."

"You?"

"Yeah."

"What makes you think that?"

"I dunno. I been down in the dumps lately, and real edgy. And I'm fagged all the time, but I have trouble sleeping. Bad dreams. They just go on and on."

"Well I'll tell you, if you——"

"And I've been thinking bad thoughts," Max broke in, "like maybe I've been lettin' the others down, or that they've been slacking off themselves, lettin' me down."

"Listen, if you——"

"And there's more. I ain't been eatin' right. I gotta force everything down. Used to be that I could eat anything they gave us, awful as it was, but now it's different. Look at me." He held both arms straight out, "Nothing but skin and bone. Hell's bells, Morgan, I ain't gonna last another month at this rate."

"Well everybody's like that, and you should see those Fritzes back at the prisoner compound. They're in worse shape than we are."

"An' one more thing. I think I'm gonna go west the next time there's action. I can feel it, Morgan. Don't some people know when things like that are gonna happen? I remember readin' about some people on the *Titanic*. They had a feelin something bad was gonna happen, and sure enough. My mother said some people know when their time is up, and by damn, Morgan, I think my time is up if I don't get outta here." There was pleading in his eyes. "Do you think I got the same thing you had?" he asked.

Max's desperation cut Morgan to his soul, but there was no easy way. Morgan leaned over and grasped Max's arm. "Max, if you can ask, you're alright."

"What?"

124

Morgan shook his arm gently. "When it happened to me, I didn't even know what it was, until afterward."

Max's thin shoulders sagged even more. "I just thought that——"

"I know. It's rough. But let me tell you something. You don't want what I had. It's the worst thing that can happen to a man. You lose control, and no matter what you do, it just makes everything worse."

Morgan knew he hadn't made much sense, and he could tell Max didn't know what he was talking about.

"A feller can get killed up here," Max stated flatly.

Morgan smiled at Max's macabre—perhaps unintended—sarcasm.

"How can anything be worse than that?" Max asked.

Morgan considered. "That's what I'm trying to tell you, Max," he answered. "Being like me is worse, because it's like being dead, only you're still alive and you have to suffer through it. But things eventually get better. Look at you."

"Yeah, look at me."

Max could not understand. He lingered for a while, and when it was apparent that he would get no more from Morgan, he left.

Later that morning Lieutenant Stafford visited the trenches. Sergeant Shepherd followed as he worked his way down the section occupied by Company D. When the lieutenant got to 1st Platoon, he stopped. He was nervous, and he obviously didn't like the smell.

"How's it going, Rhodes?"

"Fine, Sir," Lansing answered. He didn't salute.

The lieutenant glanced at Morgan, who was sitting cleaning his rifle.

"Been getting all the ammo you need, Rhodes?"

"Yes, Sir."

"How's the food?"

"Same as always, Sir."

"Um. Yes, I suppose so. Anything else we can do for you boys?"

"No, Sir. We're getting by fine."

Sergeant Shepherd seemed uneasy.

"Good," Lieutenant Stafford said. "Well, then, I'd like to talk to Feeney."

"Yes, Sir."

"Alone."

"Alright."

Lansing and Sergeant Shepherd moved away. Morgan got up.

"Ah, yes, Feeney. Saw your name on the medical report. How you doing?"

"Fine, Sir. And you?"

"Um, alright. Ah, Feeney, I'm afraid I've got some bad news."

"Oh?"

"Yes, I, ah . . . Oh hell, I always hate this. It's about Jacob Hermann. He was a friend of yours, I gather."

"Jake? Sure, I know Jake." Morgan's voice was flat and low.

"Then I'm supposed to give you this."

The lieutenant reached into his pocket and took out a handkerchief that he handed to Morgan. Morgan unwrapped it, and inside were a gold pocket watch and a ring. The ring had a strange design on it. Morgan thought it was Jewish.

"How'd he get it?"

"Accident. A Mills bomb blew up. Hell of a deal."

Morgan went numb. "And he wanted me to have this?"

"Oh, well, there was this note." Lieutenant Stafford handed Morgan a dirty, tattered piece of paper. Morgan's name, rank, and unit was scrawled on the back.

Dear Morgan,

If anything happens to me, please see that Sydney gets my watch and my ring. If you never see him again, keep them. Thanks, and so long.

Your friend,
Jake

"I'll do what I can."

"Right, Feeney. Who's Sydney, anyway?"

"Friend of his. Used to be his fight manager."

"A prizefighter?"

"Yeah. They were real good friends."

"Oh."

"I'll see that he gets it."

"Alright. See you later, Feeney."

"Yes, Sir."

Lieutenant Stafford about-faced and strode away. Morgan's body tingled, and his legs went rubbery. He had been in France since right after Christmas. Now it was the end of July—he couldn't remember the exact date—and nothing ever seemed to change.

CHAPTER EIGHTEEN

Lansing handed his open diary to Morgan. "Read the page I just wrote." They were sitting in the bottom of the shallow trench they had just helped dig.

Sept. 11th, 1918

I think we're somewhere near St. Mihiel. Sergeant Shepherd says we're an all-American army now. 1st Army, under General Pershing. Things have been pretty easy the last month or so, but there's something big in the air. I know we aren't supposed to keep diaries, but I'm signing my name in case I pass. God be with us when we push off tomorrow.

Lansing Rhodes
Corporal, A.E.F.

Morgan tried to return the diary.

"Keep it," Lansing said. "If something happens to me, see that my father gets it. But don't read any more."

Morgan put it his pack. The trouble with Lansing's reasoning was, of course, that they each had an equal chance of getting killed, so he could just as well have kept the diary. Maybe Lansing thought if someone else got killed with it, he could always take it back. Hard to tell. Lately there was no reasoning with him. Something had happened. Not shell shock. Something else. Maybe when the war was over he'd snap out of it.

Morgan sat hunched over, refusing to look up. It was all the same: farm after farm, field after field, village after village. Dirt, filth, misery. Leafless trees, bloated cattle, wrecked vehicles. Day after day, mile after mile. Burned-out tanks, discarded rifles, unexploded artillery shells. Trenches, craters, foxholes. Lice, fleas, rats, flies . . . . The wounded, the gassed, the half dead, the dead . . . .

"About time?" Lansing asked Horace Gray. Horace had been chatting with two men from a trench mortar crew.

"Yeah."

"Sure you won't come?" Lansing asked Morgan.

"To listen to a sky pilot? No thanks. Say, you two aren't turning into Holy Joes, are you?"

Lansing reddened. Going to the services had been his idea. "Naw, but I guess a guy has to keep his options open."

"Sounds like we're in for quite a scrap tomorrow," Horace added. His wandering eye seemed straighter than usual. "A little insurance wouldn't hurt you either."

"No thanks."

"Well, off we go."

"Right. See yuh."

As Lansing and Horace faded into the evening mist, Morgan moved away from the mortar crew and found a soft spot in the dirt. He sat, hugging his knees under his chin with both arms, thinking of his mother. How she had tried to give him religion. The comfort she had found in it. But in the end, it hadn't helped her a bit. Worked herself to death cleaning people's homes. Sold eggs and butter, trying to keep from losing the farm. Trying to keep her besotted husband from drinking everything up.

As Lansing and Horace shuffled back, cool dampness descended, and far to the east a lone star shell rose, bloomed, floated, and died. A shot rang out, and someone shouted. Then it was quiet again.

"How was the service?" Morgan asked.

"You didn't miss much," Lansing replied.

"Oh?"

"Those chaplains are pretty good at giving us big send offs, but I wonder how they'd like to jump off with us sometime. I bet they'd shit their drawers just the same as everyone else."

"Haw!" Morgan felt better.

"Still, there was a big crowd."

"What'd he talk about?"

"The usual. How we have to have faith, and all that. Talked about the *Angels of Mons*."

"Who?"

"At the beginning of the war, in Belgium, angels appeared over a battlefield."

"Horseshit."

"No, really. A lotta British soldiers saw them."

"Huh."

"Well, I dunno, but I talked to a Tommy who talked to a guy, who swore it was true."

Silence.

"Maybe it really happened," Lansing murmured. "I don't know what to think anymore."

Silence.

"Well, I'm really whacked," Morgan said. "I'm gonna try to get some sleep. Good luck tomorrow."

"Thanks. Good luck to you too."

They rolled up in their blankets.

Five minutes later Lansing sat up.

"What's wrong?" Morgan asked.

"Can't sleep. Damn, I ate too many bullets."

"Ha! Well get away from me. I told you not to eat so many beans on an empty stomach."

"You'd think the Krauts would be about ready to go kaput. Maybe it won't be so bad tomorrow."

"Maybe not."

"The last time we tangled with 'em it was a humdinger though."

At one o'clock in the morning three thousand Allied guns opened, pounding German positions with drum fire for over three hours. Then came a creeping barrage, behind which riflemen—some with wire cutters and Bangalore torpedoes—advanced. When the first wave had passed, the second wave jumped off, then a third.

Morgan's company was in the third wave. As he scrambled out of the trench, he was thankful for the fog that hung over the battlefield. But the fog—both natural and man-made—was mostly a psychological advantage. Again Morgan heard the familiar whisper of bullets, and occasionally he felt puffs of air. He never heard the really close ones; he only felt them.

It took Morgan a while to hit his stride. Lansing was on his right, then Tom Livingstone. Morgan could see, even through the fog, that Tom was terrified, as usual. To Morgan's left were Pat Fitsimmons, Simon Madsen, and John Dempsey. Simon showed no emotion whatever, plodding sullenly and determinedly straight ahead. Pat—compact and muscular, with rusty hair and ruddy complexion—was the same. Morgan couldn't make out John's face, but it didn't matter. They had all been alone for a long time. Islands. Morgan wished he could pray, but he no longer could, and he had no atonement to make.

Morgan saw someone drop. Pat. Morgan charged, and he felt another puff of air on his cheek. Time slowed, and it was like he was walking in tar. A trench mortar shell landed in front of him, making a shallow hole in the ground; blowing dirt and debris high into the air. Morgan saw an arm. It spun slowly, then it slid sideways and landed at his feet. The fingers were still moving. There was a wedding ring on one finger, and, curiously, Morgan's only reaction was that it was the man's left arm. Hell of a thing to be without a left arm, he thought, and he moved on, around the newly-formed crater in front of him.

131

That evening Morgan's platoon found themselves huddled in a road ditch near Thiaucourt. The emanations of death enveloped them like a burial shroud.

"German," Elmer Sitwell said. Elmer, the butcher's assistant, who claimed he could tell death by its smell. Humans from animals, and even Germans from French, British, and Americans. Elmer looked ghoulish as sat he sniffing the stagnant air.

"Looks like soldier's supper tonight," Francis Cook complained.

"What's soldier's supper?" one of the new men asked. Morgan didn't even know his name. No name, no face, nothing. Only a voice.

"Nothin'," Francis chortled. "That's what soldier's supper is: nothin'. Even the rats are startin' tuh look good."

"How many missing?" Lansing asked abruptly.

"Just Pat," Morgan said. "I saw him go down not long after we jumped off."

"Me too," John said.

John's dark eyes had dulled to a pallid brown. Morgan wished he and John and Lansing could go back to the little tavern and get drunk again.

"How bad?" Lansing asked.

"It was bad," John answered. "Couldn't a' lasted five minutes." John tried to spit to show his disgust, but he was too dry.

"Alright then, it coulda been worse," Lansing said. "It looks like we're in line with the rest of the company, so we might as well stay here for the night unless we're told otherwise."

He glanced at Morgan, and Morgan nodded almost imperceptibly.

Lansing continued, "I'll see if I can find Sergeant Shepherd. Maybe he'll know what the hell's going on. You guys sit tight." He motioned for Morgan to follow him.

When they were away from the others, Lansing stopped. "I don't feel very good," he said.

"What's the matter?"

"I . . . I just don't feel worth shit, Morgan." He rapped his helmet with his knuckles. "Up here."

"Like me?"

"I don't think so. Something else."

"I thought something was wrong."

"Well, I'd better go." Lansing hurried off.

A mortar shell landed nearby, and Morgan ducked.

CHAPTER NINETEEN

Morgan fought his way through the maelstrom of dust, smoke, and noise; searching desperately for shelter. Rifle fire cut the air, and artillery shells erupted. Through it all came shouts, and screams.

Morgan dropped to his hands and knees, and as he crawled, his only compass was the din of battle. When it seemed that he had crawled for over a mile, he came to a stone fence. He followed it to a depression in the ground, fell to his stomach, snaked the last few yards to the rim, and peeked in.

The depression was fifteen feet in diameter, and nearly ten feet deep. In the bottom, on one side, was a German soldier. Across from him was an American. The German lay face down, and the American lay on his side with his back to Morgan.

"Hello," Morgan called.

Morgan aimed his rifle at the gray form of the German and called again. Still there was no answer. He slid over the top and down the side, pointing his rifle.

"Hey!"

Neither of the occupants moved. Morgan crabbed his way toward the German and kicked hard. The body was stiff. Morgan heard a moan behind him. He spun on his buttocks, put down his rifle, and crawled forward.

"Hey, bud, you alright?" The man rolled over, and Morgan blanched. It was Sydney Berman, Jake's fight manager. "Sydney? That you?"

Sydney looked at him uncomprehendingly.

"Sydney! What the hell you doing out here?" Morgan stammered.

Sydney lay with his arms together, between his legs, tight against his groin. He was pale, and his eyes didn't seem to focus. "Oh, God, who is it? Is that you, Jake?"

134

"No, it's me, Morgan. Morgan Feeney. You remember me don't you?"

"Morgan? Oh, Morgan. Oh, God, it's good to see you. God, I got it bad, Morgan. Yuh gotta help me."

"Sure thing, we'll get you outta this mess. Just hang on." Morgan looked around. He had at first thought he was in a shell crater, but the hole was grassed over. Maybe it was a natural depression, or something from centuries ago. Whatever it was, it was a good refuge. A burst of machine gun fire passed overhead.

Sydney moaned again.

"Where'd you get it, Sydney?"

"Unnnh. Downstairs. Got it in the guts. Ripped me wide open."

"Let me see." Morgan tried to pull his arms away.

"No! No, leggo, it's worse than you think." He began to cry. "I'm all done, but the worst part is, everything below the belt is gone."

Morgan was getting sick, and he was glad he hadn't had anything to eat all day. Even so, he started to throw up. He turned and forced himself to swallow until the acid taste subsided.

"I can't even piss, Morgan. Ain't that a laugh, when a guy can't even take a piss? Nothing to piss with." Sydney started coughing, and when he stopped, Morgan thought he had passed out, or died.

"Sydney?"

"Yeah," came the weak reply.

"How'd it happen?"

"Well, things were really hot, and I got lost, and then I came across this hole, and suddenly things were lookin' pretty good. I was happy as all get out, then that Boche over there decided to join me, and . . ."

He started coughing again. Morgan found the German's blanket and made a pillow.

"Anyway, he came rolling in and landed right on top of me. I guess he panicked, 'cause he pulled out a potato masher. We tossed it back and forth a few times, and that's all I remember. Jeez, Morgan, why the hell'd he hafta do that? Oh, God. An' I can't see very good either." He stiffened and started shaking. Morgan put one hand on Sydney's forehead.

"Why the hell didn't he just shoot me?" Sydney groaned.

"I don't see a rifle."

"Oh. You got your rifle though, don't yuh?"

"Yeah."

"Ahhh, good. I lost mine." He relaxed slightly. "Morgan, first I hafta ask one thing. Have you seen Jake? You remember my friend, Jake Hermann, the fighter. You seen anything of him?"

"Sure, I saw Jake not so long ago."

"You did? You saw him? How was he?"

"Fine. He was fine, Sydney." Morgan felt the lie stick in his throat. "He was an orderly at headquarters."

"Was?"

"Sure."

"He's alright, isn't he?"

"He's fine. Good, cushy job. Easy duty. Why, he has it so easy I was kidding him about re-upping and making the army his career."

"Heh. What'd he say to that?"

"You don't wanna hear it. He didn't think much of it. He wants to get out of the army and start fighting again."

Sydney smiled, then he grimaced and clinched his arms tighter, and a greenish-brown fluid seeped out. "Did he ask about me?"

136

"Sure. Of course he did. He's already making plans for him and you to go back on the road once this is over. He said it'd be just like old times."

Sydney relaxed a little, and again a faint smile crossed his face. "Yeah, those were the good old days. Me and Jake never did get rich, but we sure did have a time. He was gettin' close to some big money too. Why, in another year we'd have——"

A mortar shell struck nearby, and Morgan flinched.

"We went all over," Sydney continued. "Coast to coast. Funny thing, Morgan, of all the places we were, I liked Montana the best. I always thought that when we were through fightin' maybe we could settle down there."

"That sounds like a swell idea, Sydney. I may do that too. Maybe a farm."

Machine gun bullets swept over, and when the firing stopped Morgan picked up his rifle and crawled up the side of the hole. He peeked out, and the firing started again. He rolled back.

"Damn. I don't think we're ever gonna get outta here."

Sydney smiled at him, and winced again. "Morgan, I sure could use a drink. Yuh got anything on yuh?" he asked.

"Yeah, sure, but I'm not supposed to give anything like that to you. It might——"

"Oh for chrissake, what's the difference? You think it's gonna kill me?" He laughed harshly. "God damn, Morgan!"

Morgan fumbled for a small bottle he had hidden. "It's rum," he said, holding it up. "I always kept it for an emergency."

Sydney eyed the bottle. "Rum's fine, and this is an emergency. Gimme a little water first, will ya?"

Morgan unhooked his canteen and took off the cap. He lifted Sydney's head and helped him drink.

137

"Ahhh." Sydney licked his lips. "Now, how about the real thing?"

Morgan put down the water and opened the bottle. "Here." He smelled it, and lifted Sydney's head. "They told me it was good stuff," Morgan said.

Sydney took four long, hard swallows, then he turned his head and coughed. "Ahhh. Oh, my, that was good." He coughed again, and looked at Morgan. "You have one. I hate to drink alone."

"Naw. You need it more than——"

"Drink," Sydney ordered. "It'd make me feel better if you had just one."

"Yeah, sure, maybe I could use a drink at that," Morgan responded. "How." He tipped the bottle and drank, trying to make it look good. "Ahhh. Pretty good stuff all right." Morgan wiped his mouth with his sleeve. "But I'm afraid I can't stand any more. Never agreed with me. Guess you'll hafta finish it." He put the bottle to Sydney's lips, and Sydney emptied it in five long gulps.

"Oh, mother," Sydney gasped. "I don't know when a drink ever tasted so good."

"Yeah."

They sat quietly, then Sydney tensed. "Ohhh."

"Sydney, lemme wrap you up. I can cut up a blanket and——"

"No."

"But at least that would——"

"No! Just leave me be. I'm S.O.L. and we both know it, so just leave me be. You can help me alright, but not that way."

Morgan was becoming uneasy.

"Lemme rest a while, and when it gets too bad, I'll let yuh know."

Morgan fidgeted, and glanced at the dead German, wondering whether he should take another look outside. A trench mortar shell exploded, and he decided not to.

"Tell me again about Jake," Sydney said. He sounded dreamy and distant.

Morgan nerved himself, pretending to do something with his equipment. "Jake looked better than ever. Looked like a real champ. There was this regimental boxing tournament, and of course Jake was too good to enter, so he was the referee, and . . . ."

Morgan embellished everything he could remember about his last time with Jake, and he invented what he could not remember. Sydney listened, only now and then stirring or moaning softly, and when Morgan started repeating himself, Sydney stopped him. He took one arm away from his groin, and held out his grimy, bloody hand.

"Here, Morgan, I want you to give this ring to Jake."

There was a plain silver ring on his middle finger. Morgan worked it off.

"You got anything to write on?" Sydney asked.

"Why, no, I don't think so."

"Well, then, you're just gonna hafta stay alive so you can tell him." He pressed both arms to his groin again, and clenched his teeth. "Tell him I . . . Jeez, Morgan, this is hard. I hope you'll understand. Promise you'll tell him, no matter what you think."

"I promise."

"Tell him . . . Tell him he's the only person that ever meant anything to me. Tell him he was a real friend. He'll know what I mean."

"I'll tell him, Sydney. Don't you worry, I'll tell him. I'll get outta here in one piece, and I'll tell him if it's the last thing I do."

Tears came to Sydney's eyes. "I know you will. You're a helluva swell guy, Morgan. I know you will."

"Is that all?"

"Yeah. I wish to hell he was here so I could tell him myself. God, I didn't want it to end this way. If we just coulda made it for a little while longer, the war woulda been over. Damn. Funny how things go, isn't it?"

"Yeah."

The gunfire was sporadic, and the sun was going down. Sydney closed his eyes. He lay for a long time without moving.

"Morgan, you know any prayers?"

Morgan started. "Eh, no, I guess not. My mother taught me some, but I can't remember 'em."

"Uh. Well I sure wish there was a chaplain here." He rolled to his side and faced Morgan. "You ever seen an angel?"

"Yeah, as a matter of fact I have. And just the other day one of the guys was telling me about the Angels of Mons."

"What's that?"

"Well, when the Brits got to Belgium, in their first big battle, a lotta them saw angels hovering overhead, and . . . ."

Morgan told the story, and Sydney seemed comforted by it.

"Morgan, you got religion?"

"Well, not really, but then I guess a guy never knows."

"Yeah, me too, but then . . . Well, you know. Anyway, I sure wish you could say a prayer for me. It'd mean a lot."

Morgan collected himself. "It's been a long time, and I'm not much at that sorta thing, but I'll do the best I can, Sydney."

He slid closer and adjusted Sydney's pillow. Then he folded his hands and placed them on Sydney's shoulder, bowed his head, and closed his eyes. "Lord, I've never been much at this, but seeing that my friend Sydney is in such a fix, here goes."

140

Morgan swallowed.

"Lord, please be with Sydney, and with his friend Jake. They're both good men, and if you can see to grant them mercy, I'd appreciate it. This war wasn't their idea. They're just regular men, same as the rest of us, caught up in something they don't know much about. They didn't ask for any of this, and look what happened.

"Maybe I'm not fit, but I'm not asking for myself, and I hope after this is all over, if I make it through, I'll get things figured out. Anyway, Lord, I'm asking you to take Sydney out easy. Please show him your goodness, and let him be with you forever.

"Guess that's about it. Amen."

Morgan kept his hands folded and his eyes shut. "Sorry, Sydney, that's the best I could do. I——"

"That was fine, Morgan. That was the best I ever heard. You don't know what it meant to me. The chaplain couldn't a' done better."

Morgan opened his tear-filled eyes and looked down at Sydney. "I'm not very eloquent, but it was from the heart. I really meant it, Sydney. I wasn't just putting on for you. I really meant it."

"Yeah, I could tell. You did real good, Morgan." Sydney rolled onto his back again. "Just gimme a few more minutes, then you can do it," he groaned.

Morgan went weak inside. "Do what?" he faltered.

"You know." Sydney fixed his eyes on Morgan. "You know what you've gotta do."

"No, you can't ask me to."

"I ain't askin' for much. Just for you to speed things up a little, that's all."

"But how could I live with myself if I——?"

"How could you live with yourself if you didn't, Morgan? What's the matter? Lost your balls too?"

141

"You can't ask a guy to do something like that."

"Why not?"

"Well, Christ, it just isn't right. How'd you like to do it to me?"

Sydney's face turned even more grim. "How'd you like to be me for a while?" he asked.

"What's that got to do with it?"

"You lie here in my place for a few minutes, you'll know." His voice had become an animal growl. "I just can't go this any longer, Morgan." Red and green slime oozed from under his arms and ran down his legs.

"No. I can't, and that's that," Morgan said.

Sydney gritted his teeth and lay looking at the darkening sky. Stars were starting to appear.

"It's too much," Morgan protested again, but there was no answer. "I've gotta live with myself," he rasped.

Sydney moaned, and tightened his arms. Morgan crawled away. For a while neither spoke.

Then, "Alright, Morgan. Gimme your rifle, and I'll do it myself. I can't take this anymore."

Morgan flinched. "No."

"If I had my own rifle, I'd do it myself. What's the difference if I use mine or yours?"

"I dunno. It wouldn't be right for you to use either one."

"Bull! You bastard, Morgan. I thought you were my friend. Oh, God, you gotta help me!"

Morgan couldn't answer.

The night wore on, and Sydney's moans became cries, and at times he was delirious, one minute calling for his mother, the next sobbing for Jake. During his quieter times he cursed Morgan in words more vile than Morgan had ever heard.

At last, after midnight, Morgan broke. He faked a coughing spell to cover himself while he opened the breech of his rifle and inserted his little finger to make sure there was a

142

cartridge in the chamber. He coughed again as he levered the bolt shut. Sydney lay facing the opposite wall. Morgan's hands shook as he raised his rifle and fired.

Morgan felt the familiar recoil, and Sydney's head slammed forward. The rifle dropped from Morgan's hands, and his chest tightened. He fell backward, and as he stared skyward, the stars started spinning, slowly, then faster, and his heart raced, and he knew he would be held accountable for what he had done.

But there was one more thing. Morgan got up and took Jake's watch and his ring from his pocket. He put the ring on Sydney's finger. Then he wrapped the watch in Jake's handkerchief and pushed it deep into one of Sydney's pockets. He lifted Sydney's arm and gently laid it across his mangled body. Then Morgan cried, for them, and for himself. Maybe theirs had been an unnatural union, but even in death it was more than he had.

CHAPTER TWENTY

"Morgan. Hey! Morgan. You alright?"

The voice sounded far away, and Morgan didn't recognize it. Then it came closer. It was Horace Gray, tall and dark, who had started out with one bad eye and a good shooting eye.

"Morgan?"

Horace's face came into focus, and both of his eyes looked good. Morgan tried to answer. His mouth moved, but nothing came out.

"Oh, shit! What happened?"

Again Morgan tried to speak, but he couldn't. He held out his arm, and Horace helped him sit up.

"Where'd you get it? Maybe you should stay down till the body snatchers get here."

Morgan didn't feel like smiling, but he did, and he gave Horace a thumbs-up.

"You're alright?" Horace asked.

Morgan smiled again, and Horace laughed.

"Why, you asshole! An' here I thought you clicked it." He picked up Morgan's rifle and handed it to him, and looked away, in the direction from which he had just come. "Say, where were you anyway? We all thought you got bumped. You're always trying to get bumped."

They were on the edge of a cow pasture, but the grass had been churned up by artillery fire, and all of the cows were dead, or in various stages of dying. On the opposite side of the pasture stood a gray stone barn with some kind of thatching for a roof, and farther back was a house. The house had been reduced to a pile of red bricks. In a nearby tree a bird sang, but Morgan recognized neither the tree nor the bird. Some kind of strange-looking poplar, and a lark, perhaps. Everything was different from back home. All mixed up.

144

Morgan moved his mouth, but only gagging sounds came. He massaged the front of his neck, but it didn't help.

A man and a woman came out of the barn, went to a well, pulled up the water bucket, and began washing themselves. Morgan couldn't tell from that distance, but they had to be old. There were no young farmers left.

"You sure you're alright?" Horace asked.

Morgan gave him another thumbs-up, but Horace looked skeptical.

"Well, they sent me back with a message, and I'd better take you with me. You really look awful."

Morgan put up both hands and tried to wave him off.

"Bullshit. You're coming with me," Horace declared. "I figure if you can't even talk, you better call it quits. Maybe we can get you outta here for a while. C'mon."

Morgan gave in and followed, and soon they were at the previous night's position; a cemetery on the outskirts of a tiny, nameless village. The stone markers were old and weather stained, and tilted at odd angles. The largest, in the center, was dated 1644-1696. Guy something or other.

They sat, resting. The sky was clear, and Morgan lay back and looked up. A faint breeze wafted over him, and a flock of crows flew overhead.

Then they were off again. They ran—through force of habit, afraid of being in the open—across a field, despite the fact that the fighting was far away. Horace was looking for brigade headquarters.

"They said it was in a bunch a' trees. Must be over here somewhere."

Horace crossed a road and commenced down a trail toward a farmhouse. Morgan followed, too tired to think. There were signs of war all around—shattered caissons, abandoned field artillery, burned-out buildings—and several bodies; some in gray, some in khaki.

145

"That looks like it," Horace called back. "I see tents."

Morgan's legs were shaking and he had to work to keep up. His head felt like it was going to fall off his shoulders.

"Yeah, that's it alright. Hurry up."

They crossed another field, through more debris, and through the stench of a dead horse. It lay on its side—still in its harness—with its legs sticking straight out, black with flies. Horace grimaced and held his sleeve over his nose, but Morgan hardly noticed.

"Whew, here we are," Horace wheezed. "Gosh, I'm tired as all get out."

They approached the largest tent. Two MPs were sitting in front on ammunition boxes. Morgan fell to the ground under a nearby tree.

"This Third Brigade?" Horace asked.

"Yeah. Who wants tuh know?" one of the MPs asked. He was a sergeant; tan and rugged, with a flat nose and close-cropped hair. He stood, as if it were a supreme effort, and eyed Horace.

"Message for General Hanson."

"Humph. He's kinda busy."

"Well, I got all day. I wonder if the general does."

The MP looked sharply at Horace. "I'll see." He went inside.

Morgan watched Horace and the other MP—a large, dull-looking type—size each other up. After a few minutes a lieutenant came out. He was tired and grim, and he looked like he had been chiseled out of wood by a bad artist. Horace saluted. "Message from Colonel Upton, Sir."

"I'll take it."

Horace opened the pocket of his tunic and pulled out the message. The lieutenant snatched it and began reading. When he was finished he started to go back inside, then he turned and squinted at Horace through his wire-frame spectacles.

146

"You're new, aren't you?" he asked.

"Yes, Sir."

"What happened to the other messengers?"

"Dead. Snipers, mostly."

"Too bad. Good men. That'll be all, er, what's your name?"

"Gray, Sir."

"Thanks, Gray. Take it easy, and try to keep outta the fireworks."

"Thank you Sir. Oh, by the way," Horace said softly, "I have a friend over there," he pointed to Morgan under the tree, "who had a close call with some mortar rounds, and now he can't talk or anything, and I was wondering if there's someplace I can take him."

Morgan pretended to sleep. No use fighting it.

"Can't talk?"

"No, Sir. He's already been in and outta the dock, er, the hospital, more than most. I'm worried about him."

"Hmm. Quite a way to the nearest field hospital, and probably not much they can do for him anyway. What's his name?"

"Morgan Feeney."

"Feeney? That name sounds familiar. Just a minute."

The lieutenant went inside, and a moment later he reappeared.

"Thought I recognized that name. Look, tell him to hang around here till he feels better. I'll officially put him on our staff so he can rest up. We were gonna call him back anyway." He pulled out a notepad and wrote something. "Here, take this to his company commander. Give this one to Feeney, and tell him if anybody asks, refer them to me, Lieutenant Sheehy."

"Thank you Sir. He's a good man, he just needs——"

"That's alright, soldier. On your way now, I've got work to do." He waved Horace away, and went back inside.

The MP with the flat nose took a drink from his canteen, and offered it to Horace. "Been over long?" he asked.

"Long enough." Horace drank deeply.

"Rough go up there?" His gruffness had melted.

"I'd rather be back in Macon, if that's what you mean."

"Haw! I'd rather be back in Chicago, too," the MP said. "What's the matter with your friend?"

Morgan remained still.

"It's a long story. He's had more than his share of knocks, and it's starting to affect him."

"Affect him?"

"Something's wrong with his head."

"Like what?" the sergeant asked.

"Well, he kinda blanks out, and just sits there staring, and then he'll snap out of it. And then he has headaches. Said he's had it ever since he was a kid. I dunno. He wasn't that bad when I first met him."

"Don't worry, just leave 'im to us."

"Sure, just leave 'im tuh us," chimed in the other MP. "He kinda reminds me of my brother back in Tennessee. Why, he even has the same——"

"I'll say goodbye." Horace started toward Morgan.

"Naw, don't do that," the sergeant said. "He'll wanna go with yuh. I've seen guys like him. Just give us his paper, and leave. It'll be best that way."

"Thanks," Horace said. "Tell him there was an emergency or something, and I had to leave in a hurry."

"Sure. Don't worry. Yuh know, funny thing. We have a hell of a time keeping healthy guys on the line. It's always the ones like this who wanna get back to the front. Can't figure it out."

Morgan struggled to keep from following Horace.

148

CHAPTER TWENTY-ONE

"Morgan."

Morgan's eyes widened, and he stared, dumbfounded. Evangeline stood at the foot of his cot. As he started to answer, she faded.

It was hot in the tent, but Morgan tried to go back to sleep.

"Awake, ain'tcha?" someone asked.

Morgan opened his eyes, and there was a scrawny red-headed soldier sitting on the next cot, staring dolefully. He had large floppy ears and a red complexion, like a puppet in a traveling show.

"Yeah."

"Corporal Feeney?"

Morgan could see that it was no use trying to sleep. He sat up and looked around, and smoothed down his hair with both hands. He felt more tired than when he had gone to bed.

"Morgan Feeney."

"That's what I thought. I'm what's left a' Edgar Bunch." The young man seemed in awe. He put out his hand and Morgan shook it. It was limp and weak.

Morgan's stomach hurt.

"Mind if I ask where yer from, Corporal Feeney?"

"Montana, mostly."

"Really? What outfit yuh with?" He sat straighter, and stared intently at Morgan.

"Company D, Ninth."

"That's what I thought. Been with 'em long?"

"Too long they say."

"Oh, yeah, I suppose."

"God, I need some air." Morgan got up and went outside, and the young man followed like a puppy.

149

"Say, I didn't mean tuh pry or nothin', in case you're sore."

Morgan stopped and turned. "Naw, I'm not sore. I'm just hot. And damn, these cooties are driving me loony. You don't notice 'em so much when you're busy. Is there anyplace I can get 'em taken care of?"

"Sure, there's a station down there a ways," he pointed, "and as a matter of fact, I'm supposed tuh take yuh over there. We'll get yuh some clean clothes too."

"That so? You work here?"

"Sure. Well, I did till I got sick. Now I just work when I can."

They walked through tall oaks and maples that looked generations old.

"What's the matter with you?" Morgan asked as he scratched his groin.

"Feelin puny, an' I can't seem tuh keep weight on. Tired mosta the time."

"Been to the sawbones?"

"Yeah."

"And?"

"They didn't have much tuh say. Gave me some papers tuh give tuh the lieut."

"What did the papers say?"

"I dunno. Couldn't read the doc's writing."

Morgan stopped, exasperated. "Well, for Christ's sake, what did the lieut say?"

"Nothin'. He didn't say nothin'. Started gettin' my discharge papers ready."

They went on. The sun was bright and warm, and birds were singing, and Morgan remarked what a beautiful day it was. He hadn't seen such a day in a long time.

"So when do you get out?" Morgan asked.

"I don't. I talked 'em into lettin' me stay."

150

Morgan stopped again, and the skinny young man bumped into him. "Stay? What the hell for?"

"No place tuh go."

"No relatives?"

"Nope. Grew up in an orphans' home in Ohio. If I got any relatives, I don't know where they are. Can't even remember my parents, just the orphans' home."

"Sounds kinda tough," Morgan said. He started walking again, and Edgar Bunch followed.

"It wasn't so bad. I liked Mr. an' Mrs. Ogden—they were swell—an' Mr. Smythe. He was the janitor. It was alright, but then I got old enough tuh where I hadda leave."

"What then?"

They came to a clearing full of trucks, but Morgan's guide waved him on. A Sopwith Camel passed overhead. By now Morgan knew all of the airplanes, and he recognized the Camel easily enough, especially with its red, white, and blue tail rudder, and the archery-like target on the fuselage. The pilot dropped a small parachute.

"Seems like more an' more a' our planes, and less a' theirs all the time," Edgar observed.

"What then, after you got out of the orphanage?"

"Oh, well, I bummed around awhile, an' worked in a meat-packing plant some, then I tried tuh join the army, but they wouldn't take me. So I waited, an' pretty soon we got into the war, an' then they were plenty glad tuh have me," he said smugly. "Never had it so good. Hell, no reason tuh get out; I'd just die in some stinkin' hospital, or in some alley somewhere. Can do the same thing right here. At least I got friends."

"Die?" Morgan turned and walked sideways. He wished Edgar would hurry up and walk beside him.

"Of course. Cripes, yuh think I'm stupid? I ain't very well educated, but I ain't stupid. If I was gonna live very long,

151

that'd be different. They wouldn't keep me. They don't want no invalids."

Morgan tripped over a stump and almost fell. They reached the far end of the clearing and entered the trees again, then they walked in silence for a few minutes.

"You know what yer really here for, don't yuh?" Edgar asked suddenly.

"Rest, I guess."

"Yuh mean yuh really don't know?"

"Know what? What're you talking about?"

"The medals! They're gonna pin medals on yuh the day after tomorrow. You're a hero, and yuh don't even know it!"

"The hell they are," Morgan said. "So that's what this is all about. I knew something wasn't right. But how could Horace have known? Hell, he just picked me outta the dirt by accident on the way back."

They stopped, and Edgar pulled out his cigarette papers and his tobacco pouch. "He didn't know, but the lieut recognized yuh and held yuh back. They were gonna bring yuh back anyway, and there yuh were." He smiled gleefully.

"So that's it. And here I thought they were giving me some rest just out of the goodness of their hearts."

"No. Better yet, they're givin' yuh medals!"

Morgan was relieved that Horace hadn't been involved. He guessed he couldn't have blamed him for being in cahoots, but he was glad he wasn't.

"Yeah, yer gettin' a medal from us, an' one from the Frogs. A crow-day-gear."

"A what?"

"A crow-day-gear. That's a big French medal. I heard 'em talkin' about it."

"Great," Morgan said.

"Say, yuh don't seem very excited about it."

"Well, that's all fine and dandy, but right now I'd rather get rid of these cooties. How much farther?"

Edgar scraped a hole in the dirt with his heel, threw his just-lit cigarette in, and covered it. They walked on. "Not far. Boy, I can't figure you out. You heros sure must be different from the rest of us. Why, I——"

"I'm not a hero."

"What?"

"I said I'm not a hero. I don't know how the hell they picked me. I just do my job and keep my mouth shut, like everybody else."

"Some lieutenant recommended you. Stafford. Yeah, Lieutenant Stafford. Know 'im?"

"Yeah."

"Well, he's the one who put yuh in."

"Swell. We about there?"

"Right over this little rise."

"Say," Morgan asked, "if you're sick, what do you do?"

"Messenger, mostly, an' some cleanin'. Things like that. Been shuffling a lot of papers lately, being I can't get around like I used to. It's real good duty. Yup, never had it so good."

A week after Morgan received his medals, he decided he did deserve them after all. They helped him put everything in perspective. His friends were getting thinned out day by day, but the war would be over soon, and maybe peacetime army life wouldn't be so bad. And, he had nothing else.

Over the next few days Morgan convinced himself that he was, or would be, more than just a mud slogger. He would re-up and become a career man, and his worries would be over. The more he thought about it, the more enthused he became, until he remembered why he was really there; because they thought he had cracked. That was the real reason, and the medals were coincidental. Then he began to worry about his

153

record. The medals would be good, but what about his hospital stays, especially the last one? They would have to be on his record. War wounds were one thing—they could even be considered badges of courage—and now he had his medals, but damn, if they had put his hospital files in his permanent record, the jig was up.

As the days passed, Morgan grew morose, but there was a slim chance. Perhaps Edgar Bunch could help, if he lived long enough.

"They keep mosta the records at division headquarters, an' it'd be tough," Edgar said.

Morgan and Edgar were sitting on the ground in front of their tent. Edgar looked gaunt, and sallow.

"You can't do it then?"

"Wait a minute, I didn't exactly say I can't do it. I said it'd be tough. Lemme think." Edgar sat scratching in the dirt with a twig.

Morgan waited. He could hear heavy artillery. Probably little Berthas. Another airplane flew over, above the low clouds, and he thought maybe it was French, from the sound. It was heading east.

"I do know a guy named Charlie."

Morgan pushed. "I suppose it'd be asking too much."

"No, hell no," Edgar bristled. "He'd do it for me. I helped 'im out once. Saved his ass. So big I can't even tell yuh about it. The thing is, I don't know if he's still there."

"He got transferred?"

"I dunno. I haven't talked to 'im in quite a while. But if he is still there, he'll take care of it, just like that." Edgar snapped his fingers.

"You don't say so?"

"Yeah. I'll see what I can do, first thing in the morning. I ain't feelin so good right now. Musta been those beans. I never could tolerate beans, and that's all we been havin' lately; beans, beans, beans. God, I get tired a' beans."

"You know," Morgan said, "I could get used to this lying around. I'm starting to enjoy not being shot at."

"Don't blame yuh. Guy could get killed."

Morgan didn't know if Edgar was serious, or if he was being sarcastic about his condition. He decided he was serious.

"That's why this is so important to me," Morgan said, "to have a clean record. Remember, I don't care what's in those hospital reports as long as they don't say anything about head problems. Shell shock they call it. Or neurasthenia. Can you remember that?"

"Yeah, sure I can remember that," Edger said indignantly. "Yuh think I'm stupid? I told yuh, I may be——"

"Alright, don't get all riled up. I just wanted to make sure."

"I'll get over there in the morning."

The next evening Edgar came up behind Morgan, who was sitting on the latrine.

"Pssst. I got it done."

"Yeow! Jeez! Do you hafta sneak up on a guy like that? Look what you made me do."

"Sorry. I was anxious tuh tell yuh. It's all taken care of."

"It is?" Morgan stopped wiping himself.

"Sure. Nothin' to it. No big deal."

"Gosh, Edgar, that's great. Thanks. I owe you."

"Naw, think nothin' of it. Glad tuh do it."

"I'm a career man now, if I live."

"Me too," Edgar said.

Morgan pulled up his trousers, and they left the latrine. Edgar walked slowly and painfully. Evidently his hike to division headquarters had taken its toll, and Morgan wished he could do something for him.

On the 24th of September Edgar Bunch got orders to report to the field hospital for transport out of the combat zone.

"I knew it was gonna come tuh this," Edgar said. "No use fightin' it."

"Anything I can do?" Morgan asked. "I owe you one, you know." He felt like he had when his childhood dog, Wolf, had been killed.

"Naw. Just think of me once in a while, that's all." Edgar took Morgan's hand and held on for a moment. "Nice knowin' a real hero," he said. He blinked back a tear, backed up, saluted, turned, and walked away.

"See you later, old-timer," Morgan said.

The next day Morgan got orders to rejoin his unit. There were rumors of another big Allied offensive.

CHAPTER TWENTY-TWO

The Meuse-Argonne offensive began on September 26th. Morgan knew, because he had been counting the days.

Morgan, Clarence Mudd, and Victor Steele had put their faith in the stout walls of the stone basement of a church. They were under heavy artillery attack, and each near miss sent dust and cobwebs filtering down on them as they sat cowering in the darkness.

"Anybody see the others?" Clarence asked. He had lost his perpetual-surprise look. Perhaps, Morgan thought, there was nothing more that could surprise him.

"I saw 'em head for the barn," Victor said. He meant Samuel Robbins and Simon Madsen. Max Stuller, the American German, had been killed during the assault on St. Etienne. Hit by a shell almost as big as he was. Horace Gray had put a bullet through his own head two days before, and Lansing had done the same thing the day before that.

The church shook again, as though it were about to come down.

"An' here I thought the Heinies were runnin' outta shells," Clarence moaned. "Gosh darn it."

Lansing had still been breathing when the stretcher bearers found him with half of his face blown away, but they had said he wouldn't last an hour.

"Fuckin' Kraut bastards," Victor snarled. "I hope I get a chance to knock off a few more of 'em before this is over."

Morgan had tried to follow the stretcher bearers, but Sergeant Shepherd had stopped him.

"Ka-wham!" The house shuddered.

Lansing. Not Lansing, who had always been so strong. Why, when it was almost over? Why?

"I sure do miss Sergeant Shepherd," Clarence said.

Sergeant Shepherd had gone down fighting the day Lansing died.

"Huh. No use bellyaching," Victor said.

"Yeah, but he was special. I ain't felt the same since."

"What was so special about him? He shit, just like the rest of us."

"Why, that's no way tuh talk about———"

"Oh, stuff it, will'ya? If your number's up, it's up. Whinin' ain't gonna do no good."

"Wham!"

Morgan ignored their bickering. Not many of the originals left. So much had happened. And it wasn't just the ones who had been killed. Francis Cook had lost both legs, and later, in the hospital, the last thing he had said to Morgan and the others was that he wished he had gone west instead. Then they had carried him out and loaded him into a truck, and that was the last they had seen of him. He hadn't even waved as the truck pulled away. Morgan had wanted to look him up after the war, but Francis told him not to. It was just as well. The rule about not forming attachments. But it was hard sometimes.

And Elmer. All he did was sit and stare, and whenever they moved out he was like a dog, following, doing what they did, eating when they ate, taking cover when they took cover . . . . They took care of him the best they could, but most of them had enough trouble taking care of themselves.

Lansing. He haunted Morgan day and night. It was like he was still alive and would return. Morgan thought he knew how the disciples had felt after the crucifixion. And each time he thought of Lansing, he wanted to start over. To turn back time to when they were young, not so long ago. Morgan's head spun. He gripped his rifle tighter, almost wishing he were dead too.

"Ka-rump."

Morgan kept his eyes closed despite the darkness. Then he heard her. Evangeline.

"What? Is that you?" Morgan said.

"Who the hell do you think it is?" Victor growled.

"Didn't you hear . . . ? I mean, did you hear someone else?"

"Yeah. General Ludendorff. He wants to have lunch with us. He's bringing beer and sauerkraut."

"Yuh know, Victor, you're startin' tuh get on my nerves," Clarence said.

"Yeah, well you guys are gettin' on mine."

"You've been awfully cranky lately."

Morgan was so tired.

"You have to persevere."

"Is it really you?"

"Yes."

"I knew you would come, but sometimes it's hard to——
"

"I am always with you."

"But how do I . . . ? I saw you in the hospital, but the other times? I can't continue, not knowing."

"It doesn't matter. If I were real, you would have images and remembrances of me. If I were not real, you would still have the same images and remembrances. Don't you see?"

More dust and dirt fell. Morgan reached into his pack and felt Lansing's diary. It was worn, and some of the writing had been smudged, but he, who had been with Lansing throughout, could still distinguish every word. The entries were brief, but there was one for almost every week since they had hit the front lines.

"Thump."

"Lettin' up a little," Clarence said.

159

Morgan remembered the first page. *"Despite everything, I have faith in humanity."*

And the optimism halfway through. *All in all I consider myself lucky to have made it this far, and we are looking forward to the end. Then perhaps we can put our lives back together.*

Then the final, terrible scrawl. *Something has gone wrong.*

Morgan closed his eyes and tried again to think of a prayer, but he couldn't. He wanted to pray, not for Lansing, or for his own safety, but for humanity. Then the feeling passed, and the familiar emptiness returned. He felt himself going to pieces again, little by little. Like the last time, when he had struggled so hard to stay afloat, and the harder he had tried, the deeper he had sunk, until all he could do was surrender.

"Sorry, Feeney, we've got to let you go."

"But don't I deserve——?"

"Better? Of course you do. You and those like you. But I don't make the rules." The major sat behind his desk chewing a cold cigar. "The war is over," he continued. "We don't need as many——"

"Balmies?"

"Men. And with your hospital records . . . ."

Outside, alone behind his tent, Morgan cried. Edgar Bunch had been just so much hot air. He would have killed him for bungling the job, except Edgar was already dead.

160

PART TWO

Morgan scratched the dirt from his face and opened his eyes. He lay still, his left leg in a pool of blood.

"Sergeant Shepherd!"

The worst was dying alone, like a stinking dog.

"Lansing? Don't leave me like this! I stuck by you!"

Nothing. No answer from his best friend, and bitterness welled up in Morgan's throat, like vomit. He had been between the lines many times, dragging men back. Where the goddamn hell were they now that he needed them?

"Over here!" Morgan clenched his teeth and tried to sit up, but the effort was too much, and he fell back. Then—before he floated away on waves of pain—he remembered he was in Montana.

"Can you hear me?"

Morgan fought to keep his eyes closed.

"Take some deep breaths. And you'll have to open your eyes sooner or later."

Morgan sucked in as much air as he could and opened his left eye. The other eyelid was stuck shut. "Evangeline?" Her face was out of focus and wavy, like the horizon on a hot day.

"No, Genevieve."

She looked troubled, and he wondered if he was dying. "Where——?"

"The hospital. You fell off your tractor and managed to get run over by your disk harrow. Your legs are hurt."

"Am I going to make it?"

"Die? Of course not. From what I heard, you're tough to kill."

"From what you heard?"

"You did some talking a few minutes ago."

162

"About what?"

A film of tears came to her eyes. "Never mind." She took his hand in both of hers, and clung to it a bit too firmly. "But I'd like to talk to you sometime."

"Umm. How did I——?"

"Lars Nordraak brought you in. Don't you remember?"

Morgan shook his head, and pain seared his neck. Lars and his wife, Caroline, were his nearest neighbors—there in the dry, flat nothingness of northeastern Montana—and Lars was his only friend. The closest to a friend he had.

"My tractor?"

"The seat broke loose. Your tractor stopped when it hit a rock pile." She moved away. "He's back, Dr. Raulsten."

Another face appeared, and a man's voice boomed down. "How are you, Feeney?"

"Am I——?"

"You'll live. Your right leg isn't broken, but there may be a hairline fracture, so I put a cast on it. No use taking any chances. And I stitched up your other leg."

The doctor's face was blurry, and he sounded old, and grumpy. Then he faded completely, and the somber nurse returned.

"Is there anyone we should call?"

"No."

"Evangeline? You said that name."

"No, thanks."

"Alright, soldier. I just thought——"

"Soldier?"

"Everyone knows you were in the war."

Morgan opened his other eye with his thumb, and he saw her clearly. She was strikingly beautiful: tall and fair, with auburn hair and a soft smile. It was her eyes that held Morgan. Brilliant blue-green. But even when she smiled her eyes were serious and penetrating.

163

"Genevieve? Your name is Genevieve?"

"I'll get Lars." She turned and almost ran from the room.

Morgan looked around. Besides the bed, there was a stand with a pitcher of water, and a straight-backed wooden chair. A chamber pot graced the floor in the far corner, and beside the window was a white-painted chest of drawers. The walls were hospital white, with—of all things—pictures of sailboats. Morgan hadn't even thought to ask which hospital, but he assumed the local one in Charity. If you could call it a hospital. More like a field hospital, there in a dusty little town of five hundred, on the vast, godforsaken prairie. No trees, no lakes, no streams . . . One could see for miles, but there was nothing to see. And by the time he'd gotten here—two years ago, in 1920—the rain had stopped. Damn Edgar Bunch. If only he'd fixed his army records like he was supposed to.

Morgan's company met columns of other infantry trudging through the mist—thin, ragged lines, and individual stragglers—in all conditions: dirty, wounded, tired . . . . Some of the French had the thousand-yard stare; a look that no civilian would immediately recognize. And vehicles—ambulances and trucks, mostly—going both ways, belching gas and oil fumes. And horses, and mules. Even a few donkeys, heads hanging sadly, panting like dogs under their loads.

Occasionally would come a staff officer in a motor car, or a courier pushing his bicycle through the mud. Or an artillery battery, men and horses with dry froth around their mouth, trying to catch their breath; officers in front, shouting and swearing in words not even Morgan had heard, trying to clear the roadway for them.

"Well," Lars said as he came in. "Figured I'd hang around so you could thank me for saving your life."

Lars Nordraak had a strange sense of humor. He was a good man, most of the time.

"Thanks."

"Don't mention it." Lars pulled the chair beside the bed and sat down. He was tall and lean, with a handsome Roman-nose profile. His grandparents had come from Norway, and Lars still had a slight *dis* and *dat* accent, and he couldn't say his *J*s. *Junior* always came out *yoonyer*.

"You don't look so hot," Lars said.

"I don't feel so hot."

"You make it through the war in one piece—a big hero—then you damn near get killed in a tractor accident."

"Huh. Big hero."

Lars played it for all he could get. "I thought you were gonna bleed to death on me before I could get you here, and——"

"How's my tractor?"

"Don't worry about your tractor. Just bunged up the front wheel a little. And of course the seat fell off. I told you not to get a Wallace. Looks like a damned overgrown tricycle. But I'll have it fixed by the time you get home."

That was what worried Morgan. Lars wasn't good with machinery.

"Who's the nurse?" Morgan asked.

"That's Genevieve Richards. Some looker, eh? Oh, I get it. You planned all this! Well I don't blame you. Every guy from here to——"

"Where's she from? I've never seen her before."

"She's kind of a loner. Came here a while ago, from out east somewhere. Caroline knows her better than I do. She comes over to play our piano. You and her have something in common. They say she was an army nurse. But don't get any big ideas; she's a strange one, and——"

"It's not that. It's just that she reminds me of someone."
The walls seemed to be darkening, the ceiling was coming down,
and the bed was rocking like a boat.

"Oh? Well I'd be a little careful . . . ."

Lars droned on, but Morgan was nauseous, and he
wished everyone would just go away, including Genevieve, or
whatever the hell her name was. Go away and let him conk.

*Morgan felt something crawl up inside of his thigh. He
threw back the dirty hospital sheet, sat up, picked off the flea,
and dropped it into a hole in the top of the lantern that glowed
softly on the small table beside his bed. The flea popped in the
flame, and evaporated.*

*A nurse appeared from the dark end of the room and felt
the forehead of a soldier who had been moaning all night. Then
she glided toward Morgan's bed, and he knew it was Evangeline;
but as she drew closer he saw that it was someone else. Rather,
it was someone else's face, with Evangeline's form. Her body,
her hair, her comportment . . . , everything else about her; but
her face had metamorphosed. Yet, beneath, it was still her: her
image, and her essence. Evangeline.*

Finally Lars talked himself out. "I hafta get home. My
cow's not gonna milk herself. I'll stop by tomorrow."

Lars left, and Morgan closed his eyes. Try to forget.
That's what the doctors had said. But it wasn't easy. Destitution
of the soul. Four years, and still the visions, the memories, and
Evangeline. The first two years had been the hardest, locked up
in the hospital in New York. Not straightjacketed or tied down
like some of the others, but told when to eat, when to sleep, and
when to shit. And the religious moralizing. Father Mulligan had
been alright though. The only one who didn't blame the victims,
and—ironically—he was the most pious looking one of the

166

bunch, with his bald head, round eyeglasses, and his serious, scholarly scowl.

The nurse returned. "I brought you a little supper. Think you can sit up?" She put the tray on the night stand: a bowl of potato soup, a slice of bread, and a glass of milk.

Morgan pulled himself up, and as Genevieve stuffed pillows behind him, he smelled her lilac perfume, and he felt a strand of hair fall from beneath her nurse's cap and brush against his cheek. Then she straightened and paused.

"You have a scar on the back of your head," she said.

Morgan felt that he was being evaluated in some way that had nothing at all to do with physical wounds.

"It's nothing."

Genevieve sat on the edge of the bed and helped Morgan eat, but he took only a half-dozen spoonfuls.

"Thank you."

"You'll feel better in the morning. That's the way these things go."

He expected her to leave, but she sat looking at him in a curious way. Finally, "Lars says that you have unique strength, and dignity."

"Lars said that?"

"Not exactly, but that's what he meant." She smiled weakly. Then she lost her smile and her eyes narrowed as if she were trying to look deep within.

"What else?" Morgan asked.

"That you have trouble, because of the war." She tapped her head with her finger.

Apparently she saw no indiscretion in what she had said, and despite his pain, Morgan laughed. "You have a way with words."

Genevieve stood and picked up the tray. "We should talk sometime. Yes. Oh, yes, we must talk, Morgan Feeney. Absolutely, we must."

She spoke desperately, and Morgan lay weak and confused. How beautiful she was, Morgan thought again. Statuesque and wholesome looking, like an ancient Greek goddess. But Lars had been right. Strange. Like she was floating through a dream, lost, trying to find her way. Grasping at reality, but never quite finding it. Walking on clouds, afraid of falling.

"I'll be back later." She backed away, as if she were afraid to turn her back.

When she was gone, Morgan slid down between the clean, smooth, white sheets and stared again at the blur of the ceiling. Full circle, from Montana to the war, and back to Montana. And always alone. A lifetime of loneliness. A community eccentric, like his neighbor, Arlen Fitzwater, who had been a machine gunner with the 86th Division. He too had been one of the best, but now he was an outcast. A recluse. The only time anyone saw Arlen was when he came to town once a month for supplies, or when he was in his fields. Or when someone would drive by and see him sitting on top of his windmill tower with an umbrella.

Morgan's legs ached. Is loneliness the same for everyone? An inherent affliction? Are we not, still and all, entire of ourselves and isolated? He got up, limped to the honey pot, and urinated; a steady, dark-yellow stream.

CHAPTER TWENTY-FOUR

In the morning the pain—and the hospital smell of urine and antiseptics—reminded Morgan of where he was. It also reminded him of the field hospitals he had been in. Wounded, gassed, influenza . . . All thrown together. Not as bad as the army hospitals though. Not nearly as bad.

"Yuh gotta help me, Morgan. I don't wanna die. I got too much tuh live for back home. The farm, and Mary, my girl. She's waitin' for me. We got everything planned."

Nurses in white wing caps and gray dresses bustled up and down the center aisle, preparing the patients for doctors' rounds. They didn't stop at Johnny's bed. Johnny Parsons from Wisconsin, lying with a tube draining pus from his guts into a bucket on the floor. The bucket contained some sort of disinfectant, but the smell was overpowering. And Johnny couldn't move his legs.

"Don't worry, I'm here," Morgan said. He sat beside Johnny's bed, holding a Bible.

Johnny's face was pure white compared to the faded white of the pillowcase. He had big, brown, innocent eyes, and fine, delicate features, marred only by a fresh, pink scar across his forehead. He liked to be read to—from the book of Revelation—when the pain was bad. He especially liked the parts about angels descending.

Morgan felt the back of his scalp, still raw and sore. They had taken the stitches out the day before, and he would be leaving soon, but he hadn't told Johnny. Johnny took strength from him.

Johnny groaned, and held his arms across his stomach. "Oh, jeez."

"Bad?" Morgan asked. He wanted to hold Johnny's hand.

169

"Ohhh. Not so bad. Not as bad as yesterday."

All around the hospital men moaned, and on the far end, in the corner, one cried, softly, and talked to himself. The evening sun glimmered faintly through the windows, and one of the nurses began lighting the mantle lanterns. Two young doctors entered and started down the rows of beds—one on each side—poking, feeling, peeking under bandages, asking questions of the nurses, and grunting orders.

Morgan waved the flies from Johnny's forehead. "Shall I read some more?"

"No, thanks. Just stay with me."

"Sure."

One night, in his delirium, Johnny told someone— perhaps his mother, or his girlfriend—that as long as he wasn't alone, he would be all right.

In the morning, Morgan left. He tried to explain to Johnny that orders were orders, but Johnny turned his head away. One of the doctors followed Morgan outside.

"It doesn't matter, Feeney. He won't last two more days. Maybe three." The young doctor was bleary eyed, and he needed a shave.

"It matters to him, Sir," Morgan said. "And it matters to me."

"I meant . . . , oh, to hell with it. Good luck, Feeney."

The harshest lessons of the war—Morgan knew—were not physical; they were spiritual. And hardest of all was the terrible realization of being alone. The war wasn't only an acceleration of death, it was an acceleration of life, driving people apart. One personal exception had been Lansing Rhodes, but even that bond had been broken. Lansing was dead.

Morgan looked at the stand beside the bed, and for an instant he thought he saw Lansing's diary. He closed his eyes,

170

and he saw it again. In reality, he kept the diary beside his bed at home. It had become his Bible, and he had read from it nearly every day since he had gotten out of the army.

Despite everything, I have faith in humanity.

Lansing had had such optimism for the future, and again Morgan tried to recall something Lansing might have said, or done, in the days before his death. And all he could come up with was: "I just don't feel worth shit, Morgan." He had rapped his helmet with his knuckles. "Up here."

And again the diary: *All in all I consider myself lucky to have made it this far, and we are looking forward to the end. Then perhaps we can put our lives back together.*

Morgan had tried to contact Lansing's relatives in Idaho, but apparently there were none. *Something has gone wrong.*

Morgan would never stop wondering. What was it that had gone wrong? Why Lansing, who had survived so much; who could see the end of the war? Who had been so optimistic. Morgan realized he would probably die not knowing, but he couldn't stop trying. Trouble was, it was hard to separate memory from reality.

Someone walked by Morgan's room without slowing, and a dog yapped outside his window.

In the same way that the ghosts of Morgan's comrades haunted him, so did the spirit of Evangeline. Once he had written to find out if there had been a nurse named Evangeline in his sector of France, but he had received no reply. He had not really expected one. So, Evangeline had become his muse.

More footsteps, and the door opened.

"Good morning." It was Genevieve. "Temperature." She sat on the edge of the bed and shook the thermometer. She was unsmiling; almost brusque. She waited, without a word. When she was finished, she stood to leave.

"You're moving pretty fast," Morgan said.

"Busy. Last night Anchor Johannsen came in. He had drunk a bottle of bad whiskey. Didn't you hear the commotion?"

"No."

"Then there was an accident early this morning."

"What happened?"

"A guy from up north shot off half of his face. And maybe it wasn't an accident."

Morgan felt sick. After Genevieve left, he got up, hobbled over, and slid the chamber pot to his bed, just in case. He took off the lid, but when he looked in, he saw Lansing's image on the surface of the urine. Half of Lansing's face was gone. Morgan put the lid back on. The piss smelled too bad anyway.

That evening Genevieve returned one last time before going home. She looked better, but tired.

"Good evening, Mr. Feeney. Temperature again." She poked the thermometer into his mouth before he could answer. "Two cases of the croup, and Mrs. Tubman sprained her ankle chasing her husband with a baseball bat. He'd been drinking. And Mrs. McDonald had a baby girl. You probably heard her carrying on. She was . . . ."

Morgan watched her put a clean bandage over his stitches. Part of her beauty was in her sturdiness. Had she been a man, she might have been a boxer, or a javelin thrower, or——

"There, all done." She plucked the thermometer from his mouth. "Umm. Good." And, as she had done the day before, she sat looking at him.

Morgan knew that he should say something, and he groped. "The man with the rotten booze?"

"Pumped his stomach and sent him home. He'll get worse from his wife."

"And the other? The man who shot himself in the face?"

172

Genevieve's smile froze, and the crinkles on the outer edges of her eyes became painted tears, as on an ancient Greek tragedy mask. "He died."

Morgan waited, but she was quiet, and still. The dog yapped again.

"Maybe it was for the best," Morgan said.

She nodded, but said nothing.

"It must be very hard, working here, seeing all of the pain and misery."

"I've seen worse. Life is hard." She looked at him searchingly, like she was trying to decide something. Abruptly she said, "I knew a man like that once. With half a face."

A chill ran down Morgan's back. "Where?"

Down the hall a child cried.

"In the war. I was a nurse in France."

"France? What happened?"

"He died." She took Morgan's hand. "He was a good man, but he died." She let his hand drop.

"I knew one like that too," Morgan said. "There were many without faces."

"What happened to him?"

"He died too."

"Someday I hope we'll have that talk, Morgan Feeney. When we're both better."

"Both?"

"Well, I have to go. There's a sick little boy."

"How long will I be here?"

"Dr. Raulsten left that to me."

"I feel good, and Lars is going making me a crutch. I think with a little practice I can——"

"Better not rush it. One more day, at least."

She stood abruptly and walked out.

Morgan lay still. The sooner he got out, the better. Guys like him had less than no chance with ladies like her. The best he could hope for would be someone like Fat Fanny Ward, and that was sinking too low even for him. Morgan rolled to his side, back to the door, and closed his eyes. Might as well go back to digging.

CHAPTER TWENTY-FIVE

Through the darkness of No Man's Land came the still, ominous sounds of death. Abruptly, on the right, a Hotchkiss chattered, and up and down the line Springfields barked. After several minutes the firing stopped, and the battlefield was quiet. Then arose an endless line of spectral, fiendish barbarians. Their putrescent faces glowed, their eyes flashed, and their maws were vivid red; and they were unstoppable.

Morgan lit the lamp beside his bed, and looked at his pocket watch. Two o'clock. He had discovered the trick a year ago. A dream so frightening he had decided to wake up, and he had been able to wake himself ever since. He got up, took his crutch, and swung to his armchair. The wind howled, rattling the windows and blowing dust through the cracks in the walls. Not much of a house; just a shack with a couple of rooms tacked on. A cookstove, a table, a few chairs, some pictures . . . The previous owner had decided he'd had enough. Maynard Anderson, who had loaded everything he could into his old truck, and moved back to Iowa to be a shoemaker. Said he should never have come in the first place. His wife had left him the year before.

The wind shook the house again, probing, penetrating . . . . . The Montana wind had driven people mad. And had killed them, in the winter. The lamp flickered, and somewhere close by a coyote howled.

Morgan remembered—every day of his life—the others. Each morning he held a sacred roll call: Thorvold Vilander, Ivan Ivanka, Bill Baldwin, Max Stuller, Philbert Wisdom Stanford, Sergeant Shepherd . . . . And always at the end of the roll was Lansing. Gone, all and forever. Haunting memories, yet sometimes in the hardest times they were comforting. He had

175

tried telling Lars Nordraak once, and Lars had told him to *snap out of it.*

John Dempsey had survived. He had ended up in Ohio after the war, but Morgan hadn't been able to tell from his letters what he had been doing. Then, last year, John had simply shown up. It had been a grand reunion, rehashing the good times they had had, like the time they'd gotten drunk in the little French tavern, after John had nearly had his head knocked off in the boxing tournament. But after a few days things had soured. The bad times had begun to surface, and it turned out John hadn't been doing much of anything back home. Morgan had suspected he was the town drunk, and his suspicions were confirmed when John began spending most of his time in The Palace—the blind pig in Charity—telling war stories and sponging illegal drinks. Then the topper.

"He's back here." The bartender led Morgan to the rear of The Palace. "He's stayin' with you, ain't he?" The bartender's name was Jack Johnson: a tall, pale, middle-aged boozer with a face like a road map; only the roads were in red instead of black. "He's been like that for over an hour."

"What happened?"

John Dempsey sat on the floor in the corner, staring straight ahead, shaking. A group of men had gathered.

"I ain't sure. He walked out the front door, and a minute later he came runnin' back in. Somebody said somethin' about a gun."

"Yeah," another of the men said, "he went out the door and bumped into Nils Anderson. Nils had just got a new gun in the mail. Well this guy, John, or whatever his name is, went sorta white, and he froze up, then a kid came down the street blowin' a whistle, and John ran back in here, and out the back door. The dray man found him crawling around in the alley. We

176

dragged him in here." He looked down at John. "Damndest thing."

"You know 'im?" someone asked.

"Yes," Morgan said. "They blew the whistles when it was time to go over the top." He went to one knee in front of John. "It's over, John. Let's go." He held out his hand, and John took it.

"Time to move out?" John asked as Morgan pulled him up.

"Yeah. But don't worry, it's an easy go this time." Morgan put his arm around John's shoulders and they pushed their way through the crowd.

After that there was nothing left between them, and John left on the train two days later. The worst of it was remembering John the way he had been. A man. A soldier. One of the best.

The wind stopped, and the quiet was even more oppressive. Just the sound of the Regulator clock on the wall above the big, fancy Zenith radio that didn't work.

Dr. Green had been the only one worth talking to at the New York hospital, other than Father Mulligan. Dr. Green had a special quality. Not sympathy. They all had that to a certain extent, or none had it. Rather, an understanding that could only have come from personal experience. Morgan had developed a special relationship with Dr. Green, and if it hadn't been for him, Morgan knew he would still be in the hospital. But Dr. Green had given him something more precious than understanding. Dignity. More precisely, he had appreciated Morgan's natural dignity.

The clock ticked Morgan's life away. Beside it hung a faded 1919 calendar, fly-specked and covered with Maynard's wife's jottings. Birthdays, meetings, crop plantings . . . . The days were wrong, but Morgan didn't care; he liked the pictures.

One day was pretty much like the next anyway. Working, fighting off the loneliness, trying to forget, clinging to dignity.

That was one reason life was so hard. Trying to maintain dignity in a community where people were intent on taking it. Stodgy Danes and Norwegians, mostly. It was hard being constantly on trial, with a stacked jury. War medals meant nothing to them. They'd grunt and sweat on their farms, and when it was time to die, they'd die in bed with their families gathered around. Not alone in some filthy trench, lucky if there was a sky pilot to say a few words. Or crawling around in No Man's Land with their guts hanging out, crying for water, hoping someone would put them out of their misery. Or gassed, lungs full, drowning in their own ichor.

Reputations are easily sullied in small towns. Morgan had managed to remain, if not unscathed, at least aloof, until the day in front of the Gladstone Hotel in Charity.

On a quiet, hot Friday afternoon, Morgan sat alone on the bench in front of the hotel. His plow had broken, and he had come for parts. His head hurt, and before heading home he had stopped to rest. The shade and the gentle southeast breeze soothed him, and as the pain dissipated, he returned to Evangeline, and the war, and Lansing and the others; then he realized he must have said something. He straightened and looked around, and there was no one, but he resolved, again, to be more careful. He walked to his car and started for home. Unfortunately—he found out later—Mrs. Jorun, the hotel cook, had heard through the front door.

A mouse scurried across the room. Morgan watched it sniff a trap in the corner, then run into the kitchen. Morgan had been trying for two weeks to catch it.

Genevieve Richards. Evangeline, and yet . . . And how extraordinary. One day in the hospital she had hardly spoken to

178

him, and the next she had lingered in his room, almost clinging to him. She had kept him in the hospital an extra day, he was sure of it. But why? What was it she wanted from him? Or was he so far gone he was imagining it? One thing for damn sure: it wasn't a romantic attraction. Hadn't helped that he had been incontinent most of the time he was there either. Pissing the bed, and trying cover it up until one of the other nurses was there; one of the homely ones.

Dignity. His only inheritance. From his mother, because that was all she had. Nothing from his father, except the old pocket watch. Nothing but bad memories. Beatings, ridicule, poverty, and watching his mother try to keep the family together by cleaning Clancy's Mercantile at night. And Lundstrom's clothing, and other places. She had cleaned them all, over the years. And people's homes.

Morgan knew there was no hope regarding Genevieve Richards. No prospects. Only pity and compassion. Only Fat Fanny Ward, farming, and digging.

Shortly after he'd gotten out of the army, someone had told him he should go to college. Back then he hadn't thought much of the idea. Now, he wished he had, but it was too late, and he couldn't have done it anyway. He was smart enough, but imagine, a crazy, beat-to-hell war hero that nobody gave a tinker's damn about; a sodbuster farmer sitting with a bunch of pink-faced college kids who don't know a hoot about life, and who are greatly convinced that there will never be another big war. "Ha, ha, ha, haw!" Morgan laughed out loud, but he clamped his mouth shut. He couldn't get in the habit of thinking out loud.

Besides, the person who had urged him to go to college had been goofy. Morgan couldn't remember who it was; he had the feeling it was some do gooder. There were a lot of do gooders after the war, but they didn't do much good, and after they threw a few big parades in some of the cities, they turned to

179

other causes, like prohibiting the sale of alcohol. "Ha." And everyone else—including the federal government—began the healing process of forgetting. Morgan had seen the forgotten, in parks and in hobo camps. He still hadn't been able to shake from his mind one poor wretch he had come across down by the tracks in Atlanta—a 2nd Division guy too, with a head the shape and color of a pumpkin—who couldn't take care of himself, and who would have died if it hadn't been for two friends. The poor devil was like a Halloween jack-o-lantern, except that his candle had gone out. Every time he heard a train whistle he ran for cover, but other than that he didn't move unless told to. Would have been better off dead. Morgan had told one of the guys that, and the guy had gotten furious. Figured no one had the right to decide life and death, and blah, blah, blah. But someone should have the right. The obligation, rather. The duty.

Morgan took his bottle of Old Crow down from the top shelf above the sink, found his cleanest glass, poured two fingers, and gulped it down. Well, if things got much worse he could go back to sheepherding. "Ha! Ha, ha, ha, haw!"

CHAPTER TWENTY-SIX

The incident in front of the hotel was not the last. And people talked; and no matter how hard Morgan tried, the talk continued. One day he overheard Nils Anderson and Jake Miller in The Palace. It was crowded, and they were too drunk to notice him.

"Sometimes he just sits there staring, like he's in a trance. I tell you, Nils, he ain't right in the head. Kinda peculiar. They oughta put him away, before he hurts somebody."

"Yeah, he's in a helluva shape," Nils said. "Another malt for me an' Jake." He lifted his mug and finished it. "And diggin' all the time. I can't figure that out."

Nils and Jake looked at each other in the large mirror behind the bar. Nils, tall and thin, with a big, red drinker's nose that hung down to his mouth. And Jake, short, dark, and nervous. Always with his straw hat pulled over his eyes.

The bartender brought the malts, and Nils pulled a bottle from his boot top and poured a shot into each mug. They had been drinking all afternoon, prohibitionists be damned.

"He was locked up, wasn't he?"

"That's what they say, but I heard he was in a hospital."

"I heard he was in a loony asylum." Jake made wet circles on the bar with his mug.

"I heard he was in the pen for killin' somebody, but I don't believe it," Nils said.

"The hell? I wouldn't be surprised. I guess killing gets in your blood. I'll bet he did in a few of those Krauts over there."

"Yeah, but war's war," Nils said. "Lars Nordraak knows 'im better'n anybody, and he never said anything about him killin' anybody else."

181

Nils took two cigars from his shirt pocket and gave one to Jake. They bit off the ends, spit them on the floor, and lit up. The smoke mixed with the blue haze overhead. In the back, a group of noisy onlookers had gathered around a poker game.

"Well what *did* he say about Morgan?"

"Nothin'. He knows, but he ain't tellin.'"

"Huh. Maybe he knows, maybe he doesn't. If he isn't telling, it must be bad. I still think he's deranged." Jake put his mug down and started for the back door. "Gotta water my horse." He staggered slightly as he headed for the outhouse.

Morgan quietly left through the back door.

". . . wheat prices are lower than ever," Lars said. "The Johnsons just pulled out. Heading back to Illinois."

Lars and Morgan sat in Morgan's kitchen, drinking coffee. All of the windows were open, but it was still hot. Sweltering. Hot from the stove, and even hotter outside.

Lars continued. "I told Johnson to think twice, but he had his mind made up, and that was that. Told the bank to take the place, then he loaded up the wife and kids and left."

Lars took a rag from his back pocket and blew his nose. He was a good man with a mean streak. Kind in deed, degrading in spirit. Indeed degrading. Kind indeed.

"Can't blame him," Morgan said. "I've wanted to do the same thing."

Lars knew about New York and the hospital, and about Morgan's Silver Star, and his Croix de Guerre. He didn't seem to appreciate any of it, but he knew.

"Say, Lars, let me show you something. Just came in the mail yesterday. Bought it from a guy I used to know in the hospital in New York."

Morgan went into the back room and came out with a strange-looking bayonet.

"Some toadstabber," Lars said.

182

The bayonet was almost two feet long, and obviously—from its cruciform cross-section—it was made for thrusting.

"Yeah. I saw a lotta these," Morgan explained. "The French called their bayonets Rosalie. Really knew how to——"

"It's a beaut."

"You know, Lars, in all my time over there, I never once saw anyone get stuck, either side. The Frogs really knew how to use their bayonets—always practicing—but when the shooting started, a bayonet was as worthless as a third tit on a boar. About the only thing they were good for was stabbing rats, and they weren't much good for that. The rats were too fast."

"I saw a rat out in the barn last night," Lars said. "They say where there's one, there are——"

"Wait. Come to think, once when we took a trench near Soissons, there was this wounded Boche. Real bad, and one of us was gonna hafta pink him. Except one a' the mopper-ups stepped in with his Jerry jabber and did it for us."

"Stabbed him?" Lars winced.

"Yeah. Claimed he had to save beans. Eh, bullets. Had to give it to him twice, and it wasn't pretty. He kept——"

"Alright!" Lars said. He slammed his coffee cup down and glared at Morgan. "My God, won't you ever give it up? Every time I come over here you go on about the war. On and on. Don't you get tired of it? Sick of——"

"Of course I do, but you're never the same. If people only knew."

"Lester Sheldon was in the war, and he's alright. And what about Morley Kline? He——"

"For chrissake Lars, Lester was a dough puncher! A cook! And Kline? Nothing but a damn supply clerk! No wonder they don't have shellitis. They could just as well have stayed home! You wanna talk to somebody, talk to your neighbor, Arlen Fitzwater. He was a riveter with the Black

Hawk Division. A machine gunner. Now he's worse off than I am. Completely napoo."

"I just meant——"

"I know what you meant. Buck up, old chum. Get on with your life. Keep a stiff upper lip. Don't look back! The War to End all Wars! Over there, over there . . . People coming and wanting me to put on my uniform and march in the Armistice Day parade."

Lars stood up. "Settle down, Morgan," he rumbled. "That sort of thing won't do."

Morgan closed his eyes.

"Time, Morgan. It just takes time."

"Time," Morgan echoed.

"You need someone. It's no good to be alone like this. I think you're suffering from melancholia."

"Melancholia?"

Lars went to the window and looked out, and Morgan waited. But Lars just stood tapping his fingers on the sink. He said something, but Morgan couldn't make it out. For several more minutes Lars tapped, then he slammed the sink with his open hand, and turned. "We're gonna hafta find you a wife, Morgan."

Morgan flinched. "A what? A wife? What the hell are you talking about? Just like that, eh? Who'd have a loony like me?"

"Haw! It might take some doing, but I'm gonna put my mind to it. Don't underestimate me. Caroline knows a schoolteacher out on Mud Creek, and then there's Alice Whipple who works at the bank." Lars put on his old felt hat. He had cut holes in the crown for ventilation. "Gonna give me a crank?"

Lars' Model T Ford sedan started on the first try. Morgan hobbled around to the side of the car on his crutch, and Lars squinted up at him. "Things are gonna work out," Lars said.

Morgan didn't like his tone.

"Of course if yer really hard up, there's always Fat Fanny." Lars chuckled, but it was such an old jape it was no longer funny, even to him.

Morgan stood hatless in the blazing sun, leaning on his crutch, watching Lars' dust. Why the hell had he gone on about the war like that? Nobody cared.

Fat Fanny Ward. Lived in town with her mother. Cleaned and baked at the Gladstone Hotel. Nice girl—smart enough, good complexion, light auburn hair, pleasant disposition—but Lord was she fat. Lose eighty pounds and she'd be alright, but it seemed like the fat ones only got fatter. Most of the eighty pounds was in her hips. Even so, maybe she'd be better than no one. Snap your fingers and she'd jump the broom the next day. In fact, Morgan worried about that: getting as boiled as an owl, then waking up in the morning married to Fat Fanny. Marrying her when he was sober would be bad enough. He'd warned Lars about not letting him do anything with Fanny, and Lars knew when he was serious. But the bad thing about it was, when he was on a bender, Lars was never around. Lars didn't drink. And it was hard to tell what some of the local souses would do if they had half a chance. Best to stay home.

The horizon shimmered, and the grass and the crops withered. The grasshoppers chewed, and when there was nothing left on the ground, they ate tree leaves, burlap bags, and anything else they could find. Flies buzzed, and birds struggled to survive. Gophers and mice dug and grubbed, and jackrabbits panted in the heat. And coyotes and foxes lay in the shade, too dissipated to chase them. Creeks and water holes dried up, and deer moved away to the Missouri River. Insects crawled, searching for sustenance.

And it was still only spring.

Notwithstanding his disillusionment, Morgan climbed the steps of the Charity Lutheran Church slowly, swinging his crutch out to the side. He had two suits—both black, both wool, both unbearable in the heat—so the choice had been easy. He wore the cleanest one. He sat in the back, and as usual, Sophia Strong settled in next to him, where she would perspire her way to salvation. Morgan had tried different rows, but it seemed like wherever he sat, there she was. Too bad she was so homely. Worse than the ones Lars kept trying to line him up with: Astrid, the buck-toothed schoolteacher from Mud Creek; Alice Whipple, the fat, old-maid bank teller whose breath was enough to kill cattle; and Sadie Gustafson, whose father—the local dentist— had been trying to get her married off for years. Lord, being lonely was one thing, but he'd have to be desperate. Lars had gotten furious when he'd told him to call off the dogs, especially regarding Fat Fanny. Stayed mad for three days. Anyway, good thing Fanny wasn't there.

Morgan loosened his tie. Aside from Sophia and Fanny, nobody had much to do with him. Good, self-righteous hypocrites. But he guessed they couldn't help it. Sophia fanned herself with her bonnet and said something to him. He answered politely. Genevieve was two rows from the front, on the other side.

Eighty-year-old Pastor Syveruud got the first hymn going. Then a prayer, the announcements, another hymn, and the sermon.

". . . caught up in the daily struggle for survival, doing our best to . . . ."

Morgan had all but lost his faith back in the trenches. Maybe he had lost it. Or maybe he had never had faith. But Pastor Syveruud was—as those in his profession go—a realist, as far as Morgan could tell. He had to be, especially now, with times so bad. Still, most preachers weren't. They lived apart, in a world of their own making, separated from their parishioners by a wall of fantasy.

"Yet we must keep our faith that things will be better. That . . . ."

It was hotter than ever, and it seemed like Sophia was snuggling closer than usual. Morgan had to fight to keep from staring at Genevieve. Not that she could see him, but others would notice.

At long, long last, the final hymn, then the benediction.

Outside, Morgan lingered. He had no chance, but . . . .

Genevieve would be one of the last ones out, and though he could no longer trust himself to distinguish sentiments, he still had enough of a grip on reality to know when someone recognized him. As Genevieve descended the front steps of the church, their eyes met. But that was all. Any further interpretation was impossible, except that perhaps she felt sorry for him.

On the way home, Morgan stopped to see Lars' friend, Karl Springer.

"It ain't fair, Morgan. It just ain't fair."

Karl stood in the middle of his hog pen. He was short and stout, and, as always, he had on a white shirt and his black derby hat. He spoke with a German accent, like Max Stuller. Max, killed at Etienne.

"Two died yesterday, and one this morning. And the rest ain't good." Karl took off his hat and wiped the sweat from his forehead with his sleeve. His coal-black hair contrasted strikingly with his clear, almost-translucent skin. He looked like he was going to break into tears.

"I'm sorry, Karl." Morgan waved away a swarm of gnats.

"First Bounder, now this."

His dog, Bounder, had died the week before, and Karl had wandered the hills for four days, drinking. Finally Lars had persuaded him to come home. Lars, the unimaginative pragmatist, and Karl, the colorful, eccentric dreamer. Best friends.

"Emma says it ain't my fault—none of it—but I dunno. It's like I'm bein' punished."

Karl and his wife had come from Chicago. Once Lars had confided to Morgan that he suspected Karl was running from something. Maybe the mob, or some moonshine deal gone sour.

Karl nudged one of the hogs with his toe, but it lay still. Morgan thought of Sergeant Alfred MacIntosh, and he hoped that the sergeant was having better luck with his hogs. If he had survived the war. Raising a few hogs wasn't too much to want from life.

Karl put his hat back on and climbed over the fence. "Lars says it don't mean nothin'. Just a streak of bad luck."

It sounded like a question, but Morgan had no answer. Karl persisted. "Don't yuh think there's more tuh life than just nothin'? That God or someone really is behind everything, and sometimes we get punished for our sins? Maybe if I went tuh church more, things would be better. It couldn't hurt, could it, Morgan? I don't know what else tuh do." He looked at Morgan as a child looks at a father, and his face sagged like melting butter.

"Maybe. I don't know, Karl."

"Oh."

"I don't believe in anything anymore, Karl, and that includes religion. Any religion. Sometimes I try to, but nothing ever comes of it, and afterward I feel cheapened and ashamed. I had enough of religion in the war. Oh, sure, to hear it back here in the States—the propaganda—we were all fighting for God and country, but that was a lie. We were fighting because we had to. We were fighting for ourselves. Fighting to live."

188

"Yuh told me yuh joined up."

Morgan thought for a moment. "I did, but I didn't know what I was doing."

"Oh."

"I have to get going. Wish I could be more optimistic."

"I'm all tired and worn out," Karl said.

As Morgan limped to his old black Maxwell and drove away, he felt empty, like Karl had drained him of something.

CHAPTER TWENTY-SEVEN

Morgan set a bottle of bootleg alcohol, his penknife, a red handkerchief, a white rag, and a pair of pliers on the bench. He had honed the knife blade to a razor edge. He leaned his crutch against the wall of the house, dropped his pants, and sat down. The nine o'clock morning sun illuminated the milk-white skin on Morgan's legs above and below the cast on his right leg, and above the bandage on his left. His hands were dark tan; almost brown.

Genevieve Richards. Genevieve, Genevieve, Genevieve . . . He couldn't stop himself. Evangeline, and not Evangeline. Partly Evangeline, and partly his mother. Strange to think. And even stranger that in some ways she reminded him of Lansing, his best friend. Dead friend, and he'd never have another. Genevieve could be that friend, if only she weren't so damn beautiful. Morgan poured alcohol over the knife blade. If she weren't beautiful there would be hope. He would have settled for plain, but the only ones ever attracted to him had been ugly. Butt ugly. And then there were the fancy women, coming through on the train, working the small towns along the way. He'd never had any dalliances with any of them. Well, only one, when he was so drunk he could hardly remember it. Drink wasn't all bad. Morgan closed his eyes and slugged down as much of the alcohol as he could in one gulp. His whole body shuddered, and his throat burned; and just as he was about to go inside for a drink of water, the burning subsided, and he tilted his head back against the wall and sucked in a deep breath of fresh air.

A meadowlark sang, and Morgan opened his eyes and took a threaded needle from his shirt pocket and placed it also on the bench. He put his thumb over the opening of the bottle and dribbled alcohol over the knife blade again, then over the pliers and the needle and thread. He dampened the handkerchief and

190

wiped around the tiny steel point that poked through the skin just above the inner-front of his left knee, then he poured alcohol over the soreness, and felt it sting comfortably.

Morgan let the sun and the breeze work. He took another drink, and it burned all the way down to the bottom of his stomach. He wished he had something else; something easier to swallow. Anything would be better.

Evangeline, Genevieve, Evangeline . . . . It wasn't easy being crazy, but now this. Genevieve. Whatever it was about her, she was serious about it. It wasn't a game. But dammit, why him? She must have heard the rumors about him, and everybody knew the rumors were mostly true. Not the rumors from before he had come to Charity, but the rumors after. Morgan squeezed his eyes tightly shut and drank again, but this time he choked most of it up. He was almost ready. Hell, maybe he was working on the wrong area. Move up about two feet, and over, and he'd be done with women forever. Not that he wasn't for all practical purposes done already, but really done. He couldn't do it himself though. Lars Nordraak could. Any farmer with a sharp castrating knife could. Get stinking drunk, hold ice on his balls for about five minutes, then have Lars do it, and his problems would be over. Morgan smiled. Lord, when he started thinking like that, it was time. He capped the bottle and picked up the knife.

Ever since he had come home from France, Morgan had felt something, but he had assumed it was only a bad knee. Shrapnel. Probably from the time he'd found the soldier with the dumdums. Not sure how big it was, but when he wiggled it, it didn't seem too big, and it didn't look like there was any infection. The war would never end.

Morgan put the tip of the knife blade at the steel point, pushed it in, and drew it up about a quarter of an inch, and blood began to flow. Now the harder cut. He turned the knife, pushed, and cut downward. More blood. He dropped the knife, and as he reached for the fragment, he remembered. He uncapped the bottle and poured alcohol on his right hand, then he pinched the metal souvenir between his thumb and his middle finger and wiggled it. He took his pliers and tried a test pull. It was difficult to tell, but the blood was coming out faster, so he grimaced, and jerked. Blood began to squirt. Morgan quickly pulled his belt from his pants, looped it around his leg above the cut, and pulled it tight. The bleeding slowed, and he began sewing. Four stitches. He doused the wound with alcohol, wrapped the rag around his leg, and released the belt. He could feel blood oozing beneath the bandage, but after a while it stopped. He leaned back and let the sun cake the sweat on his face. Good thing Lars was doing his farming for him.

Genevieve. Maybe she was loonier than he was.

Morgan watched an old, stray horse trod through his field. It looked like it was lame. Sometimes when their owners didn't have the guts to shoot them, they'd just turn them loose. For the first time in his life Morgan felt old. Old. And for the first time he felt alone. He had been lonely forever, but now he felt alone. There was a huge difference, and alone was worse. The horse stopped and regarded him, and Morgan wished he could do something for it, but he couldn't shoot it. He just didn't have it in him. He waved his handkerchief and the horse gave him a sad look and plodded on.

Morgan wondered how long it would be before he could start digging again.

A MINE OF HEALTH!
By Using the Kickapoo Remedies
Kickapoo Indian Oil, a Quick Cure for All Pains
Kickapoo Salve
Kickapoo Worm Killer

The Adult's Friend, The Children's Savior . . . .

Morgan, Jake Miller, and Jake's wife, Mable, stood in front of the Gladstone Hotel in Charity, reading the Healy and Bigelow Kickapoo Medicine Company traveling show poster.

Kickapoo Indian Sagwa
For the Kidneys, Liver, and Stomach . . . .

"What's sagwa?" Mable asked.

Jake was Morgan's batty neighbor from three farms east, and Mable was Jake's rock-stable wife. Jake was good-enough looking, except for his eyes, which were so deep-set and dark. He'd been a drinker years ago, but Mable had pulled him out of the gutter and spent the rest of her life keeping him out. She was a looker—dark and buxom—and nobody could ascertain why she had taken Jake on as a project.

A stray plowhorse–strong and gray—walked along the edge of the street, stopping now and then to nibble tufts of grass, working around the wild sweet peas. A lean, brown, short-haired dog that looked like a German shepherd mix was slinking after the horse, keeping its distance, waiting; trying to decide whether to rush in for a nip at one of the horse's hocks.

Jake turned his head, and he seemed to be taking in the newly-baked-bread aroma coming down the alley from the kitchen in back of the hotel. Then he looked all around, and, like God after the creation, he seemed to Morgan like he was going to declare the world good. Of course Jake didn't believe in God. Better put, he didn't believe in religion of any kind.

"Don't know what sagwa is," Jake replied. "Must be some kind of Indian word for medicine."

"Maybe you should try some of it." Mable looked hopefully at Jake.

"Don't need it."

193

And by Special Arrangement
Clark Stanley's Snake Oil Liniment
For Rheumatism, Neuralgia, Sciatica, Lame Back,
Lumbago, Contracted Cords, Toothache, Frost Bite,
Chill Blains, Bruises, Sore Throat,
Bites of Animals, Insects, and Reptiles.
Good for Everything a Liniment Ought to be Good For.

"Perhaps some of that liniment would be alright though," Mable said. "Seems like you've always got a sore back, and——"

"Jake! When's the show?" Karl and Emma Springer. Karl had on his perennial white shirt and black derby hat, and Emma—heavy and perspiring—wore a faded black dress, and her dark hair was in a bun. Morgan guessed she had once been attractive, and she would be still if she lost some weight. A lot of weight, actually. And it would help if she got some new dresses to replace the ones like she had on; heavy and homespun looking, similar to what he had seen the Amish women wear. The time he had run away from home. The only time he had been away from his hometown, until he left for good. Should have stayed away the first time, but he had been only eleven.

"Seven o'clock tonight," Mable said. "Did you see the tent west of town?"

"Saw it two miles away," Karl said. "Say, that there sagwa might be just the thing. My stomach's been actin' up some, and I——"

Emma stiffened and glared at him. "Oh, for heaven's sake, Karl."

"Well, how do you know that it——?"

"Balderdash! You just hope there's alcohol in it, Karl Springer. Or that it's mostly laudanum . . . ."

Morgan, Jake and Mable, stepped back to let them argue. "You never can tell," Mable whispered to Jake. She referred to the sagwa.

"Bunk."

A fresh, sweet-smelling spring breeze wafted over them, and Morgan believed that it carried hope. It had been a long time since he had been able to see past life's misfortunes, into the bottom of Pandora's box, beneath the evils there, down to where hope remained. He had confidence that he could forget. Could focus on the here and now. Be a realist. Repudiate the snake oil and sagwa of life.

"Maybe you're right," Karl conceded to Emma. He turned to Morgan. "I had some a' that snake oil once. No alcohol in it at all, far as I could tell. It tasted like coal oil."

"How do you know what coal oil tastes like?"

"Cause I drank some once. Came in outta the field and saw a cup on the kitchen counter, and took four or five big gulps before I knew it wasn't water. Emma was fillin' the lamps."

Emma wrinkled her face. "Every time he belched, he held a match up to his mouth. He walked around the house for hours blowing flames like a dragon."

"Lucky I didn't die."

TONIGHT
The Little Merry Maker
Louise Hamilton in "Fogg's Ferry."
Produced with special scenery and effects.
Cast of Characters:
Gerald Black . . . .

That evening, at home, Morgan again resolved to repudiate the sagwa of life. No more illusions about snake oil, or anything else. Or about Genevieve.

195

Morgan limped to the trench on the hill behind his house. A long trench—maybe thirty yards—with parapet, firing step, duckboards, and two sandbag loopholes. Now he was working on a dugout. Well, he would be working on a dugout, but for his legs.

It was frightful being crazy, but it was terrible being crazy and knowing he was crazy. That was the *thick* part, as the Brits had put it; the intolerable part. Intolerable, but he had to tolerate it, for there was no recourse. Drinking certainly hadn't helped—once he had come close to waking up married to Fat Fanny Ward—and after sobering up, he had gotten into a dreadful row with Lars, whom he suspicioned had been in on the prank. And later he could tell by Caroline's demeanor—the way she glared at Lars whenever one of them mentioned Fanny—that he was right. Blasted Lars. And darned Fat Fanny; she'd trap him any way she could. Another time she had found him drunk, and had sneaked him home with her, and when he woke up the next morning he had to tiptoe down the back stairway so her mother wouldn't hear. Not until three days later—after he had fully recovered from his bender—had he realized that her mother had probably put Fanny up to it. For months he pussyfooted around doing a balancing act, trying to dodge Fanny, and at the same time sizing her up to see if he had gotten her into a delicate condition. With her that was hard to tell. He had kept his bags packed in case he had to leave in the middle of the night. To hell with the farm.

Morgan sat down gingerly on the rear parapet—the one nearest the house—and looked out over No Man's Land.

Morgan crawled over the parapet and slogged forward, inured to everything except the fatigue. He only wanted to lie in the mud and sleep. He couldn't put sleep out of his mind. It was

easy to tell from the sound when the bullets were close, and
when they were too close he didn't hear them at all. He felt
them. And if he got pipped, he probably wouldn't know it
anyway. Unless he got it below the waist, then heaven help him.

After a while nothing mattered. There were only so many close calls: like the time a bullet had grazed his forehead just above his eyebrow, or finding bullet holes in his uniform. And there was a limit to the carnage inflicted on others; a set number of ways for the human body to be maimed, dismembered, or vaporized. From then on, and even now, it was mostly a blur, except for one image: a human heart lying in the dirt, still beating. Curiously, it had reminded Morgan of a calf heart.

Work was Morgan's one extrication, and now he couldn't do that. Couldn't farm, couldn't dig, couldn't do much of anything but sit around and think, and he had come to disdain thinking.

The awfulness had affected men differently, of course. Most pushed on. A few simply sat down and quit, like mules, taking their chances on being shot by the blue funk squad. Some got dugout disease, and did the least they could. Others just got windy. The farts. Others worked their ticket, trying any ailment they could to get out. Some pinked themselves, usually in the foot, and a few others did the same, only in the head. Then there were the shell shock cases, and the most pitiful of those were the ones who kept doing whatever they had been doing when they had snapped. Morgan remembered one Kiltie who forever sat and sharpened his bayonet. It took five orderlies to take his bayonet away, but, unfazed, the Scotchman had sharpened an imaginary one. The Germans had called the Scotch *The Ladies From Hell.*

"Haw, haw, haw!" Lars stood looking into Morgan's trench. "Hee, hee, hee! That's a little too much, even from you." He wiped a tear from his eye with his little finger. "The neighbors are gonna talk."

"Let 'em talk," Morgan said under his breath. "Who gives a hoot?"

Lars continued. "That shell shock of yours is supposed to go away, not get worse."

How the hell would Lars know? All he'd ever done was farm and milk cows. Have kids and pick rocks. Sit around bullshitting with his neighbors, and——

Lars suddenly got serious. "This isn't right, Morgan. You've gotta stop this craziness. I mean it. You're worse than Arlen Fitzwater, and Arlen's bad."

"I may be bad, but I'm not as bad as Arlen."

"So what? People think you're both daft." Lars took off his hat and poked his fingers through the holes in it. He had turned grave. "You've gotta pull yourself together."

Big drops of rain—as big as blowflies—started to pelt them. Thunder, far away, made Morgan shiver. German big stuff limbering up. No, just thunder. Lars was either or. Nominal, that was the word. Nominal. It was a word Morgan had committed himself to remember. No in between. Everything was black and white to Lars. Every judgment, every opinion, every decision, every value, was uncomplicated. Simple, with no regrets, and no looking back. And of course it was easier for him to pass judgment on others than on himself. Human nature, but Lars carried it to a greater fault than most people did.

"Gonna rain," Morgan said.

"It is raining," Lars snarled though the large raindrops.

Morgan stood rigidly, feeling the cold rain on his shoulders and back. Lars' face suddenly twisted in a spasm of rage, and he looked like he was about to leap forward and strike him. What difference did it make to Lars? Why was he so infuriated? What had he dredged from the bottom of Lars' soul?

Morgan gazed off to the northwest, looking for rain. If worse came to worst he could always shoot himself. His trench would be a good place. Damn Lars, forever going on about his trench. When he was a friend, he was a good friend, but when he wasn't, he was dirty rotten. Maybe if Lars found him laid out, the remorse would stick with him for the rest of his life. Not a good plan though, since he wouldn't be around to appreciate Lars' guilt.

Genevieve. Why does a man with no prospects torture himself? Morgan balled up another lump of dirt and threw it. There must be something in the Bible, or in Shakespeare that would cover it; some appropriate line or verse about men's follies and . . . , what was the word? Morgan had excelled in school, for the short time he had attended. Foibles? Follies and foibles. Foibles, follies, and . . . what else? Aha! Foibles, follies, and frailties! Ha, ha! He had them all! If that line wasn't in Shakespeare, it should be.

At the far end of the trench a gopher was starting a new hole, trying to reclaim his territory, but after a while he gave up attempting to dig in damp, grassless soil. He cast Morgan a dirty look, then climbed out of the trench and away, to look for a more solid location. "Haw." Even gophers could repeat Biblical follies, like building a house upon the sand. Not that Morgan had ever read much of the Bible, but everyone knew that part. Everyone probably knew more than they thought they did about the Bible, and that probably wasn't a good thing for humanity. Religion in general wasn't a good thing, as far as he could tell. But church was a good place to meet women. Would be a good place, for someone who wasn't cracked. Nevertheless, he went

199

occasionally, to check for new prospects, and because he was afraid not to go, in case there were something to it, and because he had nowhere else to turn.

Genevieve. Fat Fanny. Why couldn't there be someone in between? Because they were all married. No average, eligible ones, and nobody in Genevieve Richards' class. Plenty of girls in Fanny's class, and a lot of men who would have been just right for her, but all of those young bloods thought they were Genevieve material. Guys like Stephen Long. There was something between him and Genevieve.

A seagull flew over and let his dropping land beside Morgan. A loose, slimy, gray deposit. What in the world was a seagull doing this far from water? But they came regularly, most often when the air was thick with moisture, usually in the afternoon a day or two before a storm.

Maybe it was time to leave. Start over. You couldn't give a farm away these days, though. Trapped. No hope.

CHAPTER TWENTY-NINE

As usual Morgan could not tell if Lars Nordraak was ridiculing him. Nor could he read Karl Springer. Karl was simple, and Lars was more complex, but not very complex. They were both simple, actually. Simple, plain, ordinary men, leading simple, ordinary lives. Farmers, who lived to farm. Married to wives who were less plain and ordinary, but not much less.

They were in the shade of Karl's barn, where Karl had hidden a bottle, but he couldn't find it. Lars stood leaning back against the barn wall, smiling at Morgan. Lars was—there was no other way to put it—mean spirited. Not always. Only in streaks, but the streaks had been coming more often, and when he was on a streak, his kindness didn't matter. It's like, Morgan thought, walking down the street with your dog, and along comes the nicest guy in town, who shoots your dog. He's a prince ninety-nine point nine percent of the time, but he kills your dog—for no obvious reason—and you don't give a damn what a wonderful person he is most of the time; all you care about is that your dog is dead. To you that's——"

"I must be losing my mind," Karl grumbled as he walked about kicking through the grass and weeds. He mumbled something in German, and all Morgan recognized was "Bounder." Karl's dog that had died. Maybe he was thinking of how dogs bury bones and then forget where they are buried.

Lars was still smiling, and Morgan thought what he needed was a good hiding, but Morgan couldn't be over-selective when it came to friends. If it weren't for Lars Nordraak, he would have no friends at all. Something was coming, and all he could do was wait. Probably Lars was going to take another stab at linking him up with someone like Fanny Ward. Lars was a dualist. Not in the philosophical sense—Morgan knew there was such a sense—rather in the common meaning. The everyday meaning that applied to everyday people like Lars and Karl, that . . . Shit. Anyway, Lars was a dualist; so good on the one hand, and so meanspirited on the other. All people are that way, Morgan knew, but Lars carried it to an extreme. With him there was no middle ground, and you never knew what to expect from day to day. Usually more good days than mean ones, but the meanness more than counterbalanced the good, and the worst of it was that Lars dictated his own whims and moods, with no influence at all from others, including Caroline. He was aloof and insulated when it came to distemper, with absolute and total disregard for——

      "I give up," Karl said. "I know I had put a bottle of—— " Then he saw Emma coming from the house, carrying a large bottle. "Verdammt," Karl said, cringing and sidling up to, then behind, Lars.

CHAPTER THIRTY

Morgan parked his Essex coach in the shade of the north side of Charity Lutheran Church. The false piety of going to church was bad enough, but to come crawling to a preacher was even worse. A new low.

Morgan shut off the engine and got out. As his left foot hit the ground the engine backfired, and his mouth began to twitch the way it always did when he was startled. As he waited for the twitching to stop, he stood regarding his new car, uncertain that he had done the right thing; spending money on something so frivolous. No, dammit, it wasn't the frivolity, it was the money itself. Money he had gotten—taken—back in his nether life, after the war and the loony hospital. Back when he had done things he knew he would never do again. Things almost as bad as he had done in the war. Things done for money. And there—rust-colored, with elegant black hood and fenders—was his payoff. Was it worth it? Well, he hadn't killed anyone for money, but that was small consolation. Anyway, he couldn't take any of it—the car or the money—back, and Father Mulligan, in the hospital lunatic ward, had said that the only way to get better was to quit the guilt. When he had asked how to do that, Father Mulligan had said to *just quit*. Let the Lord wash his sins away. It wasn't that easy—not if you didn't believe there was a Lord—and now here he was, with his shiny new Essex to remind him. He still believed in sin, even if he didn't believe all of the other religious nonsense. Sin was part of everyone, whether they accepted the mythology of religion or not. But he hadn't killed anyone after the war. He was through with that. Unless he had to, and he couldn't imagine having to.

Something splatted on Morgan's head. A big lump of brown-and-white pigeon shit. He wiped it away, and wiped his hand in the grass, then he went behind the church and pumped water onto his hands. The pump wasn't far from the graves in the cemetery, and he imagined he was pumping the spirit of the deceased onto his hands, in some kind of symbolic cleansing ritual. He glanced in the direction of the parsonage. Pastor Syveruud was going to wonder what was going on, and Morgan supposed he'd have to go in, but he dried his hands on his pants and returned to the shade of the church. He'd sworn off preachers long ago, and here he was. Sworn off preachers, but at least they were good listeners. The only one who wasn't was Father Mulligan. Father Mulligan had been a talker, not a listener, but he was the only one who had ever made sense. Well, not much sense, but more than most others, and to be fair, more than most regular people. How could that be, that a preacher could make sense? They didn't live in the real world, so how the hell could they help people solve real problems? And right now his main problem was Genevieve Richards. Ha! Problem? She wasn't exactly a problem, but he couldn't think of the right word. The best he could come up with was *obsession*, but that wasn't it either. *Overpowered* wasn't right, and *captivated* sounded like he was some twenty-year-old ninny coming courting, with hair slicked back, carrying flowers.

Morgan shifted his feet, and grasshoppers scattered away from him. They liked the green, well-watered grass beneath the eaves. A car passed by on the other side of the church, and Morgan was glad he had parked where he had. He saw someone pull aside the curtain in one of the parsonage windows. It looked like the pastor's wife. The house was a good fifty yards away, but he could see her smile.

To hell with it. Morgan got back into his car. His stomach had been bothering him. Better see Dr. Raulsten.

"What now?" Dr. Raulsten grumped. He looked like President Lincoln, but shorter, and he wore thick, rectangular spectacles. "Your leg?"

Morgan sat on a tall stool in the doctor's office, with his leg cast sticking straight down and out. The place smelled like ether. He was sure Genevieve worked on Thursdays. "No, it's my——"

"Your what? Speak up! Your leg bothering you?" Dr. Raulsten looked down at Morgan's cast.

"No, I've been having these stomach pains and——"

"Huh." Dr. Raulsten backed to his desk and sat on it, half leaning, looking at Morgan.

Morgan knew not to continue, so he waited. Two of the walls were covered entirely by shelves, and it seemed like there were more bottles and pillboxes than ever. The wall above and around the doctor's desk was posted with a half dozen charts of various sections of the human anatomy, and Dr. Raulsten had inked out the private parts. The fourth wall was lined with drawers, in which—Morgan knew—were the doctor's dreaded instruments. He had once peeked into one of the drawers, and the first thing he had seen was a saw, just like the ones in the butcher shop, only shiny and clean. There were other instruments too, and he had no inkling what most of them were for, and he hoped he would never find out.

"Feeney, I don't have the time, but I'm going to make time." Dr. Raulsten went over and closed the office door, gently and quietly. He came back and stood directly in front of Morgan. He was smiling, but it didn't seem like a smile. There was a warning beneath it. Morgan could see something other than medical advice coming.

Dr. Raulsten poked Morgan in the stomach with two fingers. "Mr. Feeney, there's not a damn thing wrong with you that drinking better whiskey wouldn't cure. What do you think I am, a gilded idiot? You're not the only one, you know. Every young buck in town finds some excuse to see Genevieve Richards, and some of them are pretty creative too. I had a guy in here last week who claimed he . . . , well, never mind. But the only thing most of you need is a good dose of saltpeter on your eggs and bacon every morning."

Morgan had never blushed easily, but he did now, darkly.

Dr. Raulsten backed to his desk and sat again, crossing his arms over his chest. Morgan still couldn't read him; only that he was taking some satisfaction in whatever he was up to.

"God dammit Feeney, I'm between the rock and the hard place here." He turned his head and directed a stream of tobacco juice into the brass spittoon on the floor beside his desk chair. "Never miss. Anyway, Feeney, if it were up to me, I'd tell all of you to get the hell out of here and leave her alone. In fact that's usually what I do, but I can't do that with you."

Morgan felt his blush fade, and he sat straighter.

"All in all I'm a pretty good judge of people, and despite your tarnished reputation I can see something in you. Looks to me like you're the best of the miserable lot."

Morgan's blush came again, starting at his hairline and washing down the sides of his face and the back of his neck. He felt like a thermometer. Still, he kept quiet.

"Genevieve isn't here. She's taking a couple of days off. Female trouble. Nothing serious." Dr. Raulsten looked down, then up at Morgan, impaling him. "Feeney, there are things you don't know about Genevieve Richards, but I have a hunch you're going to find out."

Morgan suddenly felt strong, like he had been when the going had gotten rough in France. "Do you have any idea of what I'm talking about?"

"No." Morgan stared firmly back at Dr. Raulsten.

"She's frequented by demons, Feeney."

"Do you know what kind?"

"No. Only that it's something about the war."

They were silent for a moment, and Morgan knew Dr. Raulsten was lying. Or, more likely, not telling the whole truth.

"I must say, Feeney, you're a better man than most of these slack-jawed sodbusters around here—notwithstanding your, eh, head problems—but that doesn't make any difference. You're all barking up the wrong tree. But I suppose you'll have to find that out for yourself."

CHAPTER THIRTY-ONE

Morgan tossed his Bible across the room at the wall. To hell with it. If there were anything holy about it, it would stick there on the wall beside the picture of his mother, but of course it didn't. It fell and crumpled face down on the floor. He got up from his armchair, picked up the Bible, went back across the room, and threw it again, this time as hard as he could at the wall. It fell to the floor, pages aflutter. Morgan laughed at the thought of someone peeking in the window. More ammunition for the gossips, but it would be, he admitted, first-class ammunition, not the bogus stuff they had already come up with. To be fair, though, about half of the gossip was true. Morgan chuckled. Being the town loony was interesting. Better than being a nonentity.

And the picture on the wall wasn't really of his mother; it was one he had cut from a magazine. An exceptional likeness that was all he had of her. Morgan had chosen the likeness because it erased the careworn weariness from her face.

Morgan fell back into his chair. The conversation the day before with Dr. Raulsten had left him perplexed.

Morgan was seated at the rear of the Gladstone Hotel dining room, next to the kitchen door, waiting for his order of chicken and dumplings. He had come early to beat the after-church crowd, who were just starting to come in for the Sunday dinner of ham with all of the trimmings, but Morgan had an image to maintain, and he had heard the cook, Mrs. Jorun, complaining in back, about how it was hard enough to cook Sunday dinner, without having to make chicken and dumplings. And, he liked chicken and dumplings.

It was always difficult to sit alone, and Morgan's only escape was to twiddle with his cloth napkin and the Sunday silverware, and to study the pictures that lined each side of the long dining room, high on the stucco wall above the oak wainscotting. The pictures were of opera singers, ballet dancers, and vaudeville entertainers. Mrs. Jorun was reputed to have been a ballet dancer years ago, but that was clearly ridiculous. No ballet dancer could have gained that much weight, even if she ate like a Japanese wrestler for the rest of her life. And Morgan had never heard her sing, but her speaking voice was that of a bullfrog. Perhaps she had been in vaudeville. Perhaps she had been a ballet dancer though; there was an attractiveness beneath her thick veneer.

Two flies buzzed around Morgan's glass of water, now that Mrs. Jorun had removed the cuspidors from the dining room, as she did every Sunday. She always called the spittoons *cuspidors*. Called their spit *spittle*, and complained that she would never have had the cuspidors in the first place, if it weren't for all of the unsavory reprobates from the bar next door that she had to put up with. It was easier to put out the cuspidors than to clean reprobate spittle from the floor. Early on Sunday mornings Flora Gooch, the dishwasher, could be seen out back emptying and washing out the spittoons. Flora was a nice girl, and attractive. Once Morgan had exited the back of The Palace, and—being only half potted—he had stopped to help her. He had pumped water while she washed, and all the while she said nothing. She blushed whenever he spoke, but he didn't say much, and on the way home he had wished she were a little older. She had a nice bottom.

The tables were taken—all but one near the front—a table for four. Then there was a slight lowering of the chatter level, and Morgan looked up to see Genevieve Richards— wearing a long, white, wedding dress—sit at the open table. He guessed it wasn't a wedding dress, but it certainly looked like one. Genevieve was as pale as her dress, and everyone tried not to stare, including Morgan.

Finally, talk became normal again. Morgan put his elbows on the table, clasped his napkin in his folded hands, and put his forehead on them, as if in prayer. He peeked through his fingers. Genevieve was looking down, and she didn't respond when the waitress brought a menu. The waitress stood for a moment, perplexed, then went to another table.

Morgan agonized. Should he join her? Likely she had enough problems without that. Then Genevieve started to tremble; probably imperceptibly to most of the diners. Morgan became lightheaded; she was shell shocked! He knew it when he saw it. They were starting to call it other things, but it was plain old-fashioned shell shock, or the after effects of it. But a nurse? How the hell could a nurse get shell shock? Maybe she was just touched. Whatever it was, she didn't look good, and the trembling was more noticeable.

The waitress, a pretty girl probably not over eighteen, returned to Genevieve's table and stood, at a loss. Then Stephen Long entered. He strode toward the waitress, pushed her a little too roughly out of his way, took Genevieve's arm, and tried to lift her to her feet, but—still without lifting her head—she pulled back. She put her elbows on the edge of the table and, leaning down, cupped her face in her hands. Stephen tried again, but this time Genevieve straightened and looked up at him with a rage Morgan had seldom seen in a woman. She pulled her arm away and grasped a butter knife—which she lifted to her neck—and Morgan could see that it was sharp enough, especially for someone who knew what they were doing.

Stephen stepped back, and as Morgan sprang up, Dr. Raulsten entered. As the doctor approached Genevieve's table, Stephen pushed him away, as he had done with the young waitress; and at that, Morgan, ignoring his crutch, strode across the room and came up behind Stephen. He hooked his right arm under Stephen's armpit, pivoted to his left while extending his right leg, and threw Stephen backward a good four or five feet,

210

where he landed on the hardwood floor and rolled under the table of an elderly couple whom Morgan had seen in church the few times he had attended. The couple teetered backward on their chairs, but they kept themselves from falling.

Morgan expected Stephen to come up swinging, but he only lay half covered by the tablecloth, moaning.

Morgan also expected Dr. Raulsten to thank him, but the doctor only threw him a dark look—almost a glower—before taking the knife from Genevieve's hand, laying it neatly on her plate in the four o'clock position, and softly gesturing, palms up, for her to come with him. Genevieve stood, and with Dr. Raulsten's arm around her shoulders, face down, she shuffled meekly toward the door, still trembling.

Morgan remained motionless as they left, then he turned again to Stephen, but there was still only quiet moaning. Someone said, "Good for you, Feeney," and one by one people began to clap, softly, almost silently. Morgan made for the door, clamping his eyes shut to hold in his tears.

Outside, in the shade of the alley, Morgan wiped his eyes. What had happened inside was worth more than gold.

CHAPTER THIRTY-TWO

Summer's splendor unfolded, hot and dry.

Morgan sat on his front porch, watching Lars Nordraak and Karl Springer emerge from Karl's black, beat-up Model T Ford sedan. They each took a rifle from the back seat.

"We're goin' deer hunting," Karl called as they approached. He had on his black derby, and he was sweating.

"It's not deer hunting time," Morgan said.

They stepped into the porch, and Morgan gestured for them to sit down.

"Don't tell anybody," Lars said. He put his lever-action Winchester 30-30 down beside his chair. "I know a place in the hills northeast of here, on Sand Creek."

Karl cradled a long military rifle on his lap.

"Where'd you get the Mauser?" Morgan asked.

"Ain't it a beaut?" Karl pulled up and aimed at a crow that was sitting on a fencepost beside the barn. "Uncle Franz in Hamburg sent it to me. It was Helmut's." He lowered the rifle and sat admiring it.

"Who's Helmut?" Morgan asked.

"My cousin. He sneaked his rifle home from the war so he could fight for the Independent Social Democrats, but he died. Got shot in the thumb two days before the armistice. No big deal at first, but he got an infection. So Uncle Franz wanted me tuh have his rifle."

"Haw." Lars swatted Karl with his hat. "During the war our friend here was good old patriotic Karl Springer. Didn't know a German from a Pygmy. Now it's uncle Franz, and cousin Helmut, and dear old aunt Inga, and the Social Democrats, and——"

"Alright!" Karl gave Lars a malevolant look. "I woulda gone into the army if they'd a' wanted me. It wasn't like I was unpatriotic or anything. Or a coward. They just——"

"Haw!" Lars laughed again. "They thought you were a spy! If it hadn't been for me, they'd have thrown you in jail! You'd have been breaking rocks."

"Thanks."

"Not at all."

Karl's jaw tightened, and he sweated even more profusely. "It wouldn't a' been right though. Me goin' over. I might'a been the one that killed cousin Helmut."

"Haw," Lars snorted.

"What's so funny about that?"

"I dunno. An irony I guess."

"Some irony."

Karl sat fingering his rifle, glaring, but Lars appeared to have gotten it out of his system. Lars had a penchant for picking at people's sores.

Rosalie walked slowly across the yard, toward her water dish in the shade of the house. A shaggy, skinny, black-and-white mongrel Morgan had named after what the French soldiers had called their bayonets. A totally inappropriate name.

Morgan looked westward, where dark clouds rimmed the horizon. Rain, perhaps. But overhead the sun beat down.

Karl left off glaring at Lars and turned to Morgan. "Wanna come with?"

"No, thanks, I've gotta——"

"It'd do you good to get off the farm," Lars said. "Hell, Morgan, all you do is sit here on your porch."

"I'd better not. My legs."

Karl waved dismissively. "Don't even hafta get outta the car. You can——"

"I can't."

"Ah, c'mon," Lars urged, "you can do the driving, and Karl and I can do the shooting."

"I've seen enough shooting."

213

A flash of light enshrouded Morgan. Lars and Karl faded, and in their place appeared Barry Saul. Barry was lean and gaunt, with hollow, blazing eyes, and he held a telescopic-sighted sniper's rifle. His hands were skeletal, and his uniform hung in rotten tatters. He raised one bony hand, pointed at Morgan, and tried to speak.

"I think he's preoccupied," Lars said.

"Preoccupied?" Karl asked.

"Something cooking with Genevieve Richards," Lars chuckled. "I told him I'd find him a wife, but he's got his eye on Genevieve. Seems like every time I see him, he's with her."

"I've only talked to her a few times," Morgan said. "That's all. Nothing wrong with that."

"Just talk, eh?" Lars winked at Karl.

Karl shifted and looked down. "I think yuh better give up on 'er, Morgan. She's seein' Stephen Long. Anyway, she's kinda peculiar."

After they left, Morgan sat on the hill behind his house, beside the shallow grave at the south end of his trench. Digging the grave had taken him three days, with his bad leg. And always the sun. Morgan watched dust devils twist across the fields to the south, and the southern horizon shimmered in the heat. Morgan had dislodged a fox from the shade of a nearby rock, but the fox had run only halfheartedly, tongue hanging, disgusted at the intrusion. Occasionally a gust of wind ruffled the grass, but mostly the air was still. Far to the west thunder boomed, like German 130s.

Morgan had, in a perverse way, found solace in his past. In memories of the war, when, despite the death and misery, he had been alive in a way that most people would never know. But at last he knew that the war was over, and that only by overcoming his past could he live.

214

Morgan stood and gripped his crutch. He went to the cream can and untied the rope that he had used to drag it up the hill. Inside were the remnants of a life now repudiated: his uniform, medals, commendations, a pistol, the French bayonet, letters . . . All except Sydney's ring—that he was to have given to Jake Hermann, the fighter—and Lansing's diary. He rolled the can into the grave with his crutch, then he sat down again. With some difficulty he pushed dirt with his shovel, until the hole was full.

After resting, Morgan placed three rocks atop the grave. They would have to do until he could add more. He stood, removed his dirty, sweat-stained railroad engineer's cap, and bowed his head.

Almighty Creator, Giver of Life, Restorer of Souls, please grant me peace. Amen.

Morgan looked up, bewildered. He was not a believer, and he had not intended to pray. Moreover, he was astonished at the words. They had come as though from someone else. Shaken, he considered the possibility of divine revelation.

The 130s rumbled louder. On the way down the hill, Morgan knew that abrogating his past was not enough. That, in order to live, he would have to win Genevieve Richards. Without her, he would perish.

But by the time he got to his house, Morgan had rejected the divine implications of his spontaneous prayer. Again he realized that he had no chance with Genevieve.

CHAPTER THIRTY-THREE

Morgan lit the fuse and swung away on his crutch. But he fell, and as he tried to get up, a white, rushing noise washed over him.

"Hey, he's wakin' up! Morgan, yuh alright?"

Someone with a German accent. Max Stuller. It must have been an ash can. Too large to have been a mortar.

"Max?"

"Max? Who's Max? It's me, Karl! Me an' Emma."

Max was dead. Morgan held up his hand, and Emma took it. "You were dynamiting a rock, and you had an accident," she said. "You're home in bed. Karl is going to call Dr. Raulsten."

With great concentration Morgan made out her huge silhouette, and there was a loud ringing noise.

"Don't worry, we'll take care of you."

Morgan had always liked Emma. Because of her kindness and compassion, she reminded him of his mother.

"Hello, Doc? This is Karl Springer. Morgan Feeney just had a dynamiting accident! He—— Yeah, he's alive. I wouldn't be callin' if—— Can yuh——?" He looked dubiously at Morgan. "I dunno, I guess he can. Emma! Can he see and hear?"

Emma let go of Morgan's hand, and said something to Karl. "Yeah, he can—— Alright, but—— Yeah, but——" Karl hung up, hard. "Damn."

"What?" Emma asked.

"He's got babies to deliver."

"Babies! This is an emergency."

Morgan could see Emma more clearly now. She was standing in the bedroom doorway with her back to him. She filled the door frame.

216

"He said if he can see and hear, and nothin' seems broke, there ain't much else he can do anyway," Karl said. "We're supposed tuh keep 'im down for three or four days. He'll get here when he can."

Emma turned and looked at Morgan. "You'll be alright." Her hair was as black as Karl's—but her olive skin was a better match than his—and she was larger than Karl. So large that she looked like her dress was about to split its seams. She whispered back to Karl, "Wait till I see that Dr. Raulsten."

The ringing in Morgan's ears seemed to be subsiding. He looked vaguely around the bedroom, at the paint peeling from the faded-white walls, and at the bare ceiling.

Karl came and leaned over the bed. "Jesus Christ, Morgan! Yuh used enough dynamite to blow your whole farm tuh Kingdom Come! It shook the ground clear over at our place, and we're two miles away. What the hell were yuh. . . ?"

The next day Dr. Raulsten came. President Lincoln with a doctor bag. Without a word he moved Morgan's arms and legs, and prodded him in a few places. Then he muttered something to himself in Latin, and left.

Morgan rolled his head so he could see the magazine picture on the wall; the one that so much resembled his mother, smiling lovingly down at him.

Every day for the next four days Emma and Karl came. Emma helped Morgan eat, while Karl did the chores. When Morgan felt better, he and Emma talked. On the third day he told her of Evangeline.

"I was in a field hospital when she first appeared. She sustained me, not only then, but through the war. And afterward. And while I knew she was probably a figment of my imagination, I held out hope."

Emma sat by the bed, holding Morgan's coffee cup while he dabbled at the vegetable soup she had prepared.

217

"If that means I'm balmy, then I am. But isn't it the same with religion? Don't we believe in what we want to, sometimes? I don't see much difference."

"Nonsense. Don't say that Morgan. It isn't the same at all." But she said it without conviction.

"Alright," Morgan laughed. "But I have to tell you this." He paused to make sure Karl wasn't coming. "Keep a secret?"

"Yes." She had her black hair in a bun, and where it was pulled tight at the sides it glistened with sweat.

"Genevieve Richards reminds me of Evangeline."

"No!"

"Yes."

"You're a strange man, Morgan." But again she spoke with little conviction. She went into the kitchen, took the slop bucket out the back door, and emptied it.

On the last day of Morgan's confinement, Genevieve Richards arrived unexpectedly, and to Emma's consternation.

"It isn't proper," Emma huffed as Genevieve came to the door. "What if Karl and I weren't here? Good gracious! No wonder people talk." Reluctantly she opened the door.

"Dr. Raulsten thought I should drop by," Genevieve said lightly. She brushed past Emma, and went to Morgan's bed. "I brought you a hot water bottle, in case you need it. And here. A tin of Dr. Atkinson's Mineral Oil Liniment."

"Thank you." Morgan struggled to sit up. "There's another chair in the kitchen," he said.

Karl brought it. Emma stood with her arms folded, glowering.

"He tried tuh blow up the whole country," Karl laughed. "I remember two years ago, when I was tryin' tuh break up a great big boulder in the field south of the house. I dug under it like a badger, and stuck in a few sticks. Damn near blew the house down. I didn't think . . . ."

Karl's story was long, and as they listened politely, Morgan tried not to look too often at Genevieve. Instead he concentrated on Karl; on his mouth moving.

"Next time I do any dynamiting, I'll . . . ." Karl went on and on.

Finally Genevieve broke in. "I should be going." She stood and patted Morgan's arm. "If you don't start feeling better, please let us know." She cocked her head to one side and looked searchingly at him. "Take care, Lieutenant Feeney."

"Corporal Feeney. I was only a corporal." He tried to get up, but Emma came and held him down with one hand while she waved goodbye to Genevieve with the other.

After Genevieve left, Emma began to sputter. "Calling on single men! Why, I never heard of such a thing." Then she said something to Karl in German, but Karl just laughed.

"Dr. Raulsten thought I should drop by," Karl lilted, holding up his bent wrist and imitating Genevieve.

"Karl!"

Karl ignored her. "She's got an eye for you. A blind man could see that! And she's the kinda girl who doesn't mess around. Why, once in front of The Palace, young Stuart Knolls said somethin' to 'er, and she knocked him cold. A sneaky uppercut right here." Karl put his finger under the point of his chin. "And he didn't wake up for five minutes. Made him bite his tongue too. He thtill talkth like thith, and thath wath three weekth ago."

"Karl Johann Springer, you take that pot of soup out to the car and wait for me, before I——"

"Alright! Ha, hah! But she's got it for Morgan, that's for sure. Ho, ho! Stephen Long better watch out."

Emma chased him out the door, then she returned to the bedroom. Despite his headache, Morgan laughed.

219

"Oh, it's not so funny when you have to put up with his shenanigans all the time," Emma said, catching her breath. "Once Genevieve told me you were a composite of some soldiers she had known during the war. Can you imagine that? What a curious thing to say." She sighed. "If only she weren't such a free spirit." She patted Morgan on the shoulder. "We'll be back tomorrow to see if we can get you out of bed."

Morgan hadn't been up since the accident, except for when Karl had half carried him to the outhouse.

Karl and Emma left, and Morgan lay wondering. Had Dr. Raulsten really sent her? Of course he had.

CHAPTER THIRTY-FOUR

"If your legs feel alright, they probably are," Dr. Raulsten said.

He had Morgan on the examining table in the room next to his office. Genevieve stood behind Morgan. The walls were decorated with medical pictures of the inner workings of arms, legs, abdomens, and all other parts of the body, and, as always, the private parts were inked out. On the floor, in the far corner, lay a black cat.

"I'll give you some exercises to do so you don't stiffen up and atrophy. Come back at the end of the month. As far as the other leg goes, you're damn lucky you didn't get blood poisoning, then I'd have had to amputate. Or would you want to do that yourself too, Dr. Feeney?"

Dr. Raulsten went into his office and closed the door, and Genevieve helped Morgan down.

"How's your tractor? Did Lars get it fixed after the first accident?"

Morgan smiled. "Well, he pulled it home for me, and took the front wheel off, but that's as far as he got. Doesn't matter; I can't use it anyway. Lucky it wasn't damaged worse than it was."

Genevieve laughed. "Lars said it's a pile of junk." She said it easily, not ridiculing.

Morgan laughed. "It's a Wallace Cub Junior. Lars never did like Wallaces. Anyway, if he had his way, we'd all still be farming with horses."

Morgan put his crutch under his arm and swung his way to the door. He turned toward Genevieve. "I, uh, well thanks. I'd better get going."

"You know, Morgan Feeney, you look like you could use a glass of lemonade."

"Lemonade? I haven't had lemonade since I was a kid."

221

"Fine. My place at five-thirty."

"I'll be there. Thanks."

On the way out, Morgan's vision blurred. He went to the bench in front of the mercantile store and sat in the shade. For three days he had prepared himself to invite her to the barn dance on Saturday night, and he had failed—through lack of nerve—only to have her invite him for lemonade. And it had happened so unexpectedly. Fortunately, or he might have frozen up, or said something stupid. His only experience had been with bar girls.

Down by the depot the train clunked and groaned to a stop, and someone shouted. Morgan couldn't see the engine, but the brakeman got out of the caboose and walked forward, waving one arm. Coal smoke blew up the street before dissipating.

Whenever he had referred to Genevieve's past—especially the war—she had acted strangely, yet she persisted in dredging up his war haunts, like she was using him in some dark way. But she didn't seem like a user. What, then? Dammit, what?

Two young boys came up the street riding an old rust-colored mare. The one in front—scrawny and scraggly, with hair the color of the horse—looked at Morgan and pointed, and they both snickered.

Genevieve was not some helpless innocent. And obviously she cared little for convention. It was easy to see who she wasn't. But who was she?

It would not have been proper for her to invite him in—even she had her proprieties—so they sat on the front step of her house. Morgan had never been glib, but he was surprised at how easily his words came.

"You make excellent lemonade," he said. He held his glass up to the evening sun, and said it with the air of a connoisseur.

Genevieve laughed and clinked her glass against his. "To warm lemonade."

"Warm lemonade."

They drank, and when Morgan lowered his glass, he realized that he had succeeded in forgetting himself, if only for a short time. Perhaps it was a moment to build on. For a while they were quiet as they watched bees make their last pass of the day at the prairie rose bushes in the yard. The roses had faded and dried up, but the bees persisted out of instinct.

"Oh, I forgot the ginger cookies I made yesterday." Genevieve moved to get up, but Morgan stopped her.

"None for me, thanks."

"No? What an insult! No one has ever refused both my warm lemonade and my hard cookies."

It was then that Morgan saw the sadness in her disappear, as it had with him. She sat looking at him, completely at ease, with her hair flowing down her shoulders, and the corners of her eyes wrinkled as though she were about to burst into laughter again. Morgan stayed longer than he should have, and when they ran out of things to talk about, they leaned against the wall and watched the sun streak the horizon with red and gold.

Genevieve broke the silence. "You are indeed unique, Corporal Feeney."

"How do you mean?"

"In many ways."

"What ways?"

"Your departures, for example."

"Departures?"

"Your epilepsy. People around here call them the *fits*."

Morgan refused to look down, or to look away. He didn't mind her asking.

"Is it bad?" she asked.

"Not so bad."

As he drove away, Morgan puzzled over how easy it had been. Like being with someone he had known all of his life. Perhaps she saw something in him. Strength of character, or some inner quality that only she could discern. He hoped so, but again he had to face the probability that her geniality was sympathy.

Karl Springer teetered from the sidewalk in front of The Palace. The rotgut in The Palace was too much even for Karl.

"Just the guy I was lookin' for," Karl called. "Can I get a ride home?"

"Sure. Jump in."

Karl, portly and thoroughly inebriated, took several tries at getting in. He had a bottle in one hand. "Home, Morgan," he commanded, waving the bottle.

Morgan felt the back of his neck turn red. People were looking. He advanced the gas lever, and they were off.

"Have a pull." Karl offered the bottle, but Morgan waved it away. They finally got out of town.

"Emma got mad and left me in town," Karl explained. "She don't tolerate drinkin'. No, Siree." He took another drink, and some of the whiskey dribbled down his chin and onto his dirty white shirt. Morgan felt sorry for him. Two more of his hogs had died. He had only six left.

"How's the crop?" Karl asked. They hit a bump, and he spilled whiskey down the front of his shirt again.

"Not so good. We need rain. I heard Goodwin Ostberg got hailed out."

"Hurrumph! Goodwin," Karl snorted. "He won't last another year. Shoulda been a butcher or somethin'. In fact I heard he was a butcher back in Mississippi. He shoulda stuck tuh butcherin'."

Karl looked at Morgan like he was trying to concentrate. "Say, I saw you comin' outta Genevieve Richards' place. I think there's somethin' goin' on."

"She invited me over for lemonade."

"Lemonade! Haw! That's a good one. I bet you got more than lemonade! And here I thought you——"

"Cut me some slack, Karl," Morgan rumbled, but he couldn't help smiling.

"Alright. None a' my business. Haw! Anyway, yuh better watch out if Stephen Long finds out."

"I'll take my chances."

Karl at last changed the subject, and as they jounced along, he continued to do most of the talking. Then he got quiet, and when they got to his mailbox, he had Morgan stop.

"No use Emma takin' after you too." He got out. "Wish me luck, Morgan. Emma don't tolerate drinkin'."

"Good luck, Karl."

As Morgan pulled away he looked back, and in the moonlight he saw Karl hiding his bottle under some rocks along the fenceline.

CHAPTER THIRTY-FIVE

Morgan parked with the other cars along the road leading to Arlen Fitzwater's farm. It was a cloudless day, and the sky was an ominous shade of lavender. The same cast, Morgan recalled, as the day the 9th Regiment had marched out of Montreuil.

Lars met him. "The sheriff thought maybe you could get him out."

225

Morgan followed Lars to where the county sheriff and two deputies were standing behind a hill, peeking over at Arlen's house.

"What's going on?" Morgan asked. All he could see was the windmill, and the weathervane atop the barn.

The sheriff was big and hard looking, and he carried a double-barreled ten-gauge shotgun. He sized Morgan up. "You Feeney?"

"Yeah."

The sheriff looked like Sergeant Shepherd, except he didn't have scars on his cheeks.

"Smith." He shook Morgan's hand. "The bank in Charity's foreclosing on 'im. One a' my deputies tried to serve the papers, and this Fitz, whatever his name is, ran 'im off at the business end of a rifle." He scrutinized Morgan again. "They say he's off in the head from the Great War. You know 'im?"

"Yeah, some."

"Yuh think he'll listen tuh you?"

"Maybe. I can try."

"Here comes the doc," Sheriff Smith said. "Just in case."

Dr. Raulsten parked and got out of his car. Genevieve was with him.

"We could smoke him out," the sheriff said, "but I don't figure there's any use to start shootin' if there's an easier way."

A group of people had gathered by the road, and some of them were armed.

"What'll you do with him?" Morgan asked.

Neither of the deputies seemed enthusiastic. One looked like he was no more than eighteen or nineteen years old; a dark, wiry kid with droopy eyelids. The other, older—maybe in his thirties, with smallpox marks all over his face—had the shakes. He kept lighting cigarettes and snubbing them out.

226

"Lock 'im up for a while, then send 'im tuh the loony bin in Warm Springs I guess."

Karl Springer and two others came running, carrying rifles.

"Let me borrow your shirt, Karl." Morgan found a stick.

"My shirt? What the devil do yuh want with——?"

"It's white," the sheriff huffed. "Give it to 'im."

"Well, for cryin' out loud," Karl complained, but he took off his shirt and handed it to Morgan.

Morgan tied Karl's shirt to the stick. "Wish me luck."

Nobody said anything, then Lars stepped forward. "Want me to go with you?"

"I'd better go alone." Morgan saw Genevieve nod at him, ever so slightly, as he started over the hill toward Arlen's house. His leg hurt, but it was nice to have the cast off.

"Morgan! Come in." Arlen appeared in the doorway, holding a British Lee-Enfield. "What brings you?" His house was an unpainted two-room homestead shack.

"What brings me?" Arlen backed in, and Morgan closed the door. "You start shooting at people, and you ask what brings me? And where'd you get the Mark Three?"

"Aw, I was only tryin' tuh chase 'em away. Why the hell can't people just leave me alone?" Arlen was Morgan's age, but he looked older. He was short, and bent, and he had the eyes of a cat. Not slitted, but yellow, and intense. He limped when he walked.

"Sit down, Morgan. I'll put on some coffee."

The kitchen table was stacked with dirty dishes, and piles of garbage reached halfway to the ceiling. The smell was staggering. Arlen pulled a handkerchief from his back pocket and coughed into it, hawking up green gobs. He had been gassed.

227

"No time for coffee, Arlen. You've got to come with me."

"With you? Where?"

"The bank," Morgan lied.

"They told me I could have more time."

The living room part of the house was as messy as the kitchen. Dirty clothes, boxes, litter on the floor. It brought to mind some of the trenches Morgan had occupied.

Morgan tried again. "Maybe you could stay with me for awhile, and——"

"You?" Arlen laughed. "No offense Morgan, but everybody knows you're a little off! Anyway, they're not gonna let me do that."

"You may be right, Arlen. But the fact remains that you're going to have to come out."

Arlen gripped his rifle tighter. "I don't think I wanna do that, Morgan." He frowned and looked away, as though he were listening to someone else.

"Otherwise I'm afraid somebody's gonna get killed," Morgan said.

"Me? No big loss there." Arlen's face fell, and he pouted like a child.

They sat at the dirty kitchen table, Arlen with his rifle across his lap, Morgan nervously checking his watch. For a half hour they talked about the war, and Arlen spoke of his loneliness.

"It isn't being crazy that bothers me so much," Arlen said. "It's being alone. That's the hard part. Hell, I'd as soon be back in the war. Even that would be better than——"

Morgan could wait no longer. "We've gotta go, Arlen. I'm just trying to help, and I'm telling you, you've got to give it up. Gimme that rifle, and let's get this over with." Morgan considered jumping him.

228

"Trying to help, eh Morgan? Some friend. You haven't been over here to see me but twice since you moved to this godforsaken country. Twice. Now here you come, in cahoots with the sheriff, tryin' tuh get me tuh let him stick me in some nuthouse."

Morgan locked eyes with Arlen. "Arlen, we're too much alike. Don't you know that? We've seen the elephant, and we're alone with it now. Part of us, anyway. You go off to war, and it's all a big, patriotic show. Then the fighting starts, and you cling to each other, except the guys next to you start getting killed, and what good did it do, hanging onto them? Dead or alive, they can't help you. No one can, so you're better off pushing them away, so they don't drag you down. That's it, isn't it? You know damn well that's it. That's why you and I will never be friends."

Arlen covered his face with his hands and mumbled something.

"What?"

"Yeah, Morgan, that's it."

Morgan waited for Arlen to look at him, then, "You've got to come out, Arlen. For your own good. God knows nobody else cares. You learned that in the trenches. You said so yourself."

"No!" Arlen shouted. "I ain't leavin'!" He lifted his rifle from his lap, and cranked a round into the chamber.

Maybe there was another way. "You don't intend to hurt some deputy—some poor guy with a wife and kids, who's just trying to do his job—do you?"

Arlen jumped up and paced back and forth, muttering to himself. "I'll never hurt anyone again. I've done enough of that to last a lifetime. A hundred lifetimes. God, I can't even stand tuh go duck hunting. It's just that sometimes a guy doesn't know what tuh do. You and I talked about that once, remember? About how hard it is to know what to do? You said how you

229

always have to try to act normal, and I said I'd just as soon stay away from people as make a fool of myself? Well that's all I want. Just to be left alone. That isn't asking for much, is it? For people to leave me alone?"

"No, it isn't. But this time you have to go by the rules, Arlen. Let's go out with dignity. Like men."

"Dignity?"

"Sometimes that's all we have. Don't you remember? We talked about that too."

"I know. Dignity. But damn."

Arlen looked away and listened again, and his lips moved, as if to answer. Then he turned back to Morgan. "Yeah, I'll go out with dignity. You're right. Sometimes that's all we have. Even if they lock us up in the nuthouse. What do these people know?"

Morgan took the rifle and leaned it in the corner. "Then chin up, old boy. Let's hold our heads high." Morgan picked up his flag, and he put his arm around Arlen's shoulders. He pushed open the door with his foot, and they went outside.

"I'll do what I can for you," Morgan said.

"Thanks."

"And the nuthouse isn't so bad. I've been there."

They walked slowly toward the sheriff. With each step they kicked up puffs of dust. Morgan again noticed Genevieve, and again she nodded, almost imperceptibly.

"I have to ask, Arlen," Morgan whispered.

"Yeah?"

"Those times you were sitting on top of your windmill tower?"

"Yeah."

"Why? What were you doing?"

Arlen stopped and looked up at Morgan, and his cat eyes brightened. "I could see forever, Morgan. The whole damn world."

Morgan's knees shook. It was like the young shell shock victim he had met in the hospital in France: *They're blowing some poor devils to smithereens. I can see it from here. Isn't that strange? Am I balmy?*

CHAPTER THIRTY-SIX

"Hey, Morgan, I hear you been sparking Stephen Long's girl." It was Wolfgang Sturm, coming out of The Palace. Wolfgang: big, dumb, mean, and drunk. He swayed, hatless, with the sun broiling his bald pate. He was attracting flies.

"That so?" As Morgan stood hanging onto the door of his car, a blast of wind drove dust and grit up the street. He closed his eyes and waited.

"That's what I been hearin'," Wolfgang taunted.

By local standards, Stephen Long was wealthy. Big two-story house, new car, the best machinery. Good looking too. Like an actor in a play Morgan had seen in New York City. Tall, dark, lean. His only flaw was that he had a nervous tic on one cheek. He was well educated; always talking about Princeton. Nobody ever thought to ask what a Princeton man was doing squatting on three hundred twenty acres of dry dirt, as far from anywhere as one could get. Morgan had seen Genevieve talking to him several times, but they always seemed to be arguing.

"Yeah, yuh better watch yer step, Feeney. If someone was sparkin' my gal, I'd have somethin' tuh say about it. If I were you, I'd . . . ." People were staring. Caroline and Lars Nordraak came out of the mercantile store and stood in the shade.

Wolfgang kept on. "I hear Long's got quite a temper. Maybe yuh better lay low for a while." Wolfgang must have sensed something was wrong. He turned and focused his bleary eyes on Lars. "Eh? Well, none a' my business." He tried to smile at Morgan as he staggered back into The Palace.

Morgan glanced at Lars, got into his car, and drove away. Lars hadn't been in a pool hall over a dozen times in his life, but last year in The Palace he had given Wolfgang the beating of his life. Nobody was sure why. The regulars had been too drunk to remember, and Lars never talked about it.

232

"Nice hole," Morgan joked. Lars was digging into the hillside south of his house. "Root cellar?"

"Yeah," Lars huffed. He leaned against the cool dirt and wiped his face. "Wanna dig awhile?" He held up his shovel.

"No, thanks. I had enough digging in France." Morgan came down. "You woulda been a good groundhog. That's what they used to call us front-liners, because of all the trenches we dug. How come you never got to play hero? Actually, with your talent, they'd have probably made a sapper out of you."

"Huh. They tried to draft me, but I was too smart. They only wanted the dumb ones. What's a sapper?"

"Like a coal miner, only they'd dig under enemy lines and plant explosives."

"Well, we need a root cellar, and I always worry about tornadoes," Lars said. "Caroline was back in Fargo once, visiting her mother, and there was a tornado. Sat it out in a root cellar. A guy should never be without one."

"Hm. I get claustrophobic."

Something slithered out the front of the hole. A small, green salamander.

"Did you hear about Patty Duffy's bull?" Morgan asked.

"No. What?"

"Struck by lightning. Deader than a doornail."

"How did he know it was lightning?"

"Who? The bull?"

"You gasbag." Lars hawked up a big glob of phlegm, and spat.

"Started a fire. That was his prize bull. Patty's been in The Palace ever since."

"Huh." Lars sat down in the moist clay.

Morgan sat beside him. The clay was fresh smelling, and cool. Morgan took off his hat and looked up. Almost dinnertime. He'd have to get to the point.

"Patty got a good rain though," Morgan said.

"We didn't get any."

"Neither did I. It was spotty." Morgan dug his heels into the clay and twisted them. Lars was a friend, but such things were hard.

"I ran into Genevieve Richards the other day," Morgan said.

"Oh."

"Literally ran into her in the store. Groceries all over the place. She was good about it though."

"That right?" Lars seemed uninterested, but he made no move to get back to his digging.

Morgan's face and neck flushed the way they always did. "I don't know quite what to make of her. One time she's friendly—inviting me to her place for lemonade, and things like that—and the next she'll hardly look at me."

"Hm."

"Once you told me she was strange. What did you mean?" Morgan asked.

Lars picked up a pebble and threw it out the top of the hole. "I dunno. Kinda different."

"How?"

"It's hard to say. It's like she's off on the clouds." Lars frowned as he picked up another pebble. "And sometimes she seems to think she's a man." He threw the pebble up, and caught it.

"A man?"

"Well, I can't think of how to say it. You know, out riding horses all the time. Wears men's clothes. They say she's better with a shotgun than most men."

"Unh."

"She seems kind of strong minded for a woman. Once she even stormed into The Palace and ordered an eye opener."

"No!"

234

"Yeah."

"They give it to her?"

"Hell yes! Then she had another, and when a crowd gathered, she stomped out."

"I'll be damned."

"And there are rumors floating around."

"Like what?"

"Like she's running from something. Or that she likes other women."

"Other women?" Morgan coughed, almost choking. "I knew these two guys in the army—a prizefighter and his manager—and they were that way. You'd never have known, at first, then . . . , there were others, too. You don't really think she——?"

Lars grinned at him.

"Damn you, Lars! You know very well she isn't."

"Never can tell."

"Wise guy."

"Hello, Morgan. Never can tell what?" It was Caroline.

Morgan thought she resembled Genevieve, but a few years older, and her hair was straw colored. The resemblance was only external.

"He's still chasing Genevieve Richards," Lars crowed.

"Now, Lars."

"Her name came up," Morgan stammered, "and I was just wondering about her, that's all."

"Morgan better be careful," Lars bellylaughed. "That highfalutin Stephen Long is quite a rake I hear."

"Lars! Stop it." With deliberate effort Caroline ignored him and looked at Morgan. "She's a pleasant girl."

Caroline—like Lars–always saw things in black and white, and she was a supreme optimist. To her, most people were pleasant.

"I should be going," Morgan murmured.

"Come up to the house, Morgan. I have a pie for you."

Lars and Caroline's house was the usual tarpaper-covered shack. Lars had added a separate kitchen to one end. Caroline shooed away their two children, six-year-old Alice, and ten-year-old Sexton.

"Here." Caroline handed the pie to Morgan. "Apple."

"Thanks. I——"

"Sit down for a minute, Morgan."

Something was up. Caroline had never really talked to him before, and he had always felt that—despite her good nature and her kindnesses—she still didn't like him much.

Caroline made no move to pour coffee. She wiped her hands on a towel. "Morgan, I don't mean to stick my nose into your business, but there's something you should know."

Flies buzzed above the sink. One of them hit the strip of flypaper Caroline had hung from the ceiling. It struggled briefly, then it was still.

"It's Genevieve. I know you'll keep this to yourself."

Morgan nodded. Here it comes, he thought.

"That girl has had a rough time, Morgan. She was a nurse during the war, and——"

"I know. It seems we share a——"

"Yes. But there are things you don't know." Obviously she had rehearsed her talk. "Genevieve was in charge of some of the most severely wounded. One was worse than the others, and she became attached to him."

She paused, but Morgan remained silent. More flies came in through a hole in the window screen, and Caroline laid her towel over Morgan's pie to protect it.

"Is he still alive?"

"Yes. Chicago, I think. She writes to him, and sometimes she goes to see him."

236

Morgan felt hope flow from him. "How . . . are they . . . ?"

Caroline continued. "I don't know. It's just that I don't want her to be hurt any more than she already is." Her face sagged, and tears came. "I've said too much. But please, Morgan, don't . . ." She wiped her eyes with her apron.

"Don't worry." As Morgan got up, he felt the same as the time an army mule had kicked him in the stomach. He paused at the door. "What about Stephen Long?" Morgan asked.

"I don't know."

Morgan put his pie on the back seat of his Essex sedan and covered it with his soiled handkerchief. But Caroline did know about Stephen Long. Morgan could feel it. Her only concern was for Genevieve.

CHAPTER THIRTY-SEVEN

Two shorts, a long, and a short. Morgan lifted himself from his armchair. He should rip the damn phone out; it seldom rang, and when it did, it was always bad news. He brushed a cobweb from the receiver and put it to his ear.

"Hello?"

"Morgan?"

"Yeah. Who did you think?" He should have been glad to hear from someone, but he wasn't. He liked Karl Springer for his childlike simpleness, but now he didn't feel like talking to anyone, let alone someone of simplicity. It had been a rocky night.

"I'm in trouble, Morgan. Yuh gotta help me."

"What's wrong now?"

Karl was always in trouble, and it was usually with his wife, Emma. Morgan waited, and he could hear background noises that weren't Karl's. There could be up to a half-dozen eavesdroppers. Well, that was Karl's problem, not his.

"It's that nurse of yours! She's over here, and there's somethin' wrong with 'er! I gotta get 'er outta here before——"

"Nurse of mine? You mean Genevieve Richards?"

Now it was his problem too. Damn wiretappers. Worse than the Krauts.

"Yeah. She's over here, and I gotta' get 'er outta here before Emma gets back. Yuh gotta' come and get 'er, Morgan. It ain't gonna look good, and there's somethin' wrong with 'er!"

"What? What's wrong with her?"

"It's like she's drunk or somethin', but she ain't. I dunno." He swore in German. "Emma's gonna' kill me." Karl had gone from shouting to a low moan.

"Dammit, Karl, what's wrong with her?"

"I said, I dunno. She's lyin' on the bed groanin' and mumblin' about somethin'. I can't make it out."

"How did she get to your place?"

"When I got home from town, there she was in the back of the truck, lyin' in a big pile of gunny sacks. She musta snuck on when I was in the pool hall. That's gotta' be it. They said she'd been in the hall earlier, and was actin' pretty queer. Himmel! This ain't gonna look good! Yuh better get her outta here, Morgan."

"Did you call Doc Raulsten?"

"He's gone. Went to——"

"How about Caroline Nordraak?"

"They're not home. Are you gonna come and——?"

"Yeah, alright, I'll be right over." Morgan hung up and sagged back against the wall. Genevieve. Was she crazier than he was?

Morgan drew himself up straight and went outside. There, staring at him, was a huge—almost gigantic—buck deer, with coal-black horns larger than any Morgan had ever seen. The buck's eyes were red, and they pulsed. Neither Morgan nor the buck moved, and Morgan questioned whether he was hallucinating, or having one of his episodes, but he didn't think so. There was something different this time; some quality in the deer that held Morgan securely in the realm of reality, as best he could discern reality. Morgan knew that if he looked down and back up, the deer would still be there. He further knew that until the moment was broken, no matter what he did, the deer would remain. And, so, he stared back, half expecting the deer to speak, and it was then that Morgan realized that, when talking with Karl, he had been afraid. He had known physical fear during the war, but now his worst fears were internal, of his own design: fears of the past that had been seared into his brain by some sort of devilish, psychic branding iron. But seeing the deer calmed him. How could it be? How could a bizarre-appearing, almost supernatural damned deer have any bearing on it?

The deer—the magnificent buck with the black horns—
turned away, walking slowly, without looking either back or
from side to side, across the field in front of the house, down a
slight dip, up again, and over the hill. Rosalie, who had been
lying at her place on the porch, stood. Normally high-strung, she
remained quiet. Morgan expected her to explode, and give chase
to the deer, but she was as if she had been carved from marble.

God-damn, it's a hell of a thing when a guy gets so bad
off he imagines a deer with glowing-red eyes. Morgan put his
hand over his face to block the glaring sun for a moment. Not
that he'd imagined the deer. Maybe the eyes. Hard to tell. Shit.

"She's in the bedroom," Karl said as he gestured Morgan
in. "Back here." They went to the rear of the house. "Think we
can get her in your car? She's breathin' okay, I made sure a'
that."

Genevieve lay on her side with her eyes half shut. She
was quiet, then her lips moved, but there was still no sound.

"Gimme a hand," Karl said. "You take her arms, and I'll
take her legs."

"Wait. What's it going to look like if I take her to my
place?" But Morgan knew that was exactly what he would do.
What he had to do. He wanted Karl's reassurance.

"Better there than here," Karl spluttered. "What the hell
does it matter to you? Your reputation is shot anyway! And so
is hers." And, as always, Karl immediately felt bad for what he
had blurted out. "Well, I didn't mean it that way. What I meant
to say was, eh, just that——"

"That's alright Karl. I know what you meant. Don't
worry, I'll take good care of her, and to hell with what people
think. And you're right, you know. My reputation is shot, but
that's not so bad. If you're at rock bottom like I am, you don't
have any further to fall, so you don't worry about it."

240

Morgan smiled to reassure Karl, and he hoped his smile was convincing, and not too stiff. The irony was, Karl's reputation wasn't much better than his. And the larger irony was Karl's concern about what Emma would think. Karl was far below Genevieve, and the only concern Emma could possibly have would be that Karl—in some depraved, immoral way, would have taken advantage of Genevieve—but that wasn't Karl, who, in his simplicity, was one of the most honorable men Morgan had ever known; who—with women—came as close to being asexual as a normal man could be. Not that Karl was normal.

Morgan wiped a film of sweat from his forehead. As for him, by now the phone lines were singing the latest scandal, and they weren't singing of Karl. They were singing a new song of Morgan Feeney: a composition in shit major. Morgan worked his arms under Genevieve and lifted her. She was lighter than he had expected, and as he looked down, he saw that her face was thin and pallid, and he felt like a father carrying a precious, ill child, who might not survive.

Early the next morning Morgan lay exhausted and distraught, only half asleep, curled in his armchair with his feet on an old, gray hassock. He had covered himself with a wool army blanket, despite the heat. He had been up most of the night checking Genevieve, who lay on his bed in the back room, and who had not stirred much in the night. Perversely—because in his state of mind he regarded it as a perversion—Morgan worried most of all that Genevieve would suspect that he had abused her. Not that he cared what could happen to him if she made accusations; rather, simply and honestly, what she would think of him. He was not a degenerate.

Morgan opened his eyes and they fell on a bit of jute stuffing that had fallen from the hassock. In the farthest corner, glowering at him, was a tar-black tomcat that had strayed.

241

Morgan had given it milk, and had been thanked in growls, but the cat had stayed. The cat was only interested in survival.

As the night had spent itself, Morgan had found himself transformed from a father to a comrade in arms. And he loved Genevieve with more feeling than he could have imagined.

Genevieve moaned, and then again, and Morgan feared the next few moments. He struggled from his chair, smoothed back his hair with his hands, straightened his shirt collar, and went to the back. His legs palsied as he walked.

Genevieve was sitting up in bed, looking confusedly around; then, when she saw Morgan, she smiled, thinly but genuinely, and Morgan found himself intoxicated with relief.

"Good morning," Morgan said with as much buoyancy as he could summon.

"Good morning," Genevieve responded, but she said nothing more, and didn't move. She only sat, still smiling weakly.

Morgan awkwardly sat on the wooden chair beside the bed, waiting for some other response, but none came. Genevieve's obvious first question should have been how she had gotten there. Morgan studied her expectantly, but nothing.

"You were in Karl Springer's wagon, and we brought you here."

"Yes, I know."

"I thought you were asleep all the time."

"Not all of the time." Her smile dissolved into a look of fatigued contentedness.

As Morgan's head began to swim, a low growl came from the doorway. The black tomcat laured at Morgan, then backed out, turned, and bounded out onto the porch and away. Morgan focused again on Genevieve, waiting for her next, obvious response: embarrassment. But there appeared to be none. Morgan fidgeted, and Genevieve sat still, barely breathing.

242

"I can take you to Dr. Raulsten," Morgan offered. She didn't look very good.

"No, thank you. I'll be fine here, if you'll let me stay until tomorrow."

"Of course. As long as you want. People will wonder, but . . ." Morgan caught himself, shrugged, and they both laughed.

There was a knock at the front door. "It's Caroline," Morgan said. He went to face her.

"I hear you have a houseguest," Caroline said. She was at her sternest, down to the long, black dress she wore. She looked like a funeral mourner.

"Genevieve's here, if that's what you mean."

"I'm here to get her."

"She's alright here. She's better now, and——"

Caroline's face darkened. "Morgan, I don't know what you've done to her, but I'm taking that girl with me before anything more happens."

Morgan was numbed by the familiar rage that welled up inside of him.

Genevieve came from the back room and stood beside Morgan. "I'm alright, Caroline. Really, I am. Don't worry. I feel better here than anywhere."

Caroline's shoulders sagged. "You can't stay here. It isn't right."

Genevieve approached her, and took her in her arms. "Of course it is. It is right. Maybe not by your rules, or church rules, or most other people's rules; but they make their own rules, and I make mine. And Morgan makes his. Or maybe we've had our rules made for us, but in the end it's all the same. As long as we're not hurting anyone, I think we're entitled to be left alone."

Carolyn pushed Genevieve's arms away. "Left alone? I'm trying to help; to get you away from this, this, man," she gasped for breath, "and all you can say is you want to be left alone?"

"Not by you personally. In general. You're just a product of society, and you mean well, and I'll always love you as a friend. If you were older, you would be like a mother, but your moral sense isn't mine."

"Apparently not." Caroline turned red faced, and bustled to her car. She was not a good driver, but she succeeded in speeding away dramatically.

Genevieve looked up at Morgan. "Don't worry about her," she said, "she'll get over it."

"She will, but I won't," Morgan laughed.

Morgan spent most of the rest of the day outside, trying to find things to do.

But that night he and Genevieve sat across the old hassock from each other, and talked.

CHAPTER THIRTY-EIGHT

"Crash."

A bolt of lightning struck a lone cottonwood tree not more than two hundred yards from where Morgan and Lars sat forlornly under the shallow embankment of a dry creek bed. Lars' Model T had run out of gas on the way home from Charity. They had been playing pool.

"I told you we should have stayed in the car," Lars complained, "but hell no."

"Sorry," Morgan said.

"Well sorry doesn't mean much, does it?" They were drenched, and Lars was shaking from the cold. The wind drove sheets of rain under the embankment, stinging their faces.

"Well I'm not the one who ran out of gas. I should be more particular about who I ride with."

"Shit."

"Let's keep walking," Morgan said.

"Did you see the lightning hit that tree?" Lars said dryly. "I don't know about you, but I don't wanna wind up like Patty Duffy's bull." He put his hands under his armpits and hunched over.

"When your number's up, it's up," Morgan replied.

"Shit."

"In the war, I don't know how many times I saw someone get it, when it should have been somebody else." Morgan began to shake, and he made himself stop. He wouldn't give Lars the satisfaction.

"The war, the war, the war. That's all you talk about." Pea-sized hail pelted the mud puddles in front of them. "Damn." Lars shook harder.

"What's the matter? I thought a good Norwegian like you could take a little cold."

"I never could stand the cold. How come it doesn't bother you?" Thunder boomed, and Lars flinched.

"Thought you were tired of hearing me talk about the war?"

Lars didn't answer. He dug in his heels, and pushed himself back against the bank. A glob of mud plopped down on top of his head.

"Most of it's in your mind," Morgan said. "If you think you're cold, you're cold."

"I think I'm cold."

"Just ignore it. That's the secret. Put it out of your mind."

"Bullshit. If a guy's cold, he's cold."

"It's in your head."

"Crap."

"Philosophical crap, or pragmatic crap?" Morgan leaned forward and looked out. Lightning struck again, but farther away.

"There you go again with the philosophy." Lars considered. "I mean practically. If somebody's cold, they're cold. And if someone's miserable, they're miserable, and that's just fact. Wishing it away isn't going to change anything."

Morgan fell back and turned toward Lars. "Willpower."

"Willpower," Lars snorted.

"Though I have to admit, when the willpower runs out, you're worse off than ever."

They sat without talking. The rain let up, and when it stopped Lars crawled stiffly from their shelter. "Let's get going," he said. "I gotta get warmed up."

They climbed back onto the road.

"A nice rain though," Lars said as they sloshed through the ankle-deep mud. "We should never complain about rain in this country."

"Well you were sure doing a lot of complaining a while ago."

"I didn't wanna get my hair parted by a bolt of lightning, that's all."

"Ha! I told you——"

"Yeah, yeah, when your time's up, it's up."

"There's more too it than that. It's been my experience that it's never what you worry about that gets you. It's always something else. Always."

"Then you go and stand in the rain, and hold your finger up."

Soon the sun came out, and they were sweating. The air was fresh, and meadowlarks sang to them as they regained their good humor.

After a quarter of a mile, Lars stopped. "Gotta rest a minute."

"Whew," Morgan said, "this mud reminds me of——"

"Pot of gold."

"Huh?"

"A pot of gold, right in your front yard." Lars pointed toward a rainbow.

"The other end's in your yard," Morgan said.

"Who's gonna' get the pot?"

"You will. You get the pot, I get the gold."

"We'll split it. Whoever gets the pot splits it with the other."

"Alright. Deal. Anyway, there's probably a pot at each end."

The shook hands, laughing like ten year olds.

"Lars, what would you do if you had a pot of gold?"

Lars tried wiping his shoes on the grass along the edge of the road, but it didn't work. "You mean a whole pot of gold?"

"Yeah." Morgan stood smiling. It was nice to smile.

"Oh, I dunno. It'd be nice to have a better house, I suppose. For Caroline. And a new plow, and a new car. Hell if I know."

"Maybe you could afford a little gas, too."

"Haw."

"No, Lars, I'm talking about real money. Say you had a million dollars. What would you do?"

Lars rubbed the dirt off his head where the lump of mud had fallen. "I don't know, Morgan. I never thought about it." He looked perplexed. "I guess I can't think that big. I don't even know what a million dollars would look like, and if a guy can't see it, how would he know what to do with it?"

"That doesn't make any sense."

"That's my point. To me it's all nonsense. My chance of having that much money is zero, so why waste time thinking about it? I'm not a daydreamer." He smoothed his hair straight back with his hands. "How about you?"

"I'd go and live in the desert. Arizona."

"The desert!"

"Yeah. No mud, no people. And it'd be warm all the time. I'd build a big castle, and I could be alone. And if anyone wanted to see me, I could either lift the portcullis, or not. Probably not. And if they kept pestering me, I could pour boiling oil on 'em."

"You're crazy! What's a portcullis?"

"That's the big iron grate in front of the door."

Morgan waited for Lars to explode, but he just stood with his arms hanging limply at his sides, staring. "Jesus Christ," Lars murmured.

"Oh, I'm just joking you," Morgan said.

Lars slowly shook his head. "I thought you'd have had enough of being alone."

"Huh. Well . . . , hey, a car." Morgan pointed behind Lars, at a blue Buick coupe plowing through the mud.

248

"Hey!" Lars shouted. He waved his arms and tried to run, but both shoes came off, and he almost fell. "Hey!"

They both waved, but the car turned away, north.

"Hell. He didn't see us," Morgan said.

"He saw us," Lars said. "That was Stephen Long. He saw us. Just didn't wanna get his new car dirty inside. And I don't think he likes you much either." Lars took off his socks and stuffed them into his shoes. "Might as well walk barefoot."

Morgan watched the car disappear over a hill.

"Wait till the next time I see him," Lars grumbled.

They started walking again. Morgan looked up. The sky was the bluest he had ever seen.

"Lars, what is it between Stephen and Genevieve?"

"I think they were married once. But I don't know."

Morgan trembled slightly. "Caroline said there's a guy in Chicago too."

"That's what I heard." Lars walked faster.

"You know anything about him?"

"No. Just that he got hurt in the war." Lars stopped, and stepped in front of Morgan. "What is it with you? Haven't you taken enough of a beating?" He put his hands on Morgan's shoulders. "Give it up, Morgan. There's something wrong with that woman. Let her go. There are things you don't know, and you're gonna get hurt."

"What things?"

"I dunno. Things."

They walked on. Maybe Lars was right. Maybe there was something wrong with Genevieve. Even if there wasn't, she had too many ghosts in her past. Both Stephen Long and the unknown soldier. And God knows what else. Morgan walked beside Lars, in step with him. Anyway, why would someone beautiful and independent like Genevieve have anything to do with him? And what was she doing out here on the desolate, windswept Montana prairie?

249

Lars broke stride, and Morgan had to give up. If he skipped to get back in step, Lars would know.

CHAPTER THIRTY-NINE

Morgan had all but given up. Apparently all of Genevieve's confidences and kindness had been of no consequence. Then, at Charlie Ingvoldson's barn dance . . . .

Though he didn't like to dance—and despite the fact that nobody but Lars and Caroline, and Karl and Emma Springer, had anything to do with him—Morgan appreciated simply being on the periphery of humanity: the colorful variety of people, the conversations, the gaiety, and the music.

Morgan had never seen the musicians before, but they were good. Far above average. A round, perhaps middle-aged drummer, perspiring from his exertions; a weathered, wrinkle-skinned accordion player; and a bony, emaciated old man named Lagerquist on the violin. Violin, not fiddle, as Morgan had found out when he had complimented the man.

Genevieve was there, dancing every dance, beautiful in her long, white, lace dress, with her shiny auburn hair flowing down her back. Not once did she so much as glance at Morgan, and not once had he expected her to.

At the far end of the barn, opposite the large front door, sat Sven Svenson and Torger Lee, young bachelor farmers who lived together on three hundred sixty acres of the best land in the area. Sven was big and blond—and boisterous—and he looked like he would have fit right in on a Viking longship, pillaging and plundering the coast of England. Torger was smaller, and craggy; brooding and quiet. The only one he ever talked to was Sven. But there was plenty of talk in the community about them. Nothing in their looks reminded Morgan of Jake, his former prizefighter friend, and Sydney, Jake's manager. But one never knew.

"Mr. Feeney." Karl plopped down. "How come yuh ain't dancin'?"

"Don't see you out there." After sitting quietly all evening, it was nice to have someone to talk to.

"I ain't much of a dancer." Karl's nose and cheeks were red, and his eyes were bleary. Emma sat across the floor glaring at him.

"You're too modest," Morgan said. "I saw you and Emma dance once."

"Yeah, well I was drunk that night."

"Oh."

The dancers whirled, kicking up straw and dust. As the dance ended, Karl leaned and whispered, "Wanna slip outside for a snort? I got some real good stuff."

"No, thanks Karl. My stomach went bad on me the other day," Morgan fibbed.

"Well, to you then." Karl got up and weaved toward the door.

The gas lanterns glowed, the crowd thinned, and the violin player announced the last number: a slow Norwegian gammaldans. Morgan found himself surrounded by single men. When the music began, they would dash across the floor, hoping for one last turn with the girl of their choice. Morgan took some slight comfort in knowing he would not thus demean himself.

As couples took to the floor, Genevieve declined her first invitation. Then another, from Stephen Long. On her way toward Morgan she turned down two more, until she was in front of him. Without a word she held out her hand. Morgan stood, stunned, and as she pulled him into her arms, he felt lightheaded. They danced as though they had been melded. The barn was a palatial ballroom of colors and shadows, and as they floated, Morgan felt Genevieve tremble, and she held him tightly.

Not once did Genevieve look up, but she put her head on his shoulder, and whispered, "Just before you woke up in the hospital, you were mumbling."

252

Morgan kept quiet, and they danced on.

"You said the name Lansing."

"My best friend. Really, my only friend. His name was Lansing. He——"

Genevieve took her hand from his arm and pressed her fingers desperately to his lips. "No, please, not now. I want to talk, but not now. I'm not ready yet. I'm afraid." She pressed her face hard against his shoulder, and he felt the wetness of her tears through his shirt.

The dance ended, and the ballroom evaporated. For an instant Genevieve clung to Morgan—in the middle of the floor with everyone staring—then she turned and ran.

"I grew up in a small town in Pennsylvania," Genevieve said. She and Morgan were walking along the Missouri River. He had ratcheted up his courage, and had asked her to go for a Sunday outing. At first she had said no, but then a strange, far-of look had come to her face, and she had changed her mind.

"My father was a Methodist minister, so we weren't wealthy, but we got by. And we were sheltered from the real world."

It had rained the night before—a cloudburst that had run off fast without doing the crops much good—and the river water was murky and laden with twigs and other debris.

"And your mother?" Morgan asked.

They picked their way through cottonwood and poplar trees. Beyond the flats, on each side of the river, the Missouri breaks sloped up and away. The breaks were parched, cut by fissures and washes, and populated only by sagebrush and stunted juniper bushes.

"She died when I was eight. Tuberculosis. She called it *pthisis*. Her father was a doctor in England." Genevieve picked

253

up a stick and threw it into the water. It swirled near the edge. "Strange," she said, "I remember very little of her. Maybe because she was away so much, at the sanitarium. But I remember the way she talked." Genevieve watched her stick disappear down river.

"Just you and your father?"

"A sister died when I was three. Dora. She was six. She went suddenly—diphtheria—and we didn't even have a photograph of her. Except for the one of her in her casket, before the funeral. I burned it. It was hideous."

They walked on, passing through a willow thicket. Genevieve found a log under a huge cottonwood tree, and she sat looking at the opposite bank.

"Your father is dead?" Morgan asked.

"He caught tuberculosis from my mother."

"I'm sorry."

"It was easier than you think. He was so sure of his divine reward. I'll never forget those last weeks with him, and how he kept talking about the Unmoved Mover, and First Cause. I didn't know what he was talking about, but it was reassuring."

Morgan sat beside Genevieve, and they watched the sun steam the rain from the ground. The mosquitoes were out, and dragonflies flitted after them. Overhead a flock of birds twittered and chirped, but Morgan didn't know what kind they were. They didn't venture onto the dry prairie.

"You've had a hard life," Morgan said.

"No harder than most. Then my grandmother took care of me. My mother's mother. Her name was Lillian. Lily. Everyone said she and my mother were so much alike you couldn't have told them apart, if you could have smoothed the wrinkles on my grandmother's face a bit. And I was told they were alike in temperament as well. Kind, and compassionate."

She brushed her hair back with one hand, and smiled at her remembrances.

"Oh, the stories my grandmother told, of how it was to be a doctor's wife, London society, my grandfather's triumphs and failures, the constant entertaining . . . She made it sound so grand, yet I always felt she was glad when it was over. But one thing that stuck with her all those years was tea time. Every afternoon we had tea, no matter that I was only twelve."

"And your grandfather?"

"He was older than my grandmother, but they had a good life. He died when he was seventy. He had retired from his regular practice, and he was helping the poor. He caught something—some disease—and had to quit, and a year later he had a heart attack."

Genevieve continued to remember her childhood, then they sat looking at the river again. Morgan took Genevieve's hand and held it in both of his. He felt the strength in it.

"It seems so long ago," Genevieve said. Her eyes narrowed and hardened, and she pulled her hand away. "And you?" she asked. "Why did you come back to Montana?"

"I don't know. We have to be somewhere, don't we?"

"Where did you grow up?"

"On a farm in Illinois."

Genevieve waited.

"Not much more to tell. My father was a drinker, and when my mother died I left home. Ended up working on a ranch over by Miles City. Got tired of that, and wound up in the army. That's about it."

"There has to be more."

"Not much more. Just a farm kid. Went to school, hunted, fished . . . , the usual. I read a lot. My mother used to tell me how smart I was, and that I should study for a profession, but we couldn't afford it. Then it was time to leave." Morgan shrugged.

"Then the war," Genevieve said. She said it bitterly. "You were wounded."

"Only slightly. That scar on the back of my head." Morgan appreciated her directness. "Took a bullet through my tin derby."

"Is that why you drift off? That and the epilepsy?" She searched his face.

"That started when I was young. My father hit me, and I guess I've never been the same, but . . . ."

Genevieve pressed him about the war, and Morgan relived parts of it. Not the horror of the trenches, but the everyday experiences. The times between battles.

"We had a few francs, and there was this little tavern. John Dempsey had just had his head knocked off in an inter-regimental boxing match. We were doing our best to cure him with wine, and I guess we all got a little zigzagged. The old dirty neck who ran the place——"

"Dirty neck?"

Morgan's face reddened. "A woman of easy virtue. Anyway, she threw us out, and——"

"Threw you out? You mean you had no dalliances with her and her ooh-la-la girls?"

"How do you——?"

"You bounder." Genevieve laughed, and she urged Morgan to continue. But such experiences comprised little of army life, and Morgan became morose.

Genevieve put her hand on his sleeve. "It's too nice a day. Let's leave the past." She pulled a flower from the grass beside her and began picking off the petals. It looked like a black-eyed Susan, but Morgan didn't know any more about flowers than he did about birds.

"That's what I'm trying to do," Morgan mused. "Leave the past. But it's hard. I keep having this dream. I'm in the bottom of a trench, drowning in mud and filth, and I'm trying to climb onto the duckboards. I know that they lead to my

256

salvation. But someone is pushing me back, kicking me, trying to keep me off. Almost every night I——"

"It'll pass. It takes time."

"The wounded and the dying. Sydney and Jake, and Sergeant Shepherd, and Bill Baldwin. Jake Hermann was a prizefighter, and Sydney Berman was his manager. I met them in a restaurant in Miles City, and they talked me into joining the army. Turned out they were, well, they liked each other. You know? You run into all manner of depravity in the army. But somehow it didn't seem so bad. At least they had each other. I think I envied them. I still have Sydney's ring."

Morgan reached beneath his shirt and pulled out a silver ring that hung on a sterling chain around his neck.

"It was Sydney's dying wish that I give this to Jake."

"Why didn't you?"

"Jake was already dead."

"I'm sorry. But you have to let go."

"I know, but there were so many. I remember this guy named Barry. He was the company goof during training. A real washout. Couldn't do anything right. Except he could shoot. The best shot I ever saw. We got split up when we went overseas. I thought I ran into him one day, but it was somebody else. A sniper. Nothing left of him; just a shell. He had no soul, only——"

"You have to forget, Morgan." Genevieve had stopped picking at her flower.

"There was another sniper, named Giardello. Only he liked killing. One killer who liked it; one who didn't. Good and evil? Except how could either of them be good?"

"Put it behind you."

"Francis Cook. Lost both legs. Wished he had died. The last thing he told us was he never wanted to see us again."

"Stop."

"And most of all, Lansing. He——"

257

"Lansing?"

"He was my best friend. We went through the war together."

"What was his last name? I'm ready now. Please, tell me his last name." Her face was translucent, and through it glowed the purest alabaster Morgan had ever seen.

"Rhodes."

Genevieve's hands began to tremble, and she let the flower fall to the ground.

"He killed himself," Morgan said. "The war was almost over, and he . . . ."

CHAPTER FORTY

"Lansing Rhodes?" Genevieve gasped. She gripped Morgan's arm. "From Idaho?" She squeezed, hard.

"Yes."

"Dark, but with blue eyes, and a small brown butterfly mark here?" She put her finger high on her right cheek.

"Yes. You knew him?"

"Knew?" She slid from the log and collapsed, sobbing, clutching at Morgan's ankles. "Oh, God in Heaven, what more?"

Morgan got up, put his hands on her shoulders, and lifted her. "I'm sorry."

Genevieve pulled away and sat again on the log, swaying from side to side, trembling, straightening her hair. Her face was a grotesque, twisted mask, painted by an invisible hand, in shades of green, red, and blue.

"For God's sake, what is it?" Morgan asked.

She looked up through the cottonwood branches and moaned; a loud, primal lament. Morgan reached for her. "No!" she said, and he let his hands fall. She seemed mesmerized by something in the clouds.

"I was assigned to Hospital Train Twenty-seven," she said. "During the fighting at Chateau-Thierry, we were sent to evacuate field hospital patients. We had wonderful facilities: four hundred beds, pharmacy car, ward cars, kitchen, mess . . . , but it was terrible. Gas victims, amputees, every wound imaginable. And having to move them. I'll never forget the cries. And the smell."

She looked at Morgan and wiped her eyes with her handkerchief.

"Later I was stationed at the base hospital at Savenay. I'm like you, Morgan. There's nothing I haven't seen. The difference is, for you, the death was fast. For us, each man's death lasted forever."

Far to the east a train whistle blew.

"After a while they were all the same. Nameless faces, if they had faces. Except some weren't the same. Not many, but some. They were the worst of the dying, who had a special will to live. To beat the odds. In the time I was there, I knew thirteen such men, and each fell in love with me. They all did, but these were special, and I loved them in a way that I can't express. Like love of a child, love of parents, and love of friends, all combined. And even, I suppose, romantic love, though it sounds strange when I say it. Twelve of the thirteen died, and because they fought harder, they died harder. I almost lost my religious faith. I didn't, but more than ever, I believed in life."

"Christ and his disciples?"

She looked past Morgan, over his shoulder. "The thirteenth was horrible. Half of his face was gone, and there was no hope. The doctors could only try to ease his pain, and I thought one doctor even tried to put him out of his misery, though I couldn't be sure." Her eyes glazed. "What made it so hard was that he had been so handsome. With bandages covering the bad half, you would never have known, except for the pain."

"Lansing?" Morgan quavered. The familiar dizziness came again.

Genevieve focused on him. "We didn't know who he was. He had no dog tags. Only later did he tell me that he had tried to kill himself. He said his name was John Gant."

"They always went off by themselves, hoping no one would see them." Morgan tried to keep from shaking. "They'd throw their tags away, and do it in the head. They couldn't bear the shame."

"I learned much about him in the days I sat beside his bed. The war had destroyed something in him, but as he grew stronger, part of him clung to me with a renewed will to live. That part—bitter and cynical—loved me."

She cried, and Morgan concentrated on her tears, trying to keep from going down.

"And the other part of him?" Morgan asked.

"The second part was an idealist who wanted to die. We never knew, from day to day, which he would be. And sometimes he would be a composite of the two."

Birds chirped overhead. Morgan struggled to stop the nervous tic on his face; the one that always preceded his trouble.

"What then?"

"The French called them the *men with broken faces*. Those so hideous that they couldn't be seen in public. After the war, when the surgeons had done all they could, artists took over. The French government hired them to make masks. Most of the masks were partials. The artists worked from what was left of the faces, and from photographs. It was horrible. A perversion. But what else could they do?"

Genevieve sobbed, then she continued. "I arranged for a French artist to make John Gant a mask, but he didn't want it. He took it, but he wouldn't wear it, until it was time for him to leave. On the way to the ship, people were horrified. Some threw things at him. After that, he put it on. Half of his face was real, half was mask. He looked like the Phantom of the Opera."

"Did you see him again?" Morgan knew the answer.

"Yes. When I got home, I tried to forget. And I did. I moved to Chicago, and worked in a hospital. Everything was fine, until one day they assigned a new patient to me."

"Him?"

"Yes. I became hysterical. Afterward, the only thing I remembered was his face without the mask. And being dragged from the room."

"What——?"

261

"He couldn't let go. I tried to hide here in Charity, but he found me. I don't know how. He has connections."

"What does he do?"

"Something sinister, I think."

"Clunk." Morgan threw another rock onto his stoneboat.
He had broken another twenty-five acres. "Clunk. Clunk." He
took Nellie's rope and moved her. Peaceful, with only a horse
and a dog for company. Good, hard work. Time to think.
"Clunk, clunk." Sweat trickled down his back and under his
arms. "Clunk." Rosalie ran past, barking at birds, but she was
getting old, and by mid morning she would be lying in the shade
back at the house. "Clunk." The backbreaking work was his
assuagement. *The Lord gave, and the Lord hath taken away . . .*
Was that it? Was there no chance with Genevieve? Was she
mad? Too damaged to ever be mended?

*"Late one night while he was sleeping, I knelt by his
bed, and I prayed for him. I bargained for his life, Morgan. I
promised that if he lived, I would stay with him, and love him
always."*

"Lansing would have lived anyway."

*"You don't understand. As I prayed, a light descended.
I looked up and I saw the face of Christ."*

"Christ?"

"I knew my prayer had been answered."

"You must have been——"

"Fatigued? Distraught? Of course."

"What then?"

"Nothing. I went to bed. But . . ." She wiped a tear
from her cheek. *"I thought he was sleeping, but he had heard
my promises."*

"And he held you to them?"

"Yes."

"You can still——"

*"Break them? No. Don't you see? I could break my
promises to him, but not to God."*

263

"Clunk." Morgan stopped and scanned the horizon. Nothing. A great void.

Morgan looked down, and Lansing's face materialized in one of the rocks. Half face, and half mask. Morgan recoiled. "Why," he sobbed. "Why? I could have helped, if only you had——" But one side of Lansing's face glared, and the other smiled, and Morgan couldn't tell which side was real.

Morgan awoke with Rosalie licking his face.

CHAPTER FORTY-TWO

"Hello! Morgan! You there?"

Morgan got up from the kitchen table and went to the door. His head throbbed.

Lars stomped in. "You look kinda peaked. Another one of your spells?"

"Um. I guess so. Oh, shit, my head." He backed to his chair and slumped down.

"Your horse is still out in the field."

"Uh."

"What the hell were you doing, picking rocks in this heat? You should know better than that."

"Can it, Lars. I needed it. The peace and quiet."

"Alright, but maybe I oughta take you to the doctor."

"I'm fine." Morgan sat with his elbows on the table, holding his head.

Lars sat down across from him. "Yeah, I can see that. Anyway, Caroline said to tell you that Genevieve went to Chicago."

Morgan jerked his head up. "Chicago?"

"Said she's gonna have it out with that guy named Lansing. Caroline said you know him."

"Lansing Rhodes. I told you about him. The guy who killed himself."

"Guess he didn't do a very good job of it. How does Genevieve know him?"

"She took care of him in . . . , oh, hell, it's a long story." Morgan looked away, and he began to cry. "What else can happen? It's too much, Lars, and it's been going on forever."

"The war?"

"Yeah, the war, but more than that. It seems like it's been one thing after another, since I was a kid. But in a way the war was the best part. I wouldn't expect anybody to understand that, but I was alive, not like now. Look at me. I know what people say. But God, Lars, I was something then. It's a feeling that you and those like you will never know. It was horrible, but there was more to it than that. The others looked up to me. I did my job, and more. And now what do I get? People who've done nothing but sit on their farms and kick pigs around in a pen, and watch their crops dry up, thinking I'm balmy. Maybe I am, but most of you'd crap your pants if someone so much as waved a rifle at you. How many of your friends have been blinded, and have been sent out into the world with a *thank you*, a pat on the back, and a white cane? How many of you have watched your friends die, blown to pieces? Gut shot, or gassed, gasping for air in some stinking trench. How many people have you seen die of gangrene, or with their arms or legs blown off? And they were better men than most of you.

And now Evangeline. I mean Genevieve. It's like having your guts ripped out, until you can't go on anymore. Some of us have had our share of pain, Lars, and after a while it gets unbearable, and we don't need righteous people like you telling us everything's alright, because it's not, and it never will be. There's a time to——"

"Oh, for Christ's sake, Morgan, knock it off!" Lars thundered. He stood and pounded the table. "You think you're the only one who ever had a tough time? Quit sniveling, and get a grip on yourself."

"You don't understand. Lansing is——"

"The hell I don't understand," Lars shouted. "Guess what? Life's tough!"

He came around the table, grabbed Morgan by his shirt, and pulled him up. "I'm gettin' tired of you and your bellyaching! Figure you've had it so hard? Maybe you have, but crying about it isn't going to help." He let go, and Morgan stood, head down. "You finally meet a nice girl like Genevieve, and look at you. What would she think of you now?"

Morgan looked up like had been slapped. "Nice? But you said——"

"Oh, don't act so surprised," Lars said. "Everybody sees what's going on with you two."

"Going on?"

"How Genevieve feels about you, you jackass."

"She pities me, that's all."

"That's not what she told Caroline."

"I see her talking to Stephen Long all the time. You told me you thought they had been married."

"Oh, horseshit! Long thought he was gonna marry her, but he's nothing but a nuisance. Forget about him! And stop feeling sorry for yourself. You're not the only one who's had it rough. And now she's got that Lansing on her back. What the hell do you expect of her?"

"I swear, I didn't know."

"Yeah. Well now you do."

"But you told me to stay away from her. That she's balmy."

"I was wrong. Caroline sat up with her all night, and Genevieve told her things. Genevieve's had a tough time, and she seems to lean on you, Morgan. She thinks you're strong. So why don't you start showing a little gumption?"

Lars stomped out, dramatically, to emphasize his point.

"Why me?" Morgan called after Lars.

"I guess because you both have the war miseries."

Morgan sat, frozen and dazed. Some of life's mysteries—like why Genevieve was drawn to him—would forever be mysteries. Not that they had the war in common—that was obvious—but personally. You can't analyze everything. Things just happen. What a wonderful platitude: Things just happen. Sometimes even good things.

"Have you no faith?" Evangeline was resplendent.

"Faith in God?"

"Faith in yourself."

"I have never had faith in myself."

"Of course you have. The faith that carried you through the war, and through all of your other travails. You are a survivor."

CHAPTER FORTY-THREE

Morgan went to his hill of buried memories. His head pounded, but now he had a reason to live. If he could be a man in war, he could be a man always. He knelt by the grave at the end of his trench, and prayed. Not to God, but to whatever vital force had given him life.

———————————

"Thwap! Thwap! Thwap." The moist dirt tried to cling to Morgan's spade as he began filling in his trench. "Thwap." Morgan stopped after only the fourth shovelful, and leaned on his shovel. Time to stop being crazy. Time to——

"Whatcha doin', Morgan?"

"Yeow!" Morgan jumped, spun in midair, and landed facing the opposite direction, holding his shovel across his chest as he would a rifle and bayonet. "Jesus, mother . . . God damn you, Karl! You scared the shit outta me." Karl Springer, in his black derby hat and sweat-stained white shirt. "You could get killed sneaking up on a guy like that!" Morgan shouted.

"Haw, haw, haw! You gonna shoot me with that shovel? Hee, hee, hee." Tears trickled down Karl's rosy cheeks.

"I should give you a few good whacks with it, that's what I should do!" Morgan waved his shovel, but he fell back down in the dirt. "Jeez, Karl."

"Well whaddyuh want me tuh do, tie a cowbell around my neck?"

"No, but you could say something, or at least cough, you asshole."

"I did say something."

"Yeah, right behind me. You should . . . Oh, shit, forget it."

Morgan slumped back and examined Karl's round face for any sign of malice, and saw none. Delight, but there had been no forethought of malice. If all of the German soldiers had been like Karl, there would have been no war. Instead, they had all been like Lars, and Lars was a lousy Norwegian, and Karl was the German. How to figure? Of course the Germans and the Norwegians were cousins, so what sense did that make? It would be easier to see Lars in a German uniform that it would Karl. Far easier.

"Whatcha doin'?" Karl asked.

"Filling in my trench." Morgan waved his hat at a swarm of flies. "Damn flies."

"I heard that the Indians used to smear bear grease on themselves to keep the flies and mosquitoes off," Karl said. "Maybe you should try that." He sat on the other side of the trench, directly opposite Morgan.

"Shit. Besides, there aren't any bears around here." Now Morgan had to figure out if Karl was teasing him.

"There used to be, till the white people came. Grizzlies. But they all moved to the mountains. I suppose buffalo grease would work too."

"You seen any buffaloes lately?" Morgan asked.

"No, but come to think, I've got some badger oil that my aunt Ingeborg gave me before we came out here to Montana. I think it's still good. Mix a bit a' turpentine in it, and I betcha it'll keep those flies off. Mosquitoes too, and every other damn thing. Women too."

Now Karl was deliberately laying it on. "Yup, badger grease! Now I've seen that big stick you carry to keep the ladies away, but this stuff of Aunt Ingeborg's is the real thing." Karl took of his hat and said something in German that sounded like "Die kleppert of crappo grandiest."

270

A huge, blue-black crow flew over, cawing three times, pausing, then cawing three more times, and on and on that way until it was gone.

"Now if that doesn't work, then we'll add some——"

"Cut it, Karl, before I put a dose of that stuff up your arschloch."

Karl squinched, then he pouted. "Heck, Morgan, I was just——"

"I'm not in the mood."

"Alright. Sorry. I didn't know you were that touchy."

———————————

"Let's walk," Morgan said. Genevieve came down the front steps of her house, and he led her to the giant cottonwood tree beside the Lutheran church. They sat in the grass. "Whatever happened, I . . ." Morgan began, but he stopped.

Genevieve broke her vacant gaze, and he heard her catch her breath. She, who had been so strong and independent. She took his hands.

"I went to him, to end it," she said.

"Did you?"

A beer-barrel-shaped lady in a long black dress stared. Morgan stared back, and she bustled away.

"I tried."

"And?"

Morgan thought she had not heard. She remained absolutely still, and the dreamy, walking-on-clouds look cloaked her. But she brushed it aside.

"He's coming here. To see you."

"Here? What does he——?"

"He wouldn't tell me. But be careful, Morgan, of his evil machinations."

"Machinations?"

271

"Schemes, and intentions. Part of him is dangerous. Brainsick and dangerous. The part you never knew."

"And the other part?"

Genevieve waited for a fat man and his wife to pass.

"You may recognize the other." She stood and smoothed her dress.

"And remember, I'll be with you in spirit, as you have been with me."

"I——"

"At my lowest point, you appeared, Morgan. And you looked exactly like . . . ."

On his way home, Morgan noticed a new building at Karl Springer's place. He turned in. He felt bad about being so sharp with Karl about the badger oil.

"Turkeys!" Karl exclaimed. He had just finished putting the roof on his new turkey shed. He leaned on the mesh fence that surrounded the shed, flushed and sweating, admiring his work. "Should never have got into hogs. Lars talked me into it, and look what happened. Last one died two days ago. But a guy hasta keep goin'. I figure there's money in turkeys."

Morgan glanced around. A ramshackle house, a chicken coop, a windmill, and a barn. And now a turkey coop. "Lars seems to be doing alright with hogs," Morgan said.

"Huh. He'll learn his lesson. Now turkeys, that's a different story! Turkeys are tough. Nothin' can go wrong with turkeys, as long a yuh give 'em plenty tuh eat. I was talkin' tuh Chester Dunlop, and he said they're a sure thing."

"I hope so." Chester Dunlop was a ne'er do well who had failed at hogs too. And cattle, and wives.

Karl took out his plug of chewing tobacco and offered it to Morgan.

"No, thanks."

272

Karl bit off a big chunk. "Morgan, I don't know much, but I do know one thing: a fellow can't give up. Yuh hafta keep tryin'. If yuh don't, you're dead. And if these here turkeys don't pan out, I got somethin' else in mind. Can yuh keep it quiet? Pha-too." He spat tobacco on the ground.

Morgan nodded.

"Moonshine," Karl chortled. "There's this guy from West Virginia who knows how tuh make it. Real good stuff. Most a' what yuh get around here'd kill a person. Pha-too! So if I can talk Lars into coming up with enough money for us tuh get started, we'll clean up. All we hafta do is . . . ."

As Morgan half-listened, he saw Karl's true nobility: the indomitability of his spirit.

". . . put a still in the hills behind Lars' place. If Emma ever finds out, it'll be curtains. As far as that goes, if Caroline finds out, that'll be worse. Maybe we can . . . ."

Karl reached down and patted his new dog, Driiter, on the head. "Pha-too!" Dritt—pronounced like *sheet*—meant *shit* in Norwegian. It had been Lars' idea. Karl didn't know what Driiter meant. Lars had told him it was the name of a Norsk god.

"You're a caution, Karl," Morgan said.

CHAPTER FORTY-FOUR

Morgan came out of the First State Bank of Charity, and before his eyes could adjust to the light, "whap," someone slapped him in the face. Stephen Long, with a white leather glove.

"I won't presume that you know the proper etiquette, but as the challenged party, you may chose the weapons. May I suggest my forty-four caliber Le Page matched pair? Single-shot percussion."

Tall, handsome, tic-cheeked Stephen Long, dressed in a gray suit and a dark-gray derby hat. At first Morgan thought it was a joke. People gathered, and someone snickered, while Stephen worked hard at looking nonchalant as he stood with the thumb of his right hand hooked in his watch pocket.

"Well?"

Morgan's real surprise was that Stephen—or anyone else—would stand up to him like that. Being the town crazy had its advantages, one of which was that people usually left him alone.

"Dueling is illegal."

"I make my own laws." Stephen spoke with an exaggerated, phony English accent.

"Fists, then."

"Oh, come now! Common fisticuffs? Really! At any rate, I'd think twice about that, old top. I was on the boxing team at Princeton."

"Then how about baseball bats."

"I should have expected as much from a craven——"

"What's this about?" Morgan asked. He saw Genevieve in the crowd.

"You know very well what it's about. Love, and honor. Now, are you going to choose, or are you going to slink away like a whipped cur?"

"Coward!" someone shouted. It was Wolfgang Sturm: big, mean, and—as usual—drunk. Morgan had never been able to figure out why Wolfgang hated him. Maybe for no reason. Sometimes there are no reasons. Morgan was so tired of it all.

"How about chess?" Morgan said. "I was always pretty good at that."

A cloud passed overhead, and in the temporary shade Morgan observed that Stephen's cheek was twitching faster.

"Indeed! I should have assumed . . . ."

Morgan glanced sideways. Lars was beside Genevieve, holding her arm. There would be no help from him this time. Not that he needed it. But what if Lars was wrong? What if there were still some attachment between Stephen and Genevieve?

". . . an abject coward."

Morgan seized Stephen's tie with his left hand and pulled him forward. As he pulled, he crouched to his right, turned, and drove his fist deep into Stephen's stomach, just as Jake Hermann, the fighter, had shown him.

"Uungh."

Morgan let go, and Stephen collapsed. He lay in the dust holding both arms across his stomach, his mouth moving, trying to breathe.

"Get up!" Wolfgang hollered.

Morgan started for him, but Wolfgang ran for life's only refuge: The Palace.

That evening Morgan and Genevieve walked along the road on the south edge of town.

"Force never solves anything," Morgan said.

Genevieve stopped and looked up at him. "Why of course it does."

Stephen Long left on the train the next day.

275

Morgan sat on his porch and watched the heat shimmer over the fields of parched wheat. He swished away a half dozen flies, but they returned. In the west, dry, white, puffy clouds appeared, and the wind was from the wrong direction for rain. Too late anyway. Sunday morning. Ninety degrees.

Neighbors who had gone to church headed home. Most waved, and Morgan waved back. He had gotten over his bitterness, though he still couldn't understand the hypocrisy. How people could be so mean spirited, and at the same time retain their everyday civility. They could just as well ignore him altogether.

A dust devil twisted across the fields, picking up weeds, working its way south. Under the windmill, by the barn, birds twittered and drank, and the chickens clucked and scratched.

A car came, and when it got closer, Morgan saw it was Genevieve's Studebaker.

Genevieve parked in the yard and got out. She had on a black dress, and the brim of her hat partially covered her face. She reached back and took the door handle to steady herself.

Morgan got up. "Lansing?"

"Yes."

His head swam, and he felt like he would fall. Genevieve approached and took off her hat, and he saw her face.

"He came last night on the train. He's staying at the Gladstone Hotel."

Morgan worked to keep his knees stiff. Genevieve came to him, and they embraced.

"Are you alright?" he asked.

"Yes. And you?"

"Yes."

Genevieve put her hand to the side of Morgan's face. "He keeps his room dark, and he never leaves it. He wants you to come tonight."

She kissed him lightly, then she backed away. "I don't know which Lansing he will be. The hard, cold one, who refuses to release me; or the other."

Morgan stood watching Genevieve's dust. Then he went inside and took his whiskey bottle and a glass from the cupboard, and poured. He looked into the whiskey, but he couldn't drink.

CHAPTER FORTY-FIVE

The lobby of the Gladstone Hotel smelled of cigar smoke and baked bread. The only wall decorations were a farm calendar behind the desk, and on the far wall, a lithograph of a lady in a long, flowing dress, sidesaddle on a black horse. A grandfather clock stood next to the door to the dining room, and three wooden armchairs faced the large, dirty front window.

"He paid for a week. He said to leave his food in the hall." The hotel clerk, Harry Glick, started to follow Morgan up the stairway. Harry was short and bald, and when he was nervous his nose twitched.

"I'd better go alone."

"Fine with me. Say . . . ," Harry lowered his voice, "what happened to his face?"

Morgan steeled himself as he read the numbers. Room six. He knocked. Someone answered, and he went in.

"Lansing?" Morgan waited for his eyes to adjust to the gloom.

"As you see, Morgan. But I've suffered grievously. Not too troubling, I hope." Lansing was sitting in the far corner. He lifted the fingers of one hand. "No closer."

Morgan stiffened as he saw the revenant before him: half real, half mask. The real side looked like Lansing, but with an unfamiliar hardness. On the other side Lansing's eye remained, but the rest was gone. The flesh-colored mask extended from the front of his ear to his nose, and down under his jaw. The artist had replicated not the man Morgan had known, but the man who had been destroyed.

"Not all injuries are outward, don't you remember, Morgan? You should. You said it." The real side of Lansing's face smiled bitterly.

The mask side cut to the depths of Morgan's soul. "I——."

Lansing shrugged. He took a pack of cigarettes from the windowsill, selected one, and tossed them to Morgan.

"No." Morgan threw them back, and fell into a padded armchair. The smell of whiskey—and of other things—lingered under the stale air.

Lansing lit up, and flipped his match on the floor. "How are you, Morgan?" His voice was cold.

"Not so good, but I guess it's been hard on all of us," Morgan stumbled. Everything was surreal and slow, like in a nightmare, and his voice seemed to be coming from someone else. "Francis Cook lost both legs. You remember Frog-Eyes Francis? And Elmer Sitwell got so that all he'd do is sit and stare straight ahead. They sent him home. And John Dempsey. He came to see me."

Lansing held up his hand. "The war is over."

Morgan concentrated on the mask. It seemed to come alive, leering at him. "Alright," Morgan said. "But . . ." He pulled Lansing's small, tattered diary from his pants pocket, and put it on the bed.

"Yes?" Lansing hesitated, then he picked it up. He opened the curtain more, and in the dim evening light he read the first page, then another. He read on, stopping on some pages, rereading them, skipping others. When he got to the end, he gently closed the book, laid it on the bed, and with the back of his fingertips he slid it back to Morgan.

"A very moving and painful diary." Lansing lit another cigarette. "But the past is the past, and we have to concern ourselves with the future."

"What happened?"

"What difference does it make now?"

Morgan stiffened in his chair. "Lansing! It's me! What the hell happened to you? You had such ideals. Plans for the

279

future. And just when we could see the end, you go and pink yourself! Why?"

Lansing took a long drag on his cigarette, and slowly exhaled. The fading light from the window made his mask glow dull yellow. "You think I should have taken the duckboard trail? The honorable way out."

"You could have tried to stick it out. I did."

"Ha! Could have tried. But instead I dishonored myself."

"It has nothing to do with honor. All I want to know is why?"

"Sometimes there are no good answers."

"Please, I——"

Lansing waved his cigarette. "Enough. We have more important matters to discuss."

"Genevieve?"

"She made promises to me."

"Not to you. To God."

"But about me. It's the same thing."

"She wasn't herself. None of us were."

"Nevertheless."

"He's in here."

Morgan woke up. He was in the back room of The Palace, tied up, lying on a pile of gunny sacks. His head throbbed.

"We had tuh do somethin'," Jack Johnson, one of the bartenders, said. Lars was with him.

"What the hell's going on?" Morgan asked. His jaw hurt, and it was hard to talk.

"Yuh went off it," Jack answered. "Somebody whacked you a good one, but you wouldn't quit, so we——"

"Ummm. Well, you can let me go."

"Yuh sure?"

"Yeah."

Jack untied him.

Morgan sat up and felt his jaw. "Somebody packs quite a wallop."

"Wolfgang Sturm."

"Figures. Oh! How long have I been drinking?"

"Three days," Lars said. He took Morgan's arm and pulled him to his feet. "Let's go." He glowered at Jack. "He didn't get any of the bad stuff, did he? I knew a guy who went blind."

"We don't sell rotten stuff, Lars. I, mean, if we did sell moonshine."

"Of course not. C'mon Morgan, we'll get you home and get you cleaned up." Lars led him out the back door.

"Three days?" Morgan asked.

"Yeah."

As they left, Morgan heard Jack talking to someone. ". . . sure is an odd duck."

"Here." Lars brought Morgan a bowl of graveyard stew: lumps of bread in hot milk, with butter, salt, and pepper.

Morgan sat in bed, propped against the wall. "Oh, mercy! I don't think I can——"

"Eat," Lars said.

Lars had thrown him in the water tank, clothes and all. Now this.

Morgan tried a spoonful. "Genevieve? Does she know I——?"

"I told her you have the flu."

281

"Unh. Thanks." Morgan took another spoonful. "Did she believe you?"

"Yeah. People believe what they want to believe."

"She won't come here?"

"Don't worry."

Morgan stopped eating. He leaned his head back and looked at the photographs on the wall across from him, that he had dug out and put up the day Lansing had arrived. They were blurred on account of his drinking, but he focused on the one of him and Lansing, side by side, in front of a café in some little town in France. Not long before the big St. Mihiel offensive. He was serious, but Lansing was smiling at the camera. Almost laughing. And Morgan remembered how they had gone into the cafe and sipped wine all afternoon while the photographer developed their photos. How Lansing had expounded on a philosophy book he had read once; one that he claimed had changed his life. David Hume, about undermining superstition. And authority, when authority is harmful. Like those running the war. And Morgan remembered how they had staggered back to their unit just in time, before their buckshee passes were up. Fake passes, and being late would have given them away for sure.

". . . about Genevieve."

"What?" Morgan asked.

Lars had moved a chair beside the bed, and he looked serious. "I said, there's something I have to tell you about Genevieve. Two days ago—the day after you started your big toot—Genevieve went to see Lansing again. Later that day, at the hospital, she had a nervous breakdown."

"She . . . ?" Morgan tried to get up, but Lars pushed him back.

"She's alright. Doc Raulsten sent her home with us. We've got her doped up on laudanum."

"Laudanum? That's terrible stuff! What the hell?"

"I dunno, but it's doing the trick. Anyway, you've got a bigger problem."

Morgan handed Lars his bowl. It was mostly full. "What?"

"I don't know what's going on, but you're gonna hafta quit monkeying around and get things settled with your old friend, Lansing, once and for all. For yourself, and for Genevieve. Before it does you in."

"I have to think."

"Fine. Tomorrow." Lars took the bowl to the sink, then he pulled down the bedroom window shade.

"Genevieve's alright?" Morgan asked.

"Right now she doesn't know which end is up, but I think she'll come around." Lars put on his hat. "I'll be back tonight."

Lars left, and Morgan lay with his eyes closed, wishing life were simpler. And easier. But from now on there would be no more relapses. Again he heard his graveside epiphany, as clearly as if it were spoken: *If I could be a man in war, I can be a man always.*

CHAPTER FORTY-SIX

Lansing stood in the doorway of his hotel room. Sunlight blazed through the window behind him, forming an aura over his head. He put his hands on Morgan's shoulders. "I want to apologize for my behavior the other night. I've had kind of a rough go of it. I have my bad days." He half-smiled at Morgan.

"Forget it."

The room was a mess, and there was a patch of something foul—like vomit—on the floor. And in the sour air lingered the smell of whiskey, and the other evil odors Morgan had been unable to identify the last time he was there.

"It's good to see you," Lansing said. "You look just the same. Put a uniform on you and . . . well, it hasn't really been that long, has it? Sit down."

Morgan started to sit on the bed.

"Here." Lansing guided him to a chair by the window, then he took a small wooden chest from the night stand and put it very carefully on the top shelf in the closet. The chest was decorated with carvings of jungle trees, and elephants. "Guess we've both seen the elephant too many times," he said. "But now it's just like old times. Only . . . ." Lansing rambled on about their first days in France, before the fighting. When they were young.

As he listened, Morgan took in the room. He hadn't really seen it the first time. Blue wallpaper with bright yellow canaries, a sagging bed, three chairs, and a dresser. Dirty clothes strewn all about, two mostly-empty suitcases, and a long, gray coat hanging from a nail on the inside of the closet door.

"The doctors did the best they could," Lansing continued. He sat on the bed and leaned against the headboard. "Genevieve saved me, Morgan. She thought she was doing the right thing, but . . . ."

Then Morgan saw the pistol. A .32 caliber Webley automatic in a shoulder holster, hanging on the bedpost.

". . . she shouldn't have. I knew what I was doing, and . . ." Small and light. Eight rounds. Not a military weapon, though Morgan had taken several from German officers.

"So," Lansing went on, I came here partly to——"

"Lansing, this is important. I asked you again about your diary."

"Diary? Yes, you showed it to me, didn't you? Sometimes I have trouble remembering. But why?"

"Why? I have to know."

"What difference does it make?"

"Please."

Lansing's shoulders sagged. "I started to tell you."

"Started to tell me? You didn't——"

"Remember the night outside of Thiaucourt?"

"Yes."

"And I told you I didn't feel good. My head felt funny?"

"Yes."

"That was it." Lansing rubbed his forehead with his fingers.

"That was what?"

"When it happened. My epiphany, if you want to call it that. Haven't you ever had an experience like that? An insight so profound that you're forever changed."

"Yes."

"I mean cataclysmically."

"Yes, but what——?"

"The rest doesn't matter. It's too hard, and personal."

Morgan came to him, and tried to touch him, but his hand shook too much. "Maybe someday you'll tell me. I wish we could go back and . . . What can I do?"

After he left, Morgan wondered about Lansing's elephant-carved chest.

Morgan went to Pastor Syveruud. He felt worse than a hypocrite, but he had nowhere else to turn. Not for this.

"Morgan. Come in."

Pastor Syveruud was tall, with wild hair and eighty years of wrinkles covering his face. He made Morgan think of John Brown, the abolitionist. He also reminded Morgan of Pastor Lundmann from his childhood.

"I used to see you in church sometimes, but we've never talked," Pastor Syveruud said. "Please, sit down." He indicated a sofa across from his large leather armchair. "A bit messy, I'm afraid." "I can make tea." He said it halfheartedly.

"No, thanks. I just loaded up on coffee."

The room was cluttered with furniture, none of which seemed to match. Religious artifacts of all kinds decorated the walls—pictures of angels, small paintings, ancient Greek and Roman statuettes on shelves—and Morgan found himself intent on a large silver crucifix. The last light of the day came through the window and illuminated it so that it radiated a halo above Pastor Syveruud's head.

"Hot," Pastor Syveruud said.

"I'll say. And grasshoppers. Lotta guys are spreading mash."

"So I heard. What are they using?"

"Arsenic, oranges, bran, molasses, and salt. Mix it with water, and let it dry."

"It works?"

"Yeah, but it's expensive, and you can't make it fast enough. A losing game."

"Hummm."

286

Morgan was surprised. Most preachers he had known were impractical dreamers. Mystics living in a different world, who assumed that anything they could not rationally account for was a miracle. Nonrealists who never had to work for a living because *the Lord will provide*. Who couldn't understand how hard everyday life was.

"And how have you been, Morgan?"

"Alright. Could be worse. But I want to ask you something."

". . . atonement," Morgan said. Not until Pastor Syveruud lit a table lamp did Morgan realize how long he had been talking.

"Only the Son of God could atone for?" Pastor Syveruud asked incredulously.

"And he wants me to kill him."

"He wants you to what?" Pastor Syveruud sat straight up in his chair, and his eyes radiated white light.

"Kill him."

"Why?"

"Because he can't do it himself. He tried once and messed it up, and now he wants me to do it."

"Why you?" Pastor Syveruud stood and glared down on Morgan.

"Because . . . ," Morgan choked, "because I killed a man once."

"In the war?"

"Yes. Many. But one was different. My friend, Sydney. He would have died anyway, and he wanted me to do it, and after all night with him pleading, I killed him. You don't know what it's like. I just couldn't stand it anymore. It was like it was someone else doing it. I . . . ."

Morgan told of Sydney.

"Abomination!"

287

"But I didn't know what else to do! I was like Victor, a guy in our outfit. A German was caught between the lines, wounded, begging for help. Victor couldn't take it. He crawled out and killed the guy. It was a mercy killing."

"It was murder!"

"No! You aren't fit to judge, unless you were there. Unless you've lived like we did."

"I'm not judging you! God is."

"I came here for help."

"Pray, Morgan! Pray that you don't . . . ."

As Morgan parked his Essex in front of his house, he knew that Pastor Syveruud was a nonrealist after all.

CHAPTER FORTY-SEVEN

They followed the fencelines mostly: Morgan head down with his hands clasped behind his back, Rosalie tagging behind. Sweat trickled from under Morgan's hat, and dust caked his face. Every mile they stopped to rest, and Morgan gave Rosalie water from his canteen.

When they had rested, they walked on, Morgan searching for a way out of his fatal dilemma. Lansing's duality. If Lansing lived, Morgan knew he could lose Genevieve. And if Lansing died . . . .

"Evangeline! I'm sorry."

"You have nothing to be sorry for, Morgan. I only want you to be happy." She was radiant and beautiful.

"I've forsaken you."

"No. Don't you see, Morgan? I have come to you at last."

"You? Genevieve? No, how can that be? I——"

She put her finger to her lips. *"I was only what you wanted me to be. I was your solace and your hope. Now you no longer need me."*

"Will I see you again?"

"Yes. Every day, as long as you are with her. Live a long, happy life Morgan. I have done all I can."

"But I'm lost. Lansing is——"

"Don't you remember the day you realized that if you could survive the war, you could survive whatever came after? That nothing could be worse."

She receded, backward and up.

"Wait," Morgan cried, but she was gone.

Morgan got out of his car. Caroline met him at the bottom of the porch steps. Her hair hung down in unkempt strands, and her face was puffy.

"I have to see Genevieve," Morgan said.

Caroline frowned. "I don't think you should."

Morgan took off his hat and fixed his eyes on her. "Caroline, I don't mean to be abrupt, but I haven't the time, or the inclination, to discuss it with you."

Caroline hesitated, then she led him inside.

"She's in there," Caroline said. She pointed into one of the bedrooms. The room was dark.

"Please leave us alone."

Caroline started to say something, but she stopped. She went outside, and Morgan saw her running toward the barn.

Morgan stepped into the bedroom. "Genevieve." He struggled to breathe the stagnant air.

"Morgan? Why did you take so long?"

"I had to think." He opened the curtain and turned to her again. She gazed at him with fevered eyes, and he saw the laudanum bottle. He put it in his pocket. "You don't have to worry," he said.

"Honestly?"

Her hair was matted, and she had aged, but she was still beautiful, and Morgan knew that she was pure of heart.

"Yes. But we have to talk."

"Yes."

Morgan came out and found Lars and Caroline standing on the front porch. They had been arguing.

"No more," Morgan said. He held up the laudanum bottle.

"But . . ." Caroline began. "Doctor Raulsten said she had a nervous breakdown again." Tears welled up in her eyes.

"No. She saw reality, and it overwhelmed her, just like it overwhelms me."

Lars put his arm around Caroline. "Can we help?"

"You won't need to help me anymore, Lars."

As Morgan walked to his car, he heard Genevieve's last words to him: *He no longer exists. Neither the Lansing you thought you knew, nor the one you never knew.* Morgan waved to Lars and Caroline. Lars waved back, but Caroline turned and went inside.

Exhaust filtered up through the floorboards of Morgan's Essex, and the engine missed and sputtered every time he hit a bump. But Morgan was aware only of the imminence of the most vital juncture of his life. Of the certainty that he must confront Lansing.

"Be careful, Morgan," Genevieve had said through her drug haze.

With the sun red and low in the west, Morgan prepared for his final battle. A contest of will. His car hit a rock and bounced, and Morgan clung to the wheel. He reached down and pushed the laudanum bottle back into his pocket. It felt warm against his leg.

They gave him drugs to kill the pain.

Morgan pulled over and stopped. He shut off the engine, took the bottle from his pocket and held it to his heart. He felt like crying, but he was strong. Then, with the concussive force of an artillery shell, the awful realization hit him. *They gave him drugs to kill the pain.* Lansing, a doper! Oh, God, that's it! The chest on his night stand! *Something sinister . . .* Opium! He's mixed up in the opium trade, and he's using it himself! Of course. What else could such a disfigured, mentally unstable unfortunate do?

Morgan tried to catch his breath. Now things weren't so simple. It wasn't just a struggle for Genevieve. Or shell shock. Morgan leaned forward and rested his forehead on the steering wheel. Lansing was fighting for his life, and he needed help, even if helping him meant——

"Morgan! Havin' trouble?"

It was Big Bill Adams, his flabby, affable neighbor from just over the hill east. Bill's wife, Effie, sat next to him, glaring at Morgan. Morgan tried to clear his head.

"No, I was just thinking."

"Hm." Bill saw the bottle.

"Let's go, Bill," Effie said. She was thin to the point of emaciation.

"You sure, Morgan? Yuh ain't drinkin' again, are yuh?"

"No."

"Bill!" Effie exclaimed.

"Alright," Bill said. Morgan heard Effie scolding Bill as they drove off. She had scolded him much in the years they had been married. Bill drank more in a month than most people did in a year, and the stories of Effie in her younger days were legendary. She had found religion later in life, but she had not succeeded in imparting her piety on Bill.

Morgan closed his eyes and tried to prepare himself. He would not let Lansing go down without a struggle.

"He's gone. He left last night."

Harry Glick stood behind the hotel desk, swatting flies.

"Where did he go?" Morgan asked. He looked across the lobby at an old man sitting by the grandfather clock, and jabbed his thumb toward the door. The old man got up and scurried out.

"Dunno. I don't ask all of my——"

Morgan reached over and grabbed Harry's wrist. "Think, Harry." He squeezed, and Harry winced.

292

"Ow! Leggo! That guy's touched, and I don't want him finding out I——"

Morgan squeezed harder, and with his other hand he seized Harry's collar.

"Back to Chicago, I think! Yeah. Chicago! Ow."

Morgan let go. "You have an excellent memory, Harry. Must be that bootleg hooch you claim you never sell."

"Hooch! What the hell are you talking about?" His face got red. "You goddamn——"

Morgan moved toward him again, but Harry jumped back and held up his flyswatter.

"Stand back, Morgan! I'll call the sheriff."

"Shit."

"Does that make any sense to you?" Morgan asked. He had brought Genevieve to the hill behind his house, where he had explained to her his repository of memories.

"Yes, of course." She looked down at the grave. "I have a few things of my own I'd like to bury here." Her eyes were clear, and some of the anguish was gone.

Morgan put his hand on the side of her neck, and when she looked up, they kissed, delicately, with a sensitivity reserved for those who have suffered beyond their capacity to endure.

"Here." He led her to the wooden bench he had made; beside a spindly poplar tree that he had planted the day Lansing had come to Charity. Neither wanted to break the quiet, fearing that doing so would send them swirling into the unknown. So they sat, listening to the doves.

But darkness came.

Morgan took Genevieve's hand. "One final battle," he said. "I have to fight for Lansing, not against him." He felt her grip tighten. "I'm starting to find out what happened to him."

293

"What?"

"It's not all clear yet. But I'm sure of one thing. He's on dope."

Her grip tightened even more. "So that's it! God! I, a nurse! How could I have not known? And . . ." She sucked in her breath. "And that's what he does? The sinister thing I suspected?"

"Almost certainly." Morgan massaged the back of her hand, and her grip loosened. "I'll leave in the morning."

"Must you?"

"At first I thought I was fighting to save us all. But now I know that no matter what happens, you and I will be redeemed. Whatever evil hold he has on you."

"But I'm free now, Morgan. The sacred promises I made? It's as you said: I wasn't myself. I can't be held accountable."

"When did you know?"

"When I was with Lars and Caroline. The laudanum." She paused. "Isn't it ironic? That I would receive such insight from the very poison that is Lansing's ruin."

"Yes, but he was destroyed long before the opium."

"Then you can't help him."

A fox howled its hunger call: a terrible, human-like scream.

"I have to do it for myself, because I was his friend."

She shuddered. "There's something else, before you go. About Stephen Long."

Morgan waited.

"Did Caroline tell you?"

"No."

"You knew?"

"No. Only that Caroline was trying to protect you from the likes of me."

Genevieve laughed. "And Lars thought I was barmy."

294

"How did you know that?"

"Don't you know when someone thinks you're napoo?"

"Yes."

Genevieve turned serious again. "Stephen was a senior at Princeton, and I was in nursing school nearby, and we thought we were in love."

She blushed. Morgan had never seen her do that before.

"No, it's not true that we thought we were in love. The truth is, we were in love." She held her head up, unashamed, waiting, but Morgan said nothing.

"Stephen and his friends on the boxing squad got war fever and signed up. They were sent to Fort Leavenworth for training. Ninety-day wonders."

"Third lieutenants."

"They couldn't wait to get overseas. We tried to stay in touch, but it was impossible." Genevieve's face shone in the moonlight.

"You didn't hear from him until after the war?"

"He looked me up in New York. He came to my door with flowers. Can you imagine? I've never liked flowers, unless they're growing. That night we went to a dance, and I tried, but it was no good anymore."

"You had changed?"

"Of course. But it wouldn't have worked anyway. He was a coward."

"Lieutenant Stafford."

"Who?"

"A lieutenant I knew. But go on."

"Stephen had found war not to his liking, and he tried to fake a back injury. They court-martialed him, and sent him home to do ten years. But he's from a family of wealthy Boston lawyers, and they got him off with a dishonorable discharge."

"A yellow ticket."

295

"Yes, but to him it was a commendation. He reveled in it, and he saw those who stayed and fought as fools."

"We were."

"Eager, and idealistic, perhaps. But not fools."

"All I know is, I wouldn't do it again. I'm not a coward. I just wouldn't do it again."

The thin air became cool.

"He wanted me to marry him," Genevieve said, "and when I refused, he became obsessed. He followed me here. Oh, it's a long story, but it's over."

"I'm sorry. You seem to be the victim of many obsessions. You've had a rough go of it."

She stood, took out the engagement ring Stephen had given her, and placed it on one of the rocks.

CHAPTER FORTY-EIGHT

The train swayed, and Morgan was mesmerized by the clacking of the wheels. It reminded him of an earlier time: the ride to LaCourtine. The splitting up of friends, and the meeting of new ones. The spirit of youth, before the disillusionment.

Just four other passengers. A man and his wife near the front. Morgan couldn't see their faces, but they were well dressed. They had with them a boy—about ten years old, quiet and serious—who fidgeted and kept looking out the window, though it was dark. The other passenger was a young lady two rows up. She had been there when Morgan had gotten on, and she had seemed either disappointed that he had not sat next to her, or relieved that he hadn't. He couldn't tell—guys like him could never tell such things—but several times she had looked back at him, and he wished she would just ignore him. She was pretty enough: blond, tall, well built. But cold, and hard, with a tight mouth and colorless lips. And—on second look—unhealthy. Pale, and thin. She was going to Chicago too, she had told the man and his wife.

Morgan folded his arms across his chest, leaned back, and closed his eyes. At last he and Genevieve were free. *The sacred promises I made? It's as you said: I wasn't myself. I can't be held accountable.* But they wouldn't be truly free until Lansing was free. Morgan was as he had been in the trenches, waiting to go *over the top,* when the fear and paralysis of the night were replaced by morning eagerness to face whatever lay ahead. To get it over with—whatever *it* was—because nothing was worse than inaction: the destroyer of souls.

"I say let's give 'em what for," a voice in the gloom said.
"Look there. See that glow in the sky?" Morgan pointed eastward, but they couldn't see him in the dark. "Can

you hear it? That's artillery fire. You guys want fighting? Well, you're gonna get it." Someone profaned him for his pessimism.

They were green then, and had not yet tasted combat.

Morgan opened one eye just enough to see the boy—red headed and red faced—staring over the back of his seat. The young lady had moved, and was sleeping with her head on a pillow against the window. The rhythm of the wheels was broken by the hollowness of a bridge, then the familiar "tack, tack, tack" resumed. Morgan stuck out his tongue at the boy, but got no response. The boy continued to stare, so Morgan closed his eye again.

Morgan cried softly. Lansing gave him a dirty handkerchief, and Morgan wiped his face. Lansing picked up Morgan's helmet and handed it to him, and the onlookers moved away.

"You're alright, old man," Lansing consoled. "You just slipped a little, that's all. Happens to all of us at one time or another."

Now it was his turn to help Lansing. If he could.

Morgan stretched and looked around. The boy was still staring, and the lady by the window reminded him of a French dirty puss who had once offered herself to him.

———————————

Morgan leaned against a lamppost and checked the address Genevieve had given him: 117 East 23rd Street. The Oxford Hotel: a drab two-story brownstone. The sun was just coming up he guessed, but it was hard to tell in a city. Not much activity yet: a few delivery trucks, and an old Negro man shuffling along carrying a big canvas bag over his shoulder. The

298

man had on dark spectacles, and he carried a cane, but Morgan didn't think he was blind. Then, as he passed, he stopped and glared at Morgan. Morgan glared back, but the old man just shook his head, mumbled something about divine retribution, and moved on. A train whistle blew three times, and a tan automobile went by, driven by another Negro in some kind of uniform. Two men in suits occupied the back seat.

It was too early, so Morgan took the time to steel himself. He took the pint bottle of rotgut from his pants pocket, opened it, and touched it to his lips, but he stopped, and tossed it into an empty wooden crate full of garbage. Not now. Maybe a drink or two with Lansing, and then only for old times. As he waited, Morgan was aware of a heavy, clammy blanket enveloping him, and he knew what he was about to attempt was futile, but he had to try, for himself, more than for Lansing. Really, it was all for himself, and if there were such things as miracles, Lansing would be the perfect test. But God doesn't exist, and there are no miracles, and that's that. The biggest miracle of all would be that there are miracles. But as it is, miracles are simply things we don't understand, Morgan philosophized.

Morgan crossed the street and went in. The lobby was small and dimly lighted, with only two stuffed armchairs, a tea table, and a fancy potbelly stove. There was no one there, so he went behind the desk and took out the register. Nothing for Rhodes, but there it was: John Gant - 205.

Morgan crept up the stairway. Halfway up, one of the steps squeaked, and he waited for a few seconds, then he continued. He stopped at the top and waited again, then he moved down the dark, musty hallway. He stopped at room 205, and listened. For more than five minutes he stood. Then, as though some inner force were directing him, he knocked. He was a spectator, and he saw himself step aside, and he felt his hand reach under his coat and pull out his Webley, cock it, and point it straight up. Time had slowed, as it had when he had charged across No Man's Land. He turned his head and looked back down the hall to see if anyone was coming, but there was no one. Then he sensed someone just inside the door, and he knew it was Lansing. And he prayed for a miracle.

CHAPTER FORTY-NINE

The door opened, and Lansing stood, also holding a Webley Mark VI, cocked and pointed at Morgan.

"Oh, good grief." Morgan lowered his weapon and let the hammer down, and Lansing did the same, and they both laughed.

"Morgan, what the——?"

"You gonna let me in?"

Lansing stepped back. His room was furnished with a bed, two leather-covered armchairs, a table heaped with dirty dishes, several steamer trunks; and on the night stand, the mysterious wooden chest. The red-and-yellow floral wallpaper reminded Morgan of his own room in the hotel back in Miles City.

"Here," Lansing said. He cleared dirty clothes from one of the chairs. "Sit." Lansing took the chair beside the night stand, and laid his revolver on the bed. "I've been expecting you, Morgan."

"You should have."

"I suppose."

They measured each other, and Morgan thought he detected something of the man he had once known.

"A drink, for old times." Lansing reached down beside his chair and came up with a bottle.

"Alright. Old times."

Lansing found two none-too-clean glasses, and poured. He handed one to Morgan. "Good stuff. From Canada." He held up his glass. "To the Second Division, and all of the brave men." He said it softly, and bitterly.

They drank. When their glasses were empty, Lansing poured again.

Morgan lifted his glass. "This time let's drink to the good times."

"Here's how," Lansing acknowledged.

"There were some good times, you know," Morgan said.

They drank, and for a long time they sat, remembering.

When they had finished, Lansing put his elbows on the arms of the chair, and folded his hands. "You and I never minced words, Morgan. We won't start now, will we?"

"No. I've come to help."

"Of course. Just as we helped each other before."

Morgan caught the irony. "Yes. I don't know you anymore. You're so different, but there must be a some of the old Lansing left that we could build on."

Lansing opened his hands, and clasped them again. "You had your demons, and I had mine. You did the best you could, and you survived. I did the best I could, and my best wasn't good enough."

"But you're alive, and——"

"Alive? Look at me! Do you want me to take this off?" He reached for his mask.

"If you wish." Morgan tightened his grip on the arms of the chair.

Lansing took his hand away. "No, believe me, you don't. I only make a point. Don't you understand, Morgan? I wanted to die, and Genevieve should have let me. Sometimes, when I think of her, or when I see you, I'm able to pull myself up, but it's false hope, and I always fall back."

"I know about the dope."

"Of course. What difference does it make? I had to do something. What do you think guys like me do for a living? You think I'd be better off selling pencils? Or maybe I could take off my mask and join the circus. Sideshows are always looking for——"

"Stop!"

They both cried.

"Then there is no hope?" Morgan asked. He wiped his face with his hand.

"None. I may be a dope fiend, but I know myself, and there is none."

"Then, dammit, tell me! What happened?"

Lansing looked at the chest on the night stand, but he reached for a cigarette. "Some people, like you, cracked up gradually. For me it was sudden. Or maybe it had been building up, and it only hit me suddenly." He shrugged and struck his match. "Regardless, all of my life I had been a naive optimist. Then, when I could see the end of the war, I knew that it had all been in vain. All of the suffering, and sacrifice . . . ."

Morgan listened quietly as Lansing revealed his final struggle. For over an hour Lansing told of his journey to hell. Of slipping slowly, bit by bit each day, trying to fight it; trying to not let it show. Holding onto the end of the war, yet knowing that it was already too late. Trying to stop what was going on inside his head. "It's hard to describe," Lansing said. "Like gears grinding. You can almost feel it, and it never stops. The same thoughts, over, and over, until you can't stand it anymore, and you have to do something, even if what you do is as bad as the malady."

Lansing stopped, placed his elephant-carved chest of dreams on his lap, and unlocked it. "Close your eyes Morgan if this offends you."

"What about atonement? What you said about humanity being lost until it has suffered enough?"

Lansing paused, reached into the top drawer of the night stand, and took out a Bible. It had several markers in it, and he opened to one and read ". . . think it not strange concerning the fiery trial which is to try you . . ." He looked up at Morgan. "First Peter, Chapter Four."

"I didn't know you had turned into a Bible pounder."

"It's not what you think." He picked another page. ". . . that you present your bodies a living sacrifice, holy, acceptable unto God."

"I don't see what you're getting at."

"You asked about atonement. Maybe I was never religious in the traditional sense, but I always believed. Then, just before I broke down, it became clear to me. I was . . . ."

At last Lansing was finished.

"For heaven's sake," Morgan stammered.

"That's just it! For heaven's sake! But I couldn't carry that great a burden, so I gave up."

Evangeline's admonition rang in Morgan's ears: *Then you can't help him.*

"Afterward?"

"As I have said, there was Genevieve."

"And now?"

"Now there is nothing." He opened the chest again and withdrew a small golden cross wreathed with vines. "Not all of my palliatives are maleficent. Please, return this to Genevieve. She gave it to me in the hospital in France, when she thought I was going to die." He leaned forward and handed it to Morgan.

Morgan—as he received the cross—considered seizing Lansing's wrist. But it would have been only a postponement.

"That cross was a comfort to me. Perhaps it was false hope. I'm about to find out." Lansing took his Webley from the bed. "I wronged you, Morgan, in the hotel in Charity. It was unfair of me to ask you to do it." He rolled the cylinder. "But you can help."

"Help?" Morgan heard his own voice echo.

"It's the loneliness. I don't mind doing it myself, as long as I'm not alone." He put the revolver to the side of his head. The side without the mask. Morgan closed his eyes and waited.

CHAPTER FIFTY

"She waits for you every day, on the hill behind your house," Lars said. He and Caroline were standing on their porch.

"Thanks." Morgan went back to his car. It was a beautiful, sunny Sunday morning.

"Morgan." Caroline followed him, stepping around mud puddles. It had rained two inches. Too late for the crops, but life was good again; filled with hope and promise.

"Yes?"

"I . . . , I want to——"

"You've been Genevieve's friend, and I appreciate that," Morgan said. He reached out his hand, and she took it. Talk about redemption. Redemption coming from Caroline Nordraak was possibly the ultimate redemption.

As Morgan got into his car, Lars called, "Price of wheat's up a nickel!"

Morgan stopped. Karl Springer was changing a flat tire. "Morning, Karl. Need any help?"

"Naw, I'm alright, thanks." Karl straightened, took off his derby hat, and kicked the spare tire. He was sweating profusely through his white shirt, but a breeze came and cooled him. "Emma wanted me tuh go tuh church this morning, but I didn't wanna go. Guess I'm gettin' paid back for not going."

Morgan couldn't tell if he was serious.

"Ol' Pastor Syveruud jumped me the other day. Said I'm gonna burn if I don't start goin'. Didn't say it exactly that way, but in so many words. Maybe I should go more often." Karl continued, "But I don't know if I believe in all that hocus pocus. There may be somethin' to it though. What d'yuh think?"

"You asked me that before, Karl. I told you I didn't believe any of it. But now I don't know. Nobody does, and if they say they do——"

305

"Yeah, but what d'yuh think?"

"Well, did you ever try to imagine all of the people in the world? Most of them are religious in some way or another. I guess it's a natural human disposition, so maybe there's something to it. Or, they could all be dunces."

"Hmm."

"I've never warmed the front pew much, and I never will, but there must be more than this." Morgan swept his hand in the air. "Maybe not the heaven and hell of the Bible, but something."

Karl lightened. "That's the way I look at it. I always thought there was something."

"I've seen a lot of evil, Karl, but it seems to me that everything in life is balanced. Hot and cold, light and dark, beautiful and ugly. Then why not good? If there's so much bad in the world, doesn't it stand to reason that there's an equal amount of good? Some divine providence?"

"I suppose so."

"I guess we have to keep hope."

"Yeah! Yuh gotta have hope." Karl stood straighter and took a deep breath. "Ah! What a day!" He leaned on his car and wiped his hands on his shirttails. "Say, you've been gone."

"Chicago. Old business."

"Yeah. Well, your new business is waiting for yuh out at your place," Karl hawed. "Yuh can see 'er for miles, up on the hill in 'er white dress."

Morgan looked toward his place.

". . . turkeys. Shit. Wish I'd never seen a turkey. They're the dumbest animal on the face of the earth. Why, they don't even have sense enough tuh come in outta the . . . ."

Morgan fidgeted as Karl railed on. Suddenly Karl's face brightened. "But tuh hell with turkeys. It looks like Lars might go in on that moonshine deal with me. Now that's a sure thing!" He lowered his voice. "Not much startup money, and a big

306

profit margin. Don't say nothin' tuh Caroline. And Emma'd kill me. But I got this still lined up, and . . . ."

"Morgan." Genevieve took Morgan's hands and held them to her cheek. He kissed her, and as he put his arms around her, Lansing's poplar tree caught his eye. It seemed greener than before, and taller.

"I was saying goodbyes," Genevieve said.

"Goodbyes?"

"To my past."

They stood looking at the southern horizon, at the gray haze that hung over the Missouri River fifteen miles away. Genevieve leaned her head on Morgan's shoulder.

"Lansing?"

"It's over," Morgan said. "He finished the job." He felt her tense, and she pulled away.

"You were there when he did it?"

"Yes. He was waiting for me. Somehow he knew I'd come. He didn't want to die alone."

"You couldn't stop him?"

"Maybe I could have, but he would have done it eventually. And for him life wasn't worth living. It never would be."

"Did you have the right to make that judgment?"

They faced each other, and Morgan thought for a moment. First Sydney, now Lansing.

"I could have made it, but it was his decision."

"The police?"

"I called them, but I didn't hang around."

"I have to know, Morgan, and then I'll let you put it to rest. Remember when you showed me the diary? The last line: *Something has gone wrong.* What was it, Morgan? What could go so wrong that he would try to kill himself, with the war almost over?"

307

"Something had happened inside his head. He said it was like gears grinding, day and night. And, as he said in his diary, he had lost faith in humanity. Without that faith, he couldn't take it anymore: the killing, the filth, the degradation."

"That's it?"

"No, that was only the beginning. He had experienced a religious conversion. One day he looked at us—sitting in the trenches, with the rats, and filth, and death all around—and he knew that humanity is lost until we have atoned for our sins. The longer he thought about it, the more convinced he was that he had to atone for the sins of mankind. To follow in the footsteps of Christ. That was the reason he was there. The reason we were all there."

"That sounds——"

"Mad? Maybe, but strange things happened in the trenches. And he tried to sacrifice himself."

"Sacrifice himself? Christ didn't commit suicide."

"No. But he could have avoided crucifixion, and to Lansing it was the same thing."

"It isn't."

"Then, after the war, the dope. Opium."

"And when he finally did kill himself?"

"The same as the first. Atonement. He gave himself for us. For you and me." Morgan fixed his eyes on the horizon, and he felt a tear, on the side away from Genevieve. "He loved you very much. No matter what he had become, you were his life."

"I was his captive."

"He told me that letting you go was the hardest thing he had ever done. Harder than dying. He knew how it was to die, because he was already half dead. And how hard it is to live. For him, living was harder." Morgan took Lansing's gold cross from his pocket and gave it to Genevieve. "Put him in your heart with the others. The other twelve who loved you."

Genevieve knelt and put the cross on Morgan's grave of memories, next to Stephen Long's engagement ring. She said a silent prayer.

Morgan knelt beside her, and put Sydney's ring with the other relics of their past.

They stood, and Genevieve took Morgan's hand. "Have you lost all faith?" she asked.

"My faith was never strong."

"But you'll try?"

"Yes. But not the religion of the people around here."

"No. I've given up on hypocrisy too. But we have to have faith in something. Some higher power."

Genevieve put her arms on Morgan's shoulders, and she felt the spot on the back of his head where he had been wounded. "We'll never forget, but now we can start adding good memories to the bad ones, until there are more good than bad."

The sun cleansed them, and nearby, on a fencepost, a meadowlark sang its summer song. Morgan could feel his mantle of suffering lift.

"Now it's our time to live," Genevieve said.

"Yes."

.

www.ingramcontent.com/pod-product-compliance
Lightning Source LLC
Chambersburg PA
CBHW031940260626
47157CB00016B/670